I0823910

THE CROSSROADS

ALSO BY C. J. BOX

THE JOE PICKETT NOVELS

Battle Mountain
Three-Inch Teeth
Storm Watch
Shadows Reel
Dark Sky
Long Range
Wolf Pack
The Disappeared
Vicious Circle
Off the Grid
Endangered
Stone Cold
Breaking Point
Force of Nature
Cold Wind
Nowhere to Run
Below Zero
Blood Trail
Free Fire
In Plain Sight
Out of Range
Trophy Hunt
Winterkill
Savage Run
Open Season

THE HOYT/DEWELL NOVELS

Treasure State
The Bitterroots
Paradise Valley
Badlands
The Highway
Back of Beyond

THE STAND-ALONE NOVELS AND OTHER WORKS

Shots Fired: Stories from Joe Pickett Country
Three Weeks to Say Goodbye
Blue Heaven

THE CROSSROADS

A JOE PICKETT NOVEL

C. J. BOX

G. P. PUTNAM'S SONS
NEW YORK

PUTNAM
— EST. 1838 —

G. P. Putnam's Sons
Publishers Since 1838
An imprint of Penguin Random House LLC
1745 Broadway, New York, NY 10019
penguinrandomhouse.com

Title page photograph by Grindstone Media Group

Library of Congress Cataloging-in-Publication Data has been applied for.

ISBN 9780593851098
Ebook ISBN 9780593851104

Printed in the United States of America
1st Printing

The authorized representative in the EU for product safety and compliance is Penguin Random House Ireland, Morrison Chambers, 32 Nassau Street, Dublin D02 YH68, Ireland, https://eu-contact.penguin.ie.

For Molly, Becky, and Roxanne,
and Laurie, always

I went down to the crossroads
Fell down on my knees
Down to the crossroads
Fell down on my knees
Asked the Lord above for mercy,
"Take me, if you please"

—*Crossroads Blues*, Robert Johnson, 1936

THE CROSSROADS

CHAPTER ONE

November 15

FOR MARYBETH PICKETT, it was the call she'd dreaded for over twenty years.

At the time it came that mid-November morning, she was standing in front of a whiteboard in her director's office at the Twelve Sleep County Library, working on the annual budget presentation she was scheduled to give before the county commissioners.

Over the speaker of the phone on her desk, the front-desk librarian said, "Marybeth, someone from the sheriff's office says he needs to speak to you immediately. He says it's urgent."

Urgent.

Marybeth felt an unseen hand grip her stomach, and a bolt of cold fear shot down her legs. It was suddenly difficult to take a breath.

Marybeth looked at the phone's base, and the single plastic button that blinked spasmodically.

She tossed the dry-erase marker aside, sat down in her chair, and punched the button. As she did, dark, frightening images and possibilities flooded her mind: car accidents involving any of the three of her daughters, crimes committed where they were the victims, a plane crash, suicide, murder, kidnapping, rape . . .

"This is Marybeth Pickett," she said. Her mouth was dry and it was difficult to speak.

"Mrs. Pickett, this is Deputy Frank Carroll of the Twelve Sleep County Sheriff's Department. I'm sorry I didn't call you on your cell phone, but I'm in my vehicle, so I put it through dispatch."

She could hear Carroll's siren whooping in the the background, which made it difficult to hear what he was saying.

"Yes, Deputy," she said.

"First, is there any chance Joe is with you?"

"No, he's not here."

"Do you know where he was headed today?"

She tried to think. Her game warden husband rarely articulated his daily patrol routes to her in the morning before he set out in his Wyoming Game and Fish Department pickup. She was pretty sure that Joe often didn't have a plan, either. Only if he thought he might be out of cell phone range or radio contact did he say something. Or if he was involved in a case that might keep him out in the field well beyond nightfall.

"I don't remember him saying where he was going today," she confessed.

"So you don't know where he is right now?"

"No," she said. "I usually don't. His district is five thousand square miles, and he could be anywhere in it, since it's still hunting season. Why are you asking me all of this?"

She knew “Fearless” Frank Carroll well enough to know that he liked to talk and that it took him a while to get to the point. Marybeth was having none of that at the moment.

“Well, we got a report,” Carroll said. “A hunter called it in a few minutes ago.”

“Frank, what was the report?”

Deputy Carroll said, “I don’t want to alarm you unnecessarily, Marybeth. I really don’t. But this hunter said he came upon a Game and Fish vehicle parked out on Antler Creek Road. He said it was in the middle of the road just sitting there, so he checked it out.”

“What are you saying, Deputy?” Marybeth asked, her voice rising.

“Well, keep in mind that none of this is confirmed yet. I’m headed out there now. But according to this hunter, the pickup is all shot up and there appears to be a body inside.”

Marybeth closed her eyes and couldn’t speak for a few seconds. Then she said, “A body?”

“Well, I should have said a ‘victim,’ I guess,” Carroll said. “The hunter didn’t check for a pulse or anything. He just said there was somebody inside the pickup and that the victim was unresponsive. He said there were bullet holes in the windshield and the glass was all cracked and it was hard to see inside very clearly.”

Her heart raced. She asked, “How long ago did the report come in?”

“Like I said, just a few minutes ago. Of course, we don’t know how long that pickup has been sitting out there. That place is a long way away from town, as you probably know.”

“How soon will it be before you get there?”

"Ten, twelve minutes more, I reckon."

"Did you call dispatch in Cheyenne?" Marybeth asked. "They might know better about Joe's location. He's not the only person driving a Game and Fish vehicle in the county, you know. There are biologists, other game wardens, fisheries people . . ."

"Like I said, I don't know anything yet," Carroll said. "I was just hoping you'd be able to rule out that it was Joe."

"God, I wish I could," she said. Then: "Hold on."

Marybeth dug into her handbag for her cell phone and she speed-dialed Joe's phone and pressed it to her other ear. While she did, she noticed that the front-desk librarian who had transferred the call was now hovering outside her office door, looking into its wide window with a concerned expression. Marybeth could see her own reflection in the glass and she looked ridiculous holding phones up to both ears. But at the moment, she didn't care.

The call to Joe went straight to his voicemail.

"*This is game warden Joe Pickett. I can't take this call right now, but please leave your name and number and . . .* "

When it beeped, Marybeth shouted, "Joe, call me back right away."

"What's that?" Deputy Carroll asked over the handset.

"Never mind," she said. "I was trying Joe on his cell phone. He didn't pick up."

"Does he usually?"

She started to say yes, then she started to say he usually did, then she got honest and said, "At times. But he always calls back when he can."

She tried not to imagine her husband shot to death inside the cab of his pickup. Or worse, bleeding out while waiting for someone to arrive.

"Where is this hunter who called it in?" she asked Carroll. "Did he just leave the scene and Joe?"

"First, we don't know it's Joe," Carroll said. "Second, I'm not sure where the reporting party is right now. I didn't get the initial call."

Marybeth reached up with her free left hand and rubbed her eyes. She tried not to take all her anger, fear, and frustration out on Deputy Carroll.

"Please call me the second you get there," she said, and slammed the receiver down onto the phone's base.

She sat back for a second, staring into space. Judith from the front desk was a stocky woman in her early sixties with close-cropped gray hair and oversized black-framed glasses who was partial to wearing Christmas sweaters any time of the year. When her worried face nearly pressed against the glass of the window, Marybeth growled and raised her voice again.

"Please, Judith, leave me be and get back to work."

Judith scurried away. Marybeth made a mental note to apologize to the poor woman later.

THE DISPATCHER IN Cheyenne identified herself as Monica Luce.

"This is Marybeth Pickett, Joe Pickett's wife," Marybeth said. "We're trying to locate Joe right now. Did he call in his location this morning?"

Luce chuckled. "Joe's a great guy, but he *never* calls in his location unless it's an emergency and he needs backup."

Which, as Marybeth knew intimately, was very rare. If a game warden requested backup in the field, it meant he was in serious trouble because backup could take hours to get there in the remote Bighorn Mountain country.

"Let me ask you another question," Marybeth said. "Did you take any calls today about violations or situations in Joe's district? Do you know if he was responding to anything?"

"I'm really not supposed to divulge that kind of information, I'm afraid," Luce said.

"I know that. But I just talked to a sheriff's deputy here. Someone called in a Game and Fish pickup that's all shot up. We don't know if it is Joe or someone else. Or if the whole situation is a false alarm."

"Oh my God," Luce said. "Why didn't you say that in the first place? No, we didn't send Joe out on anything this morning. I know that for sure because I've been here the entire shift. It's been quiet this morning. Oh, I hope he's okay."

"Thank you," Marybeth said. "I hope so, too."

MARYBETH SAT BACK in her chair and looked at the ancient clock above her door. It was 10:42 a.m.

She heard a siren outside and immediately recognized its distinctive whooping sound. It was the lone local EMT ambulance emerging from its bay next to the county building two blocks away from the library. She swiveled around in her chair in time to see the vehicle speed past her window, its flashers on.

It was headed west.

Antler Creek Road was also west.

THE CROSSROADS

WHEN HER CELL phone burred, Marybeth nearly knocked it off her desktop lunging for it. But when she held the screen up, it didn't say Joe. The call was from Deputy Frank Carroll.

"It's Joe's pickup, Marybeth," Carroll said with emotion in his voice. "He's inside."

Marybeth gasped. "Is he . . . ?"

"I don't know yet. I called for the EMTs and they said they're on their way."

"What does he look like?"

After a pause, Carroll said, "There's a *lot* of blood."

CHAPTER TWO

MARYBETH GRABBED HER handbag and jacket. She didn't take the time to close her door as she left her office. She strode through the nonfiction stacks and made a turn at the endcap displays and headed for the lobby doors. As she passed the front desk, she suddenly stopped. Judith looked up, concerned.

"Is everything okay?" she asked.

"I don't know. Joe might be hurt. Please cancel all my calls and meetings for the rest of the day."

Judith gasped and raised both of her hands to her mouth. Her eyes got big. "What happened?"

"I don't know yet."

"But isn't the budget hearing tonight?"

Marybeth glared at her, and Judith dropped her eyes to the top of the desk. "Sorry," she said. "I wasn't thinking."

Marybeth let it go. Several of the newly elected county commissioners were dead set against increased funding for the library, and there were rumors among the staff that they may try to defund it entirely. One of the commissioners had even recently speculated in an article in the Saddlestring *Roundup*, "Why do we need libraries when we've got the internet? Besides, I've never even set foot in the place."

Which was true, as far as Marybeth knew. Her staff was nervous, and she didn't blame them. But now was not the time to discuss it.

As SHE PULLED out of the library parking lot, Marybeth inadvertently intercepted a convoy of two sheriff's department SUVs, a Saddlestring Police Department cruiser, and a Wyoming Highway Patrol car. They were headed west with their wigwag lights flashing and their sirens on. She pulled over to the side of the road to let them pass.

As she did, she nearly foundered in a deep bank of snow that had been plowed into a furrow several days before. Remnants of a surprise November blizzard were all around her: furrows on the sides of roads, and mountains of plowed snow slowly melting in the centers of parking lots. The high-altitude sun would make short work of the snow that remained—until another blizzard hit.

Marybeth eased back onto the street and followed the officers with her cell phone on her lap. She wished she had a radio tuned to the mutual aid channel, like Joe did in his pickup. She'd like to hear what the law enforcement officers were saying to each other, and to hear the first reports from the EMTs when they arrived at the scene.

As she followed, Marybeth glanced down at her speedometer when the convoy cleared the city limits. She was going eighty-five in a fifty-mile-an-hour zone, and she had to press on the accelerator of her Ford crossover to keep up.

Marybeth was grateful that the roads were clear after the blizzard that had shut down the area the week before. There were still big snowdrifts in the swales of the terrain and impassable roads in the mountains. There was enough snow on the ground in patches that it created perfect camouflage for the large herds of brown and white pronghorn antelope, which melded into the landscape.

Should she call her three daughters? she asked herself. Sheridan, twenty-seven, was local, working as the CEO of Yarak, Inc., a bird abatement firm owned by Nate Romanowski. April, twenty-five, was in Bozeman, Montana, at a private detective agency. Lucy, the youngest at twenty-three, had just returned to Laramie and the University of Wyoming after a semester abroad in France.

Sheridan, of course, could probably get there first if she was working within cell phone range.

Marybeth decided against it. She didn't want to alarm them with incomplete information.

At that moment, her phone lit up with a call. Sheridan. Marybeth enabled the Bluetooth feature in her car and the call appeared on the dashboard's screen.

Sheridan said, "Mom, what's going on? Is Dad okay? My cell phone started blowing up a few minutes ago."

She'd heard. Marybeth said, "Let's not panic, Sheridan. We don't know what's happened yet or if your dad is even involved."

"My God," Sheridan said, her voice trembling. "I got a text saying he was shot to death and found in his pickup."

"Ignore it," Marybeth said. "Don't even look at any more texts until we know for sure. We don't even know if your dad is injured, or if it's somebody else in a Game and Fish truck."

"Who the hell else could it be?" Sheridan said, her voice rising.

"Don't lose it until you hear from me," Marybeth said. "I'm following the first responders out to the scene right now. I should be there in fifteen minutes, or sooner at the rate we're going."

"I'm scared. This could be awful," Sheridan said. "I can't even wrap my head around it."

"Just stay calm. That's what I'm trying to do."

"You don't sound calm," Sheridan said.

"Don't call your sisters just yet," Marybeth said. "Not until we know something."

"That's going to be hard," Sheridan said.

"I know. It's hard on me as well."

"Okay. For now."

"Stay off your phone. I'll call you the minute I know what's happened," Marybeth said. "I promise."

After a beat, Sheridan said, "Growing up, we all knew something might happen someday. I mean, just about everybody Dad runs across out in the field during hunting season is armed. But . . ."

"I know. I know, believe me. Honey, I'll call you the second I know something," Marybeth said, disconnecting the call and wiping hot tears from her cheeks with the heel of her hand.

Marybeth was untethered.

If it was Joe in that shot-up pickup on Antler Creek Road, she needed to know what happened and why. And she needed to know if she could hold it together.

But there had always been a lingering fear, she admitted to

herself. A fear that Joe would encounter a situation that he couldn't reason his way out of. A situation where he was ambushed, overwhelmed, or outgunned.

As a law enforcement officer, and one who had been called a "shit magnet" for his propensity to attract trouble and controversy for doing his job by the book and without qualms, Joe had made enemies over the years. He also had a knack for walking into—or bumbling into—situations that put his life in danger. It was a trait she both loved and hated about her husband. Joe seemed unable to understand that it was possible, at times, to simply walk away.

ANTLER CREEK ROAD was an anomaly of sorts, Marybeth had learned from Joe. It started out near Saddlestring as County Road 402, and it coursed along the base of Wolf Mountain, where the foothills flattened out into sagebrush prairie. It ended abruptly at a junction near an ancient buffalo wallow, where it split off into three forks that looked from the sky like the foot track of a wild turkey.

At the junction, the public road ended and the three roads emerging from it were private. Each was posted with signs to warn the public that to proceed on them amounted to trespassing. The road that went to the north led eventually to the magnificent Double Diamond Ranch, one of the largest landholdings in the Twelve Sleep River Valley. The middle road continued on to the Bucholz Cattle Company. And the southern spur led to the McElwee Land and Cattle Ranch holdings.

All three ranches were longtime, multigenerational properties with distinct characteristics. The Double Diamond was owned by a wealthy southern mogul and his much younger wife. The Bucholz place was run by a fourth-generation couple who, rumor had it, had acquired the ranch in a shady transaction that was still whispered about. The owners of the McElwee Land and Cattle Ranch were sisters who were notorious for committing hunting and fishing violations, bending the law to fit their needs, and being involved in large-scale criminal schemes, though they'd never been charged. Joe said he hated going out there.

Although Joe and Marybeth had lived in the valley for over twenty years, they still felt like newcomers when it came to the personalities, backgrounds, and conflicts that had erupted between the principals of the three ranches. What Marybeth had heard about the three ranches often had dark and gothic overtones. Rumors of water wars, cattle rustling, spouse-swapping, missing ranch hands, cut fences, and feuds spanning several generations.

MARYBETH WAS UPON Antler Creek Junction when she topped a hill and the swale with the roads cutting through it appeared before her. A green Game and Fish Department pickup sat squarely in the middle of the road where the three ranch road spurs began. At first glance, there was no hint which fork the truck was going to take before being shot at. Beside the pickup was the EMT van, its lights flashing. The law enforcement vehicles ahead of her sped to the location and surrounded it.

The scene before her made her take in a sharp breath and hold it. Her heart raced and her mouth went dry.

She followed the LE vehicles to the junction and parked away from them. No one seemed to notice her back there.

Marybeth climbed out of her car and hugged herself tightly against the icy wind. Her eyes teared up from both the sharp wind and what she saw as she walked toward the pickup, her hair whipping around her face. The sheriff's deputies, a town cop, and a state trooper had already emerged from their vehicles to jog to the scene.

It was Joe's truck. Clearly stenciled on the side panel was GF-10, his call signal. As if to underscore her terrible realization, their black Lab, Biscuit, appeared at the back of the pickup frantically hopping up and down. Marybeth knew she did that when she was scared or stressed-out. Biscuit had likely been in the cab when it happened and she hoped the dog wouldn't be forever traumatized.

The windshield was shattered and had turned white with bullet impacts, but the glass had held together. There were three large holes in the glass on the driver's side, as well as concave dents in the hood and side doors that were clearly made by bullets. Two of the holes were centered at eye level to a driver.

EMTs huddled around the driver's side. They were shouting and moving quickly. One of them motioned to the driver of the EMT van to bring a stretcher. She heard the word "stat."

As she neared the pickup, Marybeth felt as if her soul were leaving her body and hovering above her and that she was taking everything in through the eyes of a dispassionate third party. It was all so surreal.

Then she felt a firm grip on her shoulder.

"Ma'am," a deputy she didn't recognize said, "I don't think you're supposed to be here."

The deputy looked as young as her daughters. He was trying to grow a mustache. His cheeks were flushed.

"I'm Marybeth Pickett," she said, her voice flat. "That's my husband's truck."

He winced at that. "Please don't get in the way of the medical professionals."

"Why can't I see him?" she asked.

The deputy shook his head. He was at a loss for words.

Deputy Frank Carroll approached her. He had been at the pickup and his face was ashen. He had a tough time meeting her eyes at first.

"It's Joe, isn't it?" she asked.

He nodded that it was.

"Is he dead?"

"Not yet," Carroll said. "The EMTs said there's a faint pulse. They've already called for a Life Flight helicopter. They're going to fly him straight to Billings and bypass Twelve Sleep County Hospital."

"Why? How bad is it?"

"Marybeth," Carroll said with empathy, "they said he's been hit at least twice. They stopped the bleeding, but . . . the worst is that it appears he's been shot in the head."

As he said it, Carroll touched his index finger to the middle of his forehead. Marybeth felt her legs wobble. The unknown deputy reached under her arms to keep her standing.

"I'm going with him," she said. "But first I need to text our daughters."

Carroll ordered the younger deputy to put Biscuit into his patrol vehicle and deliver the dog to the Pickett home.

Airborne, with the Twelve Sleep River meandering through snow-choked hayfields below them, Marybeth reached under the sheet and grasped Joe's hand. He didn't respond.

Plastic bags of fluid were suspended above him and fed into both arms. She could see only the bottom half of his face because his head was wrapped in thick bandages. Joe's lips were parted and he breathed softly.

They'd been accompanied on the flight by an EMT, who sat on a stool on the other side of the gurney and kept a close eye on the monitor apps on his iPad.

"Where exactly was he hit in the head?" Marybeth asked him.

"I don't know exactly, ma'am."

"I mean, was he grazed or . . ."

"I'm sorry. I don't know."

Deputy Carroll was also on the flight. He was crowded into the rear of the compartment near Joe's feet.

"Did you locate the hunter who called it in?" she asked.

"I didn't get a name," Carroll said. "Whoever it was, was gone when we got there."

"Gone? Where did he go? There's only one road out and we were all on it."

Carroll shrugged.

She said, "That means the hunter probably went to one of the three ranches. I wonder which one?"

"We'll find out," Carroll said. It was obvious he hadn't thought that far. Then: "Do you have any idea which ranch Joe was headed out to this morning?"

"No, you already asked that. I know he's had business with all of them over the years. But if I were to guess, I'd guess it was the Mac Ranch."

"Why them?"

"They're poachers and it's hunting season," she said.

"I'll call the sheriff," Carroll said, pulling his phone out of his breast pocket. He looked at it and said, "Crap, I don't have a cell signal up here."

He yelled across Joe's body to the front of the chopper. "Captain, how long before we land in Billings?"

"Twenty-three minutes," the pilot responded.

Marybeth looked at Joe and stroked his chin gently. She prayed to God he had that long.

THEY'D FIRST MET in college at the University of Wyoming in Laramie. Thirty years ago, but Marybeth could remember it as if it had just happened.

Although Joe said he'd been well aware of Marybeth for the entire school year and they'd even been in a couple of classes together, she had to honestly admit that she'd never noticed *him*. It was an anecdote that he brought up from time to time, but always with a wry smile.

Back then, Marybeth was popular, good-looking (she was told), and on track to graduate and move on to law school. She was invited to all the parties and events, and her sorority was located in one of the finest and largest Victorian-era buildings on campus. Her life was a swirl of highly structured obligations and social events overseen by her mother, Missy, who had been on her second husband at the time. Missy could keep close track of her daughter because Loren, the stepfather, was on the board of trustees at the state's only university.

Joe entered Marybeth's life the night after the Wyoming Cowboys football team upset the mighty Brigham Young University Cougars during a night game at War Memorial Stadium. Students had charged the field after the game and tore down the goalposts, although Marybeth had remained in the stands with her boyfriend, Colin Hughes, and her sorority sisters. But they'd joined in with the crowd as the students hoisted the hardware and paraded it into downtown Laramie to the Buckhorn Bar.

After the wild celebration at the Buckhorn and too many red Solo cups of Coors, they all wound up at a rambling rental house in West Laramie packed with students. Marybeth couldn't recall for sure how she got there.

One of the residents of the house, a handsome but slick fifth-year senior nicknamed Cooter had pinned her against a cinder-block–and–board bookcase. Cooter was the son of a well-known rancher and politician from Jackson Hole, and he was the kind of boy Missy wanted Marybeth to end up with. When Marybeth turned away from him, he jammed his tongue into her ear and told her that a lot of girls really liked that.

She didn't. But when she looked frantically at the crowd for Colin to come to her rescue, she saw him furtively glance away and make his way to the keg in the next room. Cooter was bigger and stronger than Colin, and it *was* his house, but . . .

That's when she noticed that there were now three of them leaning against the bookcase: Cooter, Marybeth, and a dark-haired student of medium height and build. The boy said to Cooter, "If you don't leave her alone, things are going to get western around here."

Cooter scoffed and glared at him. He said, "Who the hell are you?"

"Name's Joe Pickett."

She was struck by his demeanor. He was calm but intensely focused on Cooter, who stood a head taller.

Marybeth braced for a fight that didn't come. Instead, Cooter stepped away from her and laughed at Joe Pickett. Joe didn't react in any way, which apparently unnerved Cooter.

Cooter said, "Later" to Marybeth, then rejoined the crowd in his front room.

When she turned to her new acquaintance, Joe breathed a visible sigh of relief and said, "That went better than I thought it might."

She asked, "Who *are* you, Joe Pickett?"

And he shrugged in response and replied, "Nobody special, I guess."

Missy was on her third husband, marrying up each time, selecting her next target based on his prominence and net wealth, when Joe asked Marybeth to marry him. It was on a dinner date at the Cavalryman Steakhouse and he'd downed two strong bourbons before he could screw up the courage to ask. They'd been exclusive for only seven months.

She'd surprised both Joe and herself by accepting. Missy was shocked most of all, and she accused her daughter of doing it out of spite. Missy found Joe ordinary and unimpressive, having researched the broken family he'd come from in northern Wyoming. The news sent Colin Hughes into a tailspin, only later to reemerge as a prominent real estate executive in Cheyenne who was accused by a series of babysitters of inappropriate behavior.

Missy referred to her son-in-law as "Average Joe" and she'd despaired when he got a job with the Wyoming Game and Fish Department as the lowest-ranked game warden in the state. As the Picketts moved from district to district and Joe moved up in badge numbers and seniority, Marybeth gave up the idea of continuing her education to be a lawyer. Instead, she took local jobs as an accountant, a business adviser, and eventually a librarian. Missy saw it all as abject failure and "settling."

Marybeth saw falling for Joe as the best decision of her life.

When the family eventually included three stong-willed and independent daughters, and their situation in the Saddlestring District stabilized with Joe as the longtime game warden, Marybeth had no regrets.

SHE LOOKED AT her watch. It was fourteen more minutes to Billings.

"How am I supposed to get home?" Deputy Carroll suddenly asked Marybeth. It had apparently just occurred to him that he'd left his SUV at Antler Creek Junction.

"I don't know," Marybeth said. "I'm sure you'll figure out something."

"When are you going back?" he asked her.

Marybeth shook her head. She had no idea.

CHAPTER THREE

DORN PEDDY AND James Dale O'Bryan were the shooters, and they'd carried out the ambush at nine thirty-seven that morning. It had gone without a hitch. A few minutes after ten, they'd returned to their cache on the shadowed side of a rocky hillside that overlooked Antler Creek Junction in the distance. The ATV they'd used to access the location was parked over the hill out of view from the road.

Peddy was a large man with wispy ginger hair and acne-scarred cheeks. He had broad shoulders and big hands with stubby, tobacco-stained fingers. He was wheezing from the long hike back to the cache from the ambush location.

O'Bryan had a thin, ferret-like face and slicked-back black hair streaked with gray. He was shorter than Peddy by six inches, and was missing his ring and little fingers on his left hand, the result of an accident involving improvised explosives years before when he worked for a homicidal mob boss in Albuquerque. Back then, he was known as "Hillbilly Jimmy D." because he was from

Arkansas originally. O'Bryan considered himself more careful and cautious than Peddy, who, it seemed to him, was irrationally confident in his own abilities, but inherently reckless. Peddy was the wrong man to set up and execute the ambush, in O'Bryan's opinion. Although there was no doubt Peddy was proficient with firearms and his lethal abilities, he was too cocky.

Nevertheless, O'Bryan had followed Peddy's directives that morning, and everything had gone smoothly. Except, he thought, for one nagging detail.

"We should have checked the body before hightailing it up here," O'Bryan said. "We should have made sure he was dead."

"He was dead," Peddy declared, his face reddening. "I know where I aimed and I know where I hit him. I've got no fucking doubts about that at all."

"Still . . ."

Peddy glared at O'Bryan and his face flushed further. "How would it look if we was caught standing down there in the middle of the road with black rifles, staring into the cab of the pickup? If some ranch hand or tourist drove up? That would be a fucking disaster. No, we needed to get the hell out of there."

O'Bryan let it go. He'd learned not to argue with "Dorn of the Mountains," as Peddy liked to call himself. The name came from a book written by Zane Grey, apparently. O'Bryan had never heard of it and he doubted Peddy had actually read it.

PEDDY HAD STASHED a large canvas duffel bag beside the gnarled trunk of a cedar tree that held tight to the gritty soil. He pulled out the bag, unzipped it, and removed two bulging white kitchen garbage bags and set them aside. Then he unslung the scoped Bushmaster .450 semiautomatic rifle chambered in .284 Winchester rounds from his shoulder and slid it into the bag. O'Bryan did the same after making sure there wasn't a round in the chamber.

"Did you get all your brass?" Peddy asked while digging into his front pocket for the spent cartridges he'd retrieved. He tossed them into the duffel as well.

"I'm pretty sure I got all of 'em," O'Bryan said.

Peddy glared at O'Bryan. "You *think* you got them all? How many times did you shoot?"

"Seven, I think," O'Bryan said. "It happened fast."

"How many spent cartridges do you have?"

O'Bryan dug a handful out of his pocket and counted them. "Seven."

"You're sure you only shot seven times?"

"Pretty sure, I think."

"Let's hope you got that right, fuckwad."

O'Bryan's face reddened and he glared at Peddy. "Leave me alone, asshole."

"We gotta do this right," Peddy said.

In a huff, O'Bryan bent down and snatched his rifle out of the duffel bag. He removed the fifteen-round extended magazine and thumbed the remaining live cartridges out one by one. There were eight of them.

"I was right in the first place," he said with triumph.

"We gotta do this right or we don't get paid," Peddy repeated.

"This isn't my first rodeo," O'Bryan grumbled while holding up his hand with the missing fingers.

THEY METHODICALLY BRUSHED snow off their clothes and then stripped down and threw each item of the tactical clothing they'd worn into the canvas bag. The cold wind produced goose bumps on their bare skin, and O'Bryan hopped from one foot to the other to try and keep warm.

"Wipe yourself down," Peddy said, handing O'Bryan a handful of antiseptic wet wipes from a container. "Get all that GSR off your hands and face."

"Yeah, yeah," O'Bryan said. He ran the squares over his skin and tossed the wadded-up remains into the bag. As he did, he looked up over Peddy's shoulder and said, "Who the fuck is *that*?"

Peddy's head snapped around. A man with a rifle on his shoulder was in the process of approaching the green Game and Fish pickup they'd just shot up. The scene of the shooting was about five hundred yards away. It was too far to clearly see the hunter's face. The man was slim and dressed in camo clothing. He wore a blaze-orange cap.

"Who is that guy?" O'Bryan asked again.

"Fuck if I know," Peddy said. "I didn't see him before."

"Where is his vehicle?"

"How would I know that?" Peddy said, irritated. He swept his arm out to indicate the horizon to the west. "This is all public land before you get to the junction. He could be parked anywhere out there."

The two of them stood there, nearly naked, looking in the distance at a strange hunter who had appeared out of nowhere. The man cautiously circled the green pickup, then approached it and peered into the driver's-side window and quickly stepped away. The hunter held his hand up to his face in a motion that was unmistakable.

"Oh shit," O'Bryan said. "He's making a call."

"That's not good," Peddy said.

"Do you think he saw us?"

"I don't know. I hope to hell he didn't." Then: "We need to take him out." As Peddy said it, he was bending back over the duffel bag and hastily retrieving his rifle.

"That would be a hell of a shot at this range," O'Bryan said. "You probably can't hit him."

"Bullshit—I'm gonna try it," Peddy said. "I'm rock-solid up to eight hundred yards."

O'Bryan made a skeptical face at that, but he didn't say anything and Peddy didn't see it.

Peddy said, "We can't leave any witnesses. If he saw us, we can't have them looking for a couple of guys with high-powered black rifles wearing tactical gear."

O'Bryan fretted with a worried look on his face while Peddy dropped to his knees so he could aim and fire from a prone position. When Peddy flopped forward, he recoiled immediately and grimaced.

"Ouch—fuck," Peddy said, rolling onto his back. "I laid down in cactus."

In fact, O'Bryan could see a dozen or so thin cactus needles protruding from Peddy's chest and white belly.

"Throw me them clothes bags," Peddy ordered while he plucked out most of the cactus needles and tossed them aside. O'Bryan did, and Peddy slid the bags beneath his body to cushion it from the cactus plants. Then he leaned forward into the rifle scope.

"I'm not so sure about this," O'Bryan said. "We don't know who he's calling. Maybe he's calling his wife."

"Shut up."

"I'm freezing and you're lying on top of my new clothes."

Peddy didn't respond. O'Bryan watched the man steady his aim and go still.

The boom of the rifle was snatched up quickly in the wind. O'Bryan watched as a plume of dirt erupted from the hill on the other side of the pickup. The impact was at least three feet to the left and a foot high from where the hunter stood.

"You missed him bad," O'Bryan said.

"Goddamn wind," Peddy spat.

The hunter didn't appear to know what had just happened. He lowered the phone from his ear and looked around, apparently confused.

Peddy fired again. The second shot was wider to the left, although it was approximately head-high to the hunter. The man definitely saw the dirt kick up on the opposite hillside this time, and he ducked and started running back up the road.

Peddy fired four more times. The bullets blew up mini-geysers of earth and rocks all around the hunter, but none of them found their mark. The targeted man ran up the road until he vanished behind a small hillock between the cache and the pickup.

Peddy rolled over again and got to his feet. He was seething.

"Should we follow him, or what?" he asked.

"Let him go," O'Bryan said. "He doesn't know who was shooting at him, and he didn't know where the shots came from. We just need to get the hell out of this valley."

Peddy agreed without saying so, and both of them went into action. They threw on the clothes that had been stored in the plastic bags as quickly as they could.

As planned, they dressed as local ranch hands, or at least what Peddy had decided local ranch hands looked like. The idea was to blend in with the locals if anyone spotted them. They dressed in snap-button western yoke shirts, Wranglers, lace-up outfitter boots, belts with buckles, and Carhartt barn coats. Peddy handed O'Bryan a wide-brimmed cowboy hat that was at least two sizes too large for his head.

"I'm not wearing this," O'Bryan said. "I'll look ridiculous."

Peddy snapped, "*Wear the fucking hat*," and grasped O'Bryan by his collar. O'Bryan didn't snap back, although he was furious. Instead, he wrenched himself away and stuffed a red bandana into the sweatband of the hat to expand it and he crammed the hat on and vowed to himself that he wouldn't forget this latest humiliation.

As THEY TRUDGED over the hill carrying the duffel bag, Peddy retrieved a disposable cell phone and punched the only number that was stored in it. O'Bryan listened to Peddy's side of the conversation while holding his hat on with his free hand so it wouldn't blow away.

"We got him," Peddy said. "It's done."

Then: "I said we got him. It's probably hard to hear me with this damned Wyoming wind."

Then, after a beat: "That's right. No problems, no complications at all. It was as smooth as a baby's butt. Just as I planned it."

After Peddy signed off, he said to O'Bryan, "We made the boss very happy. Now let's go get paid."

"What about that hunter?" O'Bryan said. "You didn't mention him."

"And you aren't going to, either," Peddy said, turning and fixing O'Bryan with a murderous glare. "You got that?"

O'Bryan nodded, but in his mind he added the latest insult from Peddy to his private vengeance list.

"We should have checked the body," O'Bryan said as they approached the ATV. Peddy tossed the duffel bag into the back of the vehicle and settled in behind the wheel.

"Would you fucking shut up about that?" Peddy said, reaching for the key.

O'Bryan didn't respond, and he quietly added another item to his list.

CHAPTER FOUR

"FIRST, MRS. PICKETT, I think it's important that you're aware of the worst-case scenarios that we're dealing with here," said Dr. Kelly Ralston in the ICU waiting room.

"Please, call me Marybeth."

"All right, Marybeth, I don't believe in sugarcoating anything, and I want you to be fully informed so you can make the best decisions in regard to your husband and his medical care."

"That doesn't sound good."

"*Then* we can talk about the best-case scenarios."

Marybeth had just returned from the women's restroom down the hall, where she'd wanted to be alone for a few minutes. The helicopter ride had been stressful, and she'd spent the entire flight watching the monitors attached to Joe that displayed his heartbeat and oxygen levels, all the time praying that he continued to breathe. Joe had not regained consciousness, although she thought for a moment that she felt a squeeze from his hand, whether involuntary or not.

Inside the restroom, she'd tamed her windblown hair from the helicopter blade wash after landing on the roof a half hour before. Then she wept uncontrollably over the sink. Her sobs were so violent and racking for a few minutes that her legs felt weak. She'd been scared to look up and see her face in the mirror.

Finally, the emotions ebbed and she was able to dry her tears and clean off the streaks of mascara that had coursed down her cheeks.

Dr. Ralston, the head neurosurgeon at St. John's Hospital in Billings and the primary reason Joe was flown there, was waiting for her when she emerged. Dr. Ralston was in her midfifties and she was petite and thin-boned, with raven-black hair and striking azure eyes. She wore green scrubs, and a pair of readers hung from a chain around her neck. Her demeanor was direct and all business. Marybeth instantly liked her.

"Let's sit," the doctor said.

When they were settled on opposite ends of an uncomfortable metal-framed couch, Ralston leaned forward and placed her small hand on Marybeth's and looked into her eyes.

"There are a few things you need to know because medicine is all about percentages," she said. "The first and most critical is that gunshot wounds to the head are fatal about seventy to ninety percent of the time without emergency room trauma care." She let that sink in before continuing.

"For victims who survive the initial trauma, about fifty percent die in the emergency room. Those are not good numbers, but they're accurate numbers. There are so many victims of gun violence in the United States and so many emergency room studies out there that I can tell you this with absolute statistical certainty. Our numbers here at St. John's aren't much better."

Marybeth felt as though icicles were being stabbed into her chest, and she took a ragged breath and held it.

"I don't want to give you false hope," Dr. Ralston said. "I don't do that to the loved ones of those who suffer traumatic brain injury. But . . ."

The word hung there until Marybeth repeated it. "But?"

"We may have some factors working for us."

"Which are?" Marybeth asked.

"He's not dead, for one thing. He's alive. He had very good care on the ground, and that probably saved his life for the time being. They put immediate pressure on the wound and stopped the bleeding. They also addressed a bullet wound to his left shoulder. I couldn't help but notice bullet wound scars on his body already. It looks like he's lived an . . . adventurous life."

Marybeth nodded. "He's a Wyoming game warden."

"Are numerous bullet wounds common for game wardens?"

"Not really," Marybeth said. "Joe's special."

Then she let out her breath and asked, "How bad is the damage to his brain?"

Dr. Ralston leaned back and her hand slipped away from Marybeth's, but not in a way that was dismissive. She said, "It's too early to tell a lot of things. There are so many variables to consider at this point. We're doing a CT scan of his head now to determine the extent of the damage. We don't yet know what his level of consciousness is, and that will be determined by something we call the Glasgow Coma Scale. And we don't yet know the degree of his brain stem neurological function.

"Like I said, there are so many variables, like the location of the bullet entry, the areas of the brain damaged by the trajectory, what kind of bullet is in there, where it's lodged, et cetera."

"When will you know all of this?"

"Soon. When the CT scan is complete, I'll leave you and go do a full diagnosis."

Marybeth said, "You said bullet entry, but not exit. Are you saying it's still in there?"

"That's exactly what I'm saying," Dr. Ralston said. "That can be a good thing. It matters that there aren't two wounds. Often, the exit wound causes much more damage than the entry because often the bullet expands on impact and mushrooms in shape, so the exit is much bigger. It also might mean that the velocity of the bullet wasn't as high-powered as it could have been from, say, a hunting rifle. But it all depends on where the bullet traveled through the brain before it stopped. Or where it is located right now."

"Will he recover?" Marybeth asked. "Will he be able to use his mind if he does?"

"I can't answer either one of those questions with any certainty," Dr. Ralston said.

Marybeth looked away, trying not to cry again.

"For now," the doctor said, "with your permission, we'd like to induce a medical coma. The purpose of the procedure is threefold: to allow your husband to rest, to reduce his blood pressure, and to hopefully stave off excess swelling of the brain caused by the trauma. In effect, we'll be tricking his body not to rush blood to his brain to try and heal it too quickly. In order for us to do this, you'll have to sign off on some paperwork that gives me permission to proceed with an emergency hemicraniectomy and an external ventricular drain."

"A medically induced coma?" Marybeth said. "I'm familiar with it."

She didn't feel the need to recount how April, their middle daughter, had once been put into a coma after she was seriously injured.

Dr. Ralston said, "You don't have to sign off on it. I'm not intending to apply pressure on you. Some family members don't agree, and that's okay. They prefer to let nature take its course."

"If it was your husband, what would you do?"

"If it was my husband," Dr. Ralston said with a mischievous grin, "I might let nature take its course. But since it's *your* husband and you obviously want to give him the best chance to survive, I'd sign the papers."

Then: "I shouldn't have said that. I'm in the midst of a nasty divorce."

"I'm sorry to hear that," Marybeth said.

"If you agree, we'll have the anesthesiologist administer propofol," Dr. Ralston said. "No drug is ever one hundred percent safe or foolproof, but we use that drug every day in the operating room."

"How long will he be in a coma?"

"Again, we don't know yet. It could be hours, days, or weeks. I've read of instances where the coma was kept up for six months. It'll depend on whether the swelling recedes and how much the metabolism of his brain has been altered. If the brain heals and the swelling goes down, we can reduce or even halt the propofol."

"I'll sign the form," Marybeth said.

Dr. Ralston acknowledged her decision with a curt nod. Then she stood up and said, "I need to get back to the OR now. The CT scan should be done. I'll keep you updated."

"Thank you."

Dr. Ralston's expression softened when she said, "There's a list of hotels at the nurses' station. You should find a nice one and book a room. It may be a few days, if you can do that."

"I'll worry about that later," Marybeth said.

After Dr. Ralston departed, Marybeth retrieved her phone from her purse. There were dozens of texts from friends, her staff, and most of all from her daughters. They all wanted to know what was happening.

She tried to summarize what Dr. Ralston had told her without putting too much spin on it either way. She first sent a quick text to her staff saying Joe was injured but alive and that she wouldn't be back in the office right away. Then she began to create a text message to send to their daughters. It took her a few moments to gather her thoughts and put them into words.

TO: Sheridan, April, Lucy

Your dad is alive. He was shot twice, once in the head. We're at St. John's Hospital in Billings and I just spoke with the surgeon. They don't know how severe the damage is yet, but they should know soon. I'll keep you updated on what I hear. I trust the doctor.

Pray for him, as I will.

I love you,

Mom

Marybeth reread the message before sending it and she made two changes. She replaced I love you with We love you. And she added and Dad to her sign-off.

It was important, she thought, that their daughters knew they were still communicating to them as a team, even if Joe was unaware of it at the moment.

Then she pressed Send.

SHE WAS SHOCKED a few minutes later to see middle daughter April pushing through the double doors into the waiting room. As she entered, April held her phone out in front of her at eye level.

"Well, thank *God* he's okay," April said. "It was killing me not to know."

"He's not okay yet," Marybeth said, rising to greet her. "But he's alive."

"I told him a while back to quit getting shot," April said, her nostrils flaring. "I wish for once that he'd listen to me."

"We all do," Marybeth responded. She embraced her daughter and April hugged back. April wasn't an immediate hugger like her two sisters were.

"Where is he now?" April asked when they separated.

"In the OR. They're inducing a coma to prevent swelling in his brain."

April said knowingly, "Dr. April was going to suggest that."

"It's good to see you," Marybeth said, wiping at her eyes again. "But what are you doing here?"

"We just happened to be in town when your first text came

up," April said. "We were surveilling an asshole who is cheating on his wife and kids."

"We?"

April turned and held the door open for an older woman in her midforties to enter. The woman was plain-looking and a bit overweight, but she had intelligent eyes, Marybeth thought. And she admired the tooled cowboy boots she wore over her jeans.

"This is Cassie Dewell, my boss," April said.

"It's a pleasure to meet you," Cassie said as she held out her hand to Marybeth.

"Likewise," Marybeth said. "April has told us she loves her job."

"I like nailing assholes," April said to her mother. "You know that about me."

Marybeth nodded. "April can be a little rough around the edges at times."

"I'm aware of that, which is just one reason I like her. But she's also a very hard worker and she's like a dog with a bone when she gets an assignment," Cassie said. "I'd say she was very well raised."

"Thank you," Marybeth said. Then: "April has told us so much about you, I feel like I know you. I thought you didn't take on domestic cheating cases."

"We rarely do," Cassie said. "But when April heard about the story, she talked me into taking it on. That's what brought us from Bozeman to Billings this week."

"They have three young children and his wife is dying of brain cancer," April said with a sneer. "And the jerk is practically living at a titty joint outside of town. But the second I saw your message, we got here as soon as we could."

"I'm glad you did," Marybeth said.

"So what happened?" April asked. "Tell me—tell us—everything."

April had grown up some since Marybeth saw her the previous summer. She'd gotten a little taller, and was now four inches taller than Marybeth. April had always been slim and flinty, but it was obvious she'd been working out and was now harder and more fit than she'd ever been. Marybeth could tell that immediately when she hugged her.

April had also changed her look. Her tawny hair was streaked with magenta and she'd shaved the right side of her head into a buzz cut and added a few more silver earrings and a thin septum ring that Marybeth instantly disapproved of. She still dressed in flashy cowgirl clothing, including a big silver belt buckle. That, and a new tattoo of the Wyoming bucking horse logo with the rider on a trout instead of a bronco on her forearm.

After the three of them sat down, Marybeth recounted all the details of the morning. April listened intently and so did Cassie, who hung back in a faux-leather chair so as not to intrude on the family interaction. As Marybeth talked, April reached up and removed the septum ring from her nose, dropping it into the breast pocket of her shirt.

"I could tell it was distracting you," she said. "Go on."

". . . So we won't know more about his condition until after the CT scan, apparently," Marybeth concluded. "We're waiting for Dr. Ralston to come out and let us know her verdict."

"Shit," April said. "This sucks. It sounds like it could go either way."

"I choose to think the best," Marybeth said. "I'll adjust that if I have to."

"So who is responsible?" April asked. "Who did this?"

Marybeth shook her head as she said, "I've been racking my brain all morning for obvious suspects, but I'm coming up empty. As you know, your dad doesn't talk a lot about the things he's working on until they really heat up and he needs my help. As far as I know, he was just doing regular game warden stuff."

"Do you know why he was out on Antler Creek Road?" April asked.

"No. I'm guessing it had something to do with McElwee Land and Cattle, since they've been implicated in a poaching ring in the past. But I simply don't know. He wasn't dispatched out there on a call, so whatever he was doing, he was doing it on his own."

"Is that unusual?" Cassie asked. "I used to be a deputy sheriff, so I know what sheriff's department employees do. But I'm not all that familiar with game wardens."

"It's not unusual at all," Marybeth said. "Game wardens tend to keep their own counsel. They operate very freely out in the field. Not until they're building a case or they need some backup do they reach out to headquarters or anyone else. Joe is typical that way."

"He's actually worse," April said. "My dad tends to get involved in situations that most law enforcement types would try to avoid at all costs. You wouldn't believe some of the things he's been in the middle of over the years."

"You've told me about some of them," Cassie said. "He does sound like an extraordinary man."

"He is," Marybeth said. "Even when it puts him in danger or pulls his family into it at times."

"And that's why we need to figure out who did this," April said. "We need to find the asshole who did this and go after him and put him down."

"*Whoa*," Cassie said, holding her hands palms-out in a show of caution. "Calm down, girl."

April looked away.

As she did, Cassie produced a spiral pad from her shoulder bag and opened it to a fresh page. She handed it to Marybeth along with a pen and asked her to sketch the crime scene as if from above.

"This will help me visualize it," Cassie said.

Marybeth started with a line through the middle of the page that ended about an inch from the right edge. At that ending point, she drew straight lines going north, proceeding straight, and down to the left. On the upper side of the horizontal line she wrote "sagebrush foothills," and on the left she jotted "rolling hills." She sketched an oblong shape just in front of the junction of the lines.

"That's his truck," she said. "The road to the north goes to the Double Diamond Ranch, the middle one proceeds on to the Bucholz place, and the southern route goes to the Mac Ranch."

Cassie studied the drawing.

"So there's no way to determine which way he was headed?" she asked.

"Not from what I could tell," Marybeth said. "He could have taken any one of those three roads."

Cassie paused for a long time, obviously sorting out what she'd just seen and heard from Marybeth. Then she asked, "What happened to the RP? Sorry, the reporting party. You didn't mention him again."

"He was gone when the EMTs arrived," Marybeth said. "They said it was strange that no one was around when they got to Joe's truck."

"Don't you find that odd?"

"I asked about it a couple of times, but no one knows who called or where he went afterward."

"How many bullet holes were in his pickup?" Cassie asked. "Not that I expect you to have counted them, but I wonder if any of the first responders brought that up?"

"There were a lot of bullet holes," Marybeth said. "Several in the windshield, but also a few in the hood and in the front fenders. I'd guess at least ten, maybe more."

Cassie nodded, then said, "That may suggest more than one shooter. Especially if the shots came from different angles. And if there was more than one shooter, it suggests—"

"An ambush," April said, finishing the sentence.

"Possibly," Cassie said.

April warmed to the theory. "If Dad bumbled upon a couple of poachers in the act or something like that, it's possible that the bad guys reacted by firing their rifles at the Game and Fish pickup. It's *possible.* But that's a crazy overreaction. Most violations are misdemeanors. Game violators rarely get the book thrown at them and they know it. So why would they react like that? It makes no sense."

Marybeth agreed with April. But . . .

"No, this sounds more like an ambush," April said. "Like they knew he was coming and they were waiting for him. And I'll bet that whoever did this was from one of those three ranches out there. I'd say that's where we start."

"We need a lot more information before making that assumption," Cassie said. She said it in a tone that suggested to Marybeth that Cassie was used to dialing April down.

Cassie said, "There are a lot of facts we need to find out before we can go much further. Otherwise, it's all speculation. We need to know if any spent casings were found in the area, or any other clues that would indicate where the shots came from. We need to know if there is a telltale blood trail or gut pile out in the field where poachers might have been. We need to know who the reporting party was and where he is now. And we need to know why Joe was out there on that particular road this morning. Marybeth, did the doctor say when Joe might be able to talk to us?"

"She doesn't know yet," Marybeth said. "And we don't know if he'll ever be able . . ." She couldn't finish.

"We're hoping for the best, right?" April said, moving close to Marybeth and dangling an arm around her. "Isn't that what you said?"

"WHO IS IN charge of the investigation?" Cassie asked after Marybeth had recovered and looked up.

"I assume it'll be our new sheriff," Marybeth said. "His name is Steve Sondergard and he just got elected. I don't know if he's even moved into his office yet."

"*Great,*" April said with derision. "Another new sheriff of Twelve Sleep County."

"He seems to be okay," Marybeth said. "I met him once and he came across as honest and dedicated."

April rolled her eyes, then fixed them on Cassie. "Most of our sheriffs have been fuckups. You know the type."

Cassie nodded. "I worked for several of them. But I also worked with some really good men."

"How can we trust a guy who hasn't even found his desk yet?" April asked. "No, this is something we need to investigate ourselves."

"April," Cassie said, "you know I'm tied up here right now. As much as I wish I could, I can't drop everything and go to Wyoming."

"That's fine."

"Then what are you saying?" Cassie asked.

April said, "I'm saying I need to take that vacation time I've built up that you keep bugging me about. And I need to get my sisters in on this."

"Hold it, April," Marybeth said. "You shouldn't involve them, unless—"

"They've already agreed to it," April said, holding up her phone and cutting off her mother. "I've been texting them. They're gonna meet me in Saddlestring."

April's eyes blazed when she said, "We have three ranch families to investigate. We're going to find out which one of them did this to Dad."

As April made her vow, Marybeth's phone lit up with a call from Wyoming governor Spencer Rulon.

"Yes, Governor?"

"What in the hell happened up there?" Rulon asked. "I just heard. Is he okay?"

"It looks like he was ambushed, but we don't know much more than that. Right now, he's being examined in the Billings hospital. That's where I am."

"*Well, goddamnit,*" Rulon roared. "They better take good care of him in Montana, or there will be hell to pay."

"The doctors are supposed to be good out here."

"What can I do?" Rulon asked. "Is there anything I can do? Do you want me to send up the state plane and fly him down here to Cheyenne?"

"I don't think that's a good idea right now," she said. "We were lucky he survived the trip north."

"Keep me on speed dial," Rulon said. "If there's anything . . ."

"Thank you."

"We can't let anything happen to Joe," the governor said. "He's stubborn as hell at times, but I need him. He's one of the good ones."

"I agree."

"I'll pray for him. We all will."

"Thank you, sir."

CHAPTER FIVE

Four Weeks Before

WYOMING GAME WARDEN Joe Pickett sat on the knob of a brushy hill twelve miles out of town with his pickup running and the heater humming and his black Labrador Biscuit's head in his lap. It was four forty-five in the morning and he'd already been up for an hour and a half. He'd had two cups of coffee from his thermos and a breakfast of elk jerky and roasted cashews. He was watching a yearly ritual, an annual parade of dozens of hunters in their four-by-fours and recreational vehicles streaming up the state highway from Saddlestring toward the Bighorn Mountains in the dark. The line of vehicles stretched for miles.

"Get ready," he whispered to Biscuit. "Here they come."

It was opening day of the general elk-hunting season. Although he knew the hunters were probably hoping for snow in the mountains to better track their prey, it was cool and still and the temperature for the next week was supposed to be in the forties and fifties. He knew that he'd spend the next several months in the mountains, working from dawn until dusk, checking hunters for proper licenses, making sure regulations weren't violated, and dealing with situations that were unpredictable at best and sometimes bizarre.

There would be hundreds of hunters spread out over thousands of square miles, and then there would be Joe Pickett, the lone game warden of the Twelve Sleep District. His badge number was ten, meaning nine game wardens in the state had seniority, and forty had been on the job for fewer years. He wore a red uniform shirt with a pronghorn antelope patch on the shoulder and worn Wrangler jeans. His green pickup with the same logo on the driver's-side door was a Ford F-150 four-by-four. His battered cowboy hat was placed crown-down on the dashboard in front of him.

The sheer volume of potential problems almost overwhelmed him when he thought about it—so many hunters, so many guns, so many potential situations that could arise—so he didn't think about it. Instead, he took solace in the fact that he'd experienced over twenty "openers" in his long career thus far and somehow he'd survived.

THE SUN HADN'T yet peeked over the craggy western summits of the mountains when Joe's cell phone lit up on the dashboard and he reached for it. Clay Hutmacher Sr. was calling. Not a massive surprise.

Clay was the ranch foreman on the magnificent Double Diamond Ranch. No doubt, Joe thought, Clay was looking through his spotting scope as opening-day hunters were attempting to access the elk-rich private land of the Double D that stretched from the state highway to the top of Eagle Mountain. It happened every year, and when it did, Clay called Joe to complain about it.

"Joe Pickett," Joe said as he took the call. "What's up, Clay?"

"Hey, Joe," Clay responded. Joe immediately noted the strange tone in Clay's voice. The foreman sounded very down. "You're being summoned."

"Say again?"

"My boss wants to talk to you right away," Clay said. "Like this morning. He's flying back to Atlanta this afternoon."

"Clay, do you realize it's opening day of elk season?"

"I know that. But the boss doesn't care. He says he needs to speak to you."

Joe felt a flush of anger and he shuffled his position in the pickup and woke Biscuit.

A game warden's duties were divided into three broad categories: law enforcement, resource management, and public engagement. Landowner relations fell squarely into the public-engagement lane.

Michael Thompson was a hedge fund billionaire who had purchased the Double Diamond Ranch less than ten years before. With his very attractive younger wife, Brandy, he flew his jet back and forth to his headquarters in Atlanta. He'd retained Clay Hutmacher, the longtime foreman of the ranch, but had fired most everyone else during fits of pique. Most of the fired ranch hands were later rehired after Thompson cooled down and realized that the labor pool in the area was very shallow.

Thompson had recently started to dabble in Wyoming politics as a means to gain influence when it came to landowner-rights issues. He was headstrong and charismatic and Joe had already tangled with him several times.

Clay had lost his only son two years before when he was killed by a grizzly bear, and to Joe his old friend had also lost his drive, ambition, and his sense of humor. The Clay Joe once knew would have pushed back on a man like Thompson. But now Clay was both broken and subservient.

"Clay, I've got a few hundred elk hunters headed for the mountains right now. I'm sure Thompson can wait."

"He says it's important, Joe," Clay said, his voice pleading. "When he says something is important, it's my job to make sure that gets across."

Before Joe could respond, Clay said, "He also said to remind you that he's very close to several of the Game and Fish commissioners and he doesn't mind calling them up. Or, in this case, having *me* call them up."

"Are you really going to play this card, Clay?" Joe asked.

"*It's not me*," Clay Hutmacher said in a whisper.

The Wyoming Game and Fish Department was overseen by a board of commissioners who were appointed by the governor. If one or more of them were carrying water for Michael Thompson, Joe knew they could make his life miserable. On top of that, Thompson was a major donor to Governor Rulon, and the director of the agency was new to the job and considered a political animal who probably wouldn't hesitate to throw an individual game warden under the bus, even if he was number ten in seniority.

Still, Joe chafed at being put in a position where he was at the beck and call of a local ranch owner.

"I'll see what I can do," Joe said after a long pause. "I'll work my way in your direction, because that's what I was planning to do anyway. If I don't get into any situations or receive any callouts in the next hour, I might be able to get there. That's the most I can promise."

"Thank you, Joe," Clay said. "I hope it'll work out for your sake . . . and mine."

Joe punched off without saying goodbye.

RATHER THAN TAKE the quicker route west on the interstate highway, Joe spent the morning working his way in that direction using Antler Creek Road. He stopped at several hunting camps that had been set up on public Bureau of Land Management land to check the licenses and conservation stamps of both in-state and out-of-state hunters, and he'd inspected the hanging carcasses of both deer and elk to make sure they were tagged correctly, which they all were.

The hunters were uniformly chatty and accommodating, with the exception of one party of five from Pennsylvania, who immediately raised his suspicions. The hunters would not shake his hand or make eye contact at first, and they spent most of the time he was there staring at their boots. Although he didn't see any violations and the hunters were all legal, Joe made a note to himself to revisit the camp in a few days to try to find out what it was the party was hiding. He planned to use his best opening line on them, which was "I guess you know why I'm here." It was an inquiry that had worked time and time again and had produced all kinds of results, many not anticipated by him.

He confirmed his suspicions after leaving the hunting camp and parking his pickup over a hill and out of view of the Pennsylvania hunters. Joe activated a radio scanner installed beneath his dashboard and listened as someone asked, “Is he gone?”

The response, presumably from the camp, was “Yeah. I think so.”

“Did he find anything?”

“Nada.”

“Is it okay to come back now?”

“Give it a few minutes. Don’t worry, we won’t drink all the beer.”

Joe nodded to himself. He scrawled in his notebook that there were more than five hunters in the group and that the sixth bore special interest when he returned.

WHEN HE REACHED Antler Creek Junction, Joe took the northern spur. Almost immediately, he was struck by the number of **NO TRESPASSING** signs and written threats of prosecuting trespassers with the full weight of the law. One large sign was practically the size of a billboard, Joe thought. He didn’t recall seeing it before.

It read:

NO TRESPASSING.

No Hunting or Fishing Allowed Except by Permit.

Unless You’re Making an Authorized Delivery to the Ranch, Do NOT Get Out of Your Vehicle.

Patrolled by Air, Vehicle, and Foot.

Violators Will Be Prosecuted to the Full Extent of the Law.

We Stop at Nothing to Prosecute You for Any Violations.

Our Lawyers Will Beat Your Lawyers.

DOUBLE DIAMOND RANCH, LLC

As if in response to the message, Joe noted, someone had shot the sign multiple times with a rifle or pistol.

THE THOMPSON HOME was spectacular: three levels burrowed into the side of a mountain with huge eastern-facing windows and protruding decks on every floor. Sixty-foot spruce trees had been placed on the slopes next to the structure to help it blend into the alpine surroundings, and the eight-car parking garage was primarily underground and accessed by a circular driveway.

All of the infrastructure that made the Double D an actual working ranch was strategically hidden away from view from the Thompson house, including the foreman's home, outbuildings for the heavy equipment and ranch vehicles, and the airstrip used for Thompson's private Gulfstream jet.

Joe took the circular driveway and avoided the huge front entrance and parked near the garage, where Clay Hutmacher's ranch pickup was parked. Clay drove a light gray Ford Raptor with the name of the ranch stenciled on both front doors. Joe knew Clay had a small office inside. He told Biscuit to stay put because he knew from an earlier visit that Brandy Thompson was allergic to dogs.

As he climbed out of the cab and clamped on his hat, Joe passed by Clay's truck and glanced inside out of habit. There was a 12-gauge propped muzzle-down on the floor between the bench seats. It was a combat model, and not the over-under that Clay often used to shoot sporting clays. There was also a scoped .17 WSM bolt-action rifle next to it.

On the dashboard of Clay's pickup were several boxes of .17 Winchester Super Mag cartridges and four boxes of 12-gauge shells in four shot. The choice of guns and ammo was particularly interesting to Joe.

He knew that guns were simply tools on a ranch, and that they were chosen for specific purposes in mind. The .17 WSM was a lethal round used for varmint control. It could also take out a coyote or fox because of its velocity. But a multi-round pump-action combat shotgun shooting four- and six-shot shells? Unlike the sporting clay shells that contained an ounce of gunpowder and tiny eight-shot pellets, the rounds on the dashboard were heavier and designed for ducks or pheasants. And it wasn't duck or pheasant season yet.

It was then Joe noticed the sound of gently pulsing electronic music coming from somewhere above him. He looked up to see Brandy doing yoga on the third-floor veranda. She was wearing a tight black tank top and skintight black yoga pants. Brandy was blond and lithe and flexible. She'd no doubt seen him drive up, but didn't wave or look down.

"You'll freeze into a block of stone if you look at her for too long, believe me," Clay said with a wry grin. He came out of his office door and extended his hand. Joe shook it.

"How long have you had that new sign out on the road?" Joe asked.

"Couple of weeks."

"It's already been shot up," Joe said. "That'll happen when you overdo it."

"As if I didn't know that," Clay said. "I tried to tell Mr. Thompson it wasn't a great idea to piss off the locals."

"Yup," said Joe.

"He's waiting for you in the garage," Clay said. "Follow me, please."

Joe followed Clay down a flagstone pathway that led to an entrance near the wide garage doors. Before reaching for the door handle, Clay paused and turned to Joe. His eyes were sad, Joe thought.

"I've got to tell you," he said, "working for a billionaire cuts both ways, you know."

"What do you mean?"

Clay started to answer, but apparently thought better of it.

"Not now," Clay said. "Like I told you, he's waiting for you."

"What have you been going after with that seventeen-cal and that shotgun in your pickup?" Joe asked.

"Later," Clay said.

MICHAEL THOMPSON HAD eschewed several tricked-out pickups, a yellow Hummer H2, a battered Range Rover, and a Chevy Suburban for the four-passenger John Deere Gator that he piloted wildly down a gravel road, with Joe hanging on as his passenger. Clay had been left back in the garage.

The Gator had a roll bar and roof, but no windshield, and the cool fall air stung Joe's eyes, making them water.

Thompson was in his late sixties, and he was in great shape, Joe thought. The man was Ozempic-lean, with finely cut facial features, thick silver hair, and sharp blue eyes. His accent was a mixture of his New Jersey boyhood and the Buckhead neighborhood in Atlanta where his headquarters were located.

While Thompson whipped the Gator around the bottom of a sagebrush knoll three miles from his mountain home and Joe held on to a stabilizing bar so he wouldn't be thrown outside the vehicle, the rancher shouted, "What do you see before you, Joe?"

Around the knoll was a very scenic view of a vast wetlands bottom with a creek S-curving through it. The stream was choked by willows and buckbrush that were turning red and orange with the season. Multicolored fingers of aspen reached out toward the bottom land from the foothills, and black Angus cattle grazed like errant punctuation on the grassy floor of the valley.

"Antler Creek," Joe shouted back. "I see Antler Creek."

Thompson quickly decelerated and the Gator came to a halt. The engine puttered and he said, "Of course it's Antler Creek, for God's sake. But do you know what I see when I look at this valley?"

Joe shook his head.

"I see a big useless valley where I lose a ton of money every year. And you know what else I see out there? Especially when I look at all the sagebrush on the side of this knoll and on top of the benches?"

"What's that?"

"I see what your damned agency has deemed 'prime sage grouse habitat.'"

"Ah," Joe said. It was true. The sagebrush hills and flatlands on the Double D were the traditional home of four to six prominent leks, or gatherings of sage grouse during their mating season. Sage grouse, which were ungainly chicken-sized birds, had not been listed as endangered species in the Mountain West, but various interests in the state were very worried that it might happen. If so, the designation would adversely affect many kinds of future development.

"Now tell me if I'm wrong," Thompson said, "but my understanding is that if a businessman wanted to offer this valley you see before you as scenic parcels for second homes or, say, an upscale hunting or fishing lodge, a sign-off would be necessary to proceed. So the precious sage grouse could strut around once a year unimpeded. Am I hearing this correctly?"

"Since your ranch contains both state and federal parcels, like all the big ranches do, it would involve a sign-off of some kind," Joe said. "This really isn't my—"

"This is *my* ranch," Thompson said, interrupting Joe. "I bought and paid for it outright. But you're saying that in order to develop this little piece of it, I need to get the approval of a bunch of bureaucrats?"

"It's above my pay grade to say," Joe said. "Every situation is different."

"Ah, the refuge of every little bureaucrat," Thompson said with a sneer. "I know how these things go. I pay attention. If you're drilling an oil well, you get killed by the feds if a bald eagle gets harmed by the process in any way. But if you're putting up windmills, you can buy your way out of it and get 'take' permits to kill a bunch of bald eagles with no penalty at all. It's all who you know, and who knows you, and if what you're doing is politically correct, right?"

Joe flushed with anger. "Look, our agency has biologists and specialists in sage grouse. So does the state in other agencies. I can't sit here and tell you what you can do or what you can't do. What exactly is it that you want to put here, anyway?"

"That shouldn't matter to you or to anyone else," Thompson said. "That's my whole point. Now tell me, is it true that if I did want to develop a parcel out there that the local game warden would be involved?"

"Probably," Joe said.

"Finally, a straight answer," Thompson said with a flourish. "So you would be asked to weigh in?"

"Probably, yes."

"Now we're getting somewhere. I wasn't sure I believed it when Clay said the local game warden might help sway the powers that be. But that seems to be the case after all."

"I don't know how much sway I'd actually have," Joe said. "These decisions get political, and I try to avoid politics as much as I can."

"Haven't you been Spencer's gun-for-hire when he asks you to be?"

Joe looked away and said, "Yup. But not when it comes to political problems. Those I stay away from, and he knows it."

Joe found it significant that Thompson referred to second-time Wyoming governor Spencer Rulon by his first name. It was a tell.

"Oh, I know your reputation, Joe Pickett," Thompson said. "Spencer has a very high opinion of you."

"Except when he doesn't," Joe said.

Thompson laughed at that for a few seconds, then bore back down. "If you weighed in on my side, it might really make a difference. A big difference. You could be very helpful."

"I'd need to know a lot more about the situation," Joe said. "And you'd need to be straight with me."

"So tell me, game warden, how many sage grouse do you see out there?"

"Now?"

"Now."

"I don't see any."

"Aha!"

Joe frowned. "It's not like they wear blaze orange like hunters do. I'd have to spend some time here observing."

"Or you could talk to your friend Clay, couldn't you? Clay knows every inch of this ranch."

"I would talk with Clay," Joe said. "I'd also need to spend some time here on my own."

"Are you always this stubborn?" Thompson asked.

"Yup."

Thompson took a deep breath and let it out slowly. Joe guessed it was so he wouldn't explode.

"I'm hoping I can count on you for your support," Thompson said finally. "I'm hoping you don't derail a project that would actually help me get some return on my investment, unlike the cattle out there. You know, every bovine is a money-suck on four hooves. No one makes money from a cattle ranch anymore, because the deck is stacked against ranchers. You wouldn't want to stack the deck even higher against me, would you, Joe?"

“I’d call it like I see it,” Joe said. “But you still haven’t told me what you’re planning out here.”

“Whatever it might be, it would be good and worthwhile and harmless. That’s all I’ll say for now.”

“Okay,” Joe said. There seemed to be no point in pushing Thompson for answers at the moment.

“But you might want to spend a little more time out here in the coming months,” Thompson said.

“Maybe I can do that,” Joe said. “But right now I’m pretty busy. I’m dealing with the opening day of elk-hunting season.”

“I’ll let Clay know that you won’t be a stranger on this ranch.

“Who knows,” Thompson said with an unreadable grin, “maybe you’ll get lucky and see Brandy doing yoga out on the deck again.”

On their return to the Thompson compound, the ranch owner called his pilots to tell them to get the jet ready. As soon as he disconnected, he turned to Joe and said, “I’ve got another damned fundraiser in Atlanta tonight. I don’t even know what it’s for—homeless people or something about race relations, probably.

“My lawyers say I have to make sure I stay visible in the business community for PR purposes. They say the best way to deal with scandal is to carry on like nothing ever happened.”

Joe wasn’t aware of a scandal involving Thompson, but he made a note to ask Marybeth about it when he got home. If she didn’t know the details of whatever it was, he knew she had the resources to find out.

Then Thompson leaned in his seat closer to Joe as he drove.

"Do you know what I think they should call homeless people? So it doesn't sound so negative?"

"What's that?"

"*Outdoorsmen!*" Thompson whooped. "We should call them outdoorsmen! Who doesn't want to be an outdoorsman?"

Joe suppressed a smile, mainly because the statement was so outrageous and unexpected.

They neared the Gulfstream on the landing strip and Thompson looked at his wristwatch and declared, "I need to get into the air. Do you mind taking the Gator back to the garage?"

"I can do that," Joe said as Thompson vaulted out of the ATV.

But before he took the stairs into the aircraft, Thompson turned and clapped Joe on the shoulder and said, "Don't let me down, Joe. It wouldn't be worth it to anyone involved."

And he was gone.

BRANDY HAD VACATED the third level when Joe approached the Thompson house and guided the ATV into the open garage. He tried to wrap his mind around all that Thompson had said to him, and tried to guess what the rancher was envisioning for his mountain valley.

Clay was waiting for him outside of his pickup. On the way into the open bay, Joe had passed Clay's vehicle once again and noted that the weapons and ammunition were no longer visible inside the cab.

"What's going on around here, Clay?" Joe asked after parking the ATV and handing Clay the keys.

Clay looked away without answering. Then he turned and said,

"Let's just say I've been doing things I never thought I'd do. I mean, back when I had some self-respect."

"Like what?"

"We'll have to talk later," Clay said. "Brandy needs a ride to town. She's out of green tea."

Clay backed out of the garage toward the open door, but he paused at the threshold. "Joe, Mr. Thompson gets what he wants. He plays by a different set of rules. My advice to you, as a friend, is to not get in his way and just do what he suggests. It isn't worth it to buck him."

"Is that what you do, Clay?" Joe asked. "Like shooting every sage grouse you see with that shotgun that's no longer in your pickup?"

Clay looked as if he'd been caught. His face drained of color and he simply glared at Joe for half a minute.

"I thought we were friends, Joe," he said.

"I have a job to do, Clay, and I'll do it."

"Then don't say I didn't warn you," Clay said as he turned away abruptly.

CHAPTER SIX

November 15

ON THE NIGHT that Joe was shot and Marybeth held vigil at his bedside at the Billings hospital, their three daughters assembled at the kitchen table at Joe and Marybeth's home on the bank of the Twelve Sleep River.

Sheridan had arrived first, since she was the closest. She'd found a frozen pizza in the freezer and was cooking it in the oven when April arrived from Montana with her dog, Boone, a Labrador/husky mix she'd adopted from a Bozeman shelter. Lucy showed up an hour later, since she had to drive all the way from the University of Wyoming in Laramie, which was four hours away to the south.

Sheridan had complained about Boone's presence immediately when the huge dog bounded through the house looking for the Pickett dogs: Biscuit, their new Labrador and Joe's daily companion who had been delivered from the crime scene by a deputy, and Bert's Dog, an unholy mixed-breed blue-eyed hound that included Catahoula. Tube, a corgi and Labrador mix, had died the previous summer at the age of fourteen. Even without Tube, the remaining dogs got along well and began chasing each other, wrestling on the floor, and knocking over end tables and lamps in the living room.

Sheridan and April managed to coax the dogs outside into the backyard before they knocked over all of the furniture.

With peace restored, April went straight for her mother's wine stash in the pantry. She opened up a red blend and poured three glasses full.

She was on her second glass when Lucy arrived, wearing a beret and a long scarf that she'd apparently purchased in France during her recent semester abroad. Her light blond hair was short and stylish, making her look like a Euro-pixie.

"Oh, give me a break," April snorted when she saw Lucy. "Please don't tell me you're going to start telling us how much better everything is in Europe, are you?"

"*Oui, ma soeur*," Lucy said with a sardonic smile. "That's 'Yes, my sister,' for you rubes from Montana."

"Please don't tell me you brought a dog, too," Sheridan said.

"*Non*," Lucy replied.

Then, as if a dam had broken, the three sisters embraced and wept together. April finally pushed away from the scrum.

"LET'S GET STARTED, then," Sheridan declared after wiping her eyes. She pulled the pizza out of the oven, scoring the slices with a pizza cutter, and sliding it onto the tabletop. "How are we going to figure out who shot our dad?"

"Who made you the boss?" April asked. "I don't remember when we had the vote to decide."

"I'm the oldest and the most organized," Sheridan replied.

"And I'm the one currently working for a private investigation firm," April countered.

Sheridan turned to her youngest sister. "Lucy, do you vote for me?"

"Sure," Lucy said with a coquettish eye roll.

"So there you have it," Sheridan said.

April said, "This election was rigged, as usual. It's always two against one."

"That's because we are the reasonable sisters in the family," Sheridan said. "We have to stick together."

"The word you were looking for is 'collude,'" April said, her voice rising. "You two *collude* together."

Lucy cut in. "Let's change the subject."

"You talked to Mom last," Sheridan said to April. "What's the latest?"

April pried out a wedge of pizza and placed it on a paper plate in front of her. She said, "The surgeon told her there's a possibility that the injury *might* not be as severe as it looked at first. Mom repeated a bunch of medical terminology I don't understand, but the bottom line is that the trajectory of the bullet *might* have just clipped a single lobe, but not gone into any more of his brain. If that's the case, he might not have the worst kind of brain damage after all. The bullet is lodged in his skull, though, and she said something about a 'meninx' that I don't understand."

Lucy said, "The meninx surrounds the brain and keeps it from sloshing around in your skull all day. I read about it in a psychology class when we were studying the human brain. But I'd need to look it up again to make sure that's the case."

"So that's where the bullet is lodged?" Sheridan asked April. "In the meninx?"

"I think that's what she said. It was confusing, and Mom is wound really tight. Bottom line, though, his condition is stable for tonight and we should know more tomorrow."

"Thank God he's stable," Lucy said. "I'm all cried out from the drive up."

"He's still in a coma and not able to talk?" Sheridan asked.

"That's the situation," April said. "How long he'll be like that, nobody knows."

"How did she sound?" Lucy asked. Lucy had always been keenly attuned to the motives and feelings of others, and she often picked up on cues her sisters missed.

"Exhausted," April said. "She said she was going to find a hotel near the hospital and try to get some sleep. I don't think we should bug her until tomorrow."

"Agreed," Sheridan said.

April said, "I could tell she wasn't very excited by the prospect of us getting together to try and figure this out."

"What are we supposed to do?" Sheridan asked. "Sit on our hands? Sometimes I think she still thinks of us as her little chickens waddling in a row behind her."

"Take it easy on her," Lucy said. "She probably sees her control slipping away. I'm sure she wouldn't admit that, but it's got to be tough to watch her husband stuck in one place in a coma and not sure if he's going to make it, and her three daughters are someplace else, going off without her. She's probably feeling a lot of things right now."

April chewed on another slice of pizza, and said to Lucy, "You're the expert on other people's feelings. I defer to you on that one. I just want to find the bad guy who did this."

"Me too," Sheridan said. "So let's make a plan."

April said, "Since we don't have Dad's phone, we need to access his office computer. We need to find out his last searches and emails."

"Do we have his password to get in?" Lucy asked.

THEY TRIED 1-2-3-4-5 but couldn't access the phone. The sisters looked through drawers and scrap paper for what could be the password, but came up empty.

"Would Mom know?" Lucy asked.

"I'll text her," Sheridan said.

In the next minute, she received a reply. Sheridan looked up and shook her head. "She doesn't know his password and he can't tell us, of course."

"Crap," April said. "It was a good idea."

AFTER A SECOND bottle of wine was opened, Sheridan said, "I know exactly where that road junction is on Antler Creek Road. The land goes from public to private at that spot. It splits off and goes in three directions from there—to the Double D, the McElwee Ranch, and the Bucholz Ranch. Dad was obviously headed out to one of them when this happened. So who is the most likely of the three to ambush him?"

Lucy looked up. "Do we need a whiteboard so we can put up photos of our suspects and draw lines between them, like they do on TV?"

"That's bullshit," April said. "I've been on dozens of investigations with Cassie Dewell, and we've never used a friggin' whiteboard."

"Just asking," Lucy said meekly.

"Anyway, Mom thinks the prime suspects are the McElwees," April said, referring to the owners of McElwee Land and Cattle. "She said they're suspected to be operating a poaching ring and that Dad had been out there before."

"Does she know that's where he was headed this morning?" Sheridan asked.

"No, she doesn't. She said she has no idea where he was going this morning at all, and neither does dispatch in Cheyenne," April said.

"That's no help," Sheridan said. Then: "So we start with the McElwees. I know they're fourth- or fifth-generation landowners, and I know the other ranchers in the area don't think much of them. The two owners are sisters named Lisa and Lainie. Both have been married a few times each, but I don't think there are any current husbands in the picture. And they're both just mean as bobcats. They've had lots of disputes over the years with all of their neighbors."

"What kind of disputes?" Lucy asked. As she did so, she was searching their names on her phone.

"Problems over water, fences, missing horses and cattle, that kind of thing," Sheridan responded. "The usual stuff out in ranch country. But since I've been back, I've heard some other things about them. I've heard they might allow shady hunters to take trophy animals on their place without licenses and out of season. And apparently a couple of the ex-husbands have just disappeared off the face of the earth. I've also heard that a few of the men who work on their place are ex-cons who might be involved in dealing. But all those things are just rumors. I don't have any firsthand knowledge that any of it is true."

"They sound fun," Lucy said, deadpan. Then: "Lisa and Lainie McElwee don't seem to exist on social media. All I can find is a crummy-looking website for 'McElwee Trophy Hunting.' There aren't any photos of the sisters that I can find, just a bunch of dead-animal shots."

"I'm not surprised," Sheridan said. "They don't strike me as social media types."

"But going forward, I wouldn't rule out the Bucholz folks," Sheridan said. "John and Shelby. They come across as really nice people at first, but the more you get to know them and the more you hear about them . . ."

"What?" April asked.

Sheridan said, "Well, I was hired last spring to go out to the Bucholz place with my falcons to chase a bunch of starlings out of their barns. They seemed nice enough. But one of their hired men pulled me aside and told me to watch out for them—that they weren't at all who they seemed.

"He went on to tell me that there had been a big fight over the ownership of the ranch between a bunch of Bucholz relatives when the elders all died. There are Bucholzes all over the state and several of them own big ranches. John and Shelby hired shady PIs to dig up dirt on all of their relatives so they could discredit them in front of the courts. They might also have been behind some car crashes and other accidents. Anyway, John and Shelby ended up with the place in the end. I don't know whether any of that is true or I was just hearing stuff from a disgruntled employee. And that's not all," Sheridan said.

"When I was out there, both John and Shelby made me sign a document that said if I wandered off the grounds and looked in any old outbuildings out there that I would forfeit my fee. They were really adamant that I stay at the ranch headquarters complex the entire time I was there. I asked them what the deal was and they refused to tell me. Then, when I was done with the job and the problem birds were gone, I submitted my bill to them and they've never paid it. They claimed I violated the agreement by snooping around their property and looking in the windows of the outbuildings, which I never did."

"Are you sure?" April asked. "The Sheridan I know wouldn't be able to help herself."

Sheridan paused for a long time and then smiled. She confessed, "I might have gotten close to those old cabins one morning. Closer than they wanted me to. There are three of them back in the trees, and they're in really bad shape. They're pretty creepy. I thought I saw someone in one of the cabins looking back at me through the window, but when I got closer, they ducked and I couldn't see them again. But I never went inside. I swear it."

"Who could it have been?" Lucy asked.

Sheridan shrugged. "I've been wondering that myself for a long time."

"What did this person look like?" Lucy asked.

"It was a man, I think," Sheridan said. "Older, probably in his fifties or sixties. He had a round face and really big eyes, but he was hard to see clearly because the window was so dirty. And then he ducked away."

Lucy grimaced and held her arms out to reveal goose bumps on the skin of her forearms.

"Have you thought about suing them for your fee?" April asked.

"I've thought about it, but I just haven't pulled the trigger on that one."

"Because you *did* violate the agreement," April said.

"Technically, yes," Sheridan admitted.

"Why not sic Nate on them?" April asked.

"Because I don't want to have him solve all of my problems in the company," Sheridan said. "I want him to know I can handle things on my own."

"I'd say they sound pretty suspicious," April said. "Just like the McElwees. What if Dad knew who was staying in their cabin, or something like that? Maybe they'd want to stop him from talking."

"It seems pretty extreme," Sheridan said. "But it's worth looking into."

April agreed, and said, "And then we've got the Double Diamond Ranch. Even I know about the famous Double D. A really rich guy from back east and his trophy wife own it. The foreman is Clay Hutmacher."

Sheridan winced and looked away. Clay Hutmacher Jr. had been set to propose to her before he was killed. He died with the ring in his pocket, and he never knew that she would have turned him down.

"I'd say the first two ranches seem more likely," April said. "But I wouldn't eliminate the owners of the Double D until we know more. Superrich guys just assume they can get away with anything. And they want everything. We've got them all over Montana."

Lucy asked, "Is there any way we can find out which ranch he was going to this morning? We've all seen him keep notes in that little spiral notebook of his. Do we know where the notebook is? Or where his phone ended up? Or the name of the hunter who called it in?"

Both Sheridan and April shook their heads.

"What do we know about the new sheriff?" April asked Sheridan

"Steve Sondergard?"

"Whatever his name is, yes."

"He seems like he'll do a good job once he gets his feet on the ground," Sheridan said.

"That's not exactly a gigantic endorsement," April said with a huff.

"He's sweet on our sister," Lucy told April. Sheridan shot a look at Lucy that Lucy deflected with a grin. "Didn't you tell us that?" she asked.

"That was a private conversation."

"Like I give a crap," April said. Lucy thought that April always feigned indifference, but it obviously stung her when she thought that Sheridan and Lucy had been communicating without her.

"You *were* included on the text thread," Lucy said defensively. "You never weigh in. I can prove it if you give me your phone. Or I can show you the thread on mine."

April rolled her eyes and poured another glass of wine. She snapped, "That's because I have a real job. I'm too busy to engage in all of this gossip crap with you two."

"Anyway," Sheridan said to break up the tiff, "I think it's not a bad idea to start with Steve. He might have information we can use, and maybe he's got an idea who did this by now. He might even have the name of the hunter who called it in—or Dad's notebook and phone."

April shushed them and held up her hand with one finger extended toward the ceiling. She turned to Lucy. "It seems to me that our older sister, the elected leader of this inquiry, should use her special *influence* on the new sheriff to find out what he knows, and what he's got that might point to the guilty party here."

Lucy and April then turned to Sheridan.

"I'll find out what I can," Sheridan said reluctantly. "But I'm not sure he'll like it if he knows we're investigating this at the same time his department is."

"Tell him whatever you have to," April said. Then: "What about Nate? Is he aware of what happened?"

Nate Romanowski owned the majority of Yarak, Inc., which was a bird abatement business that Sheridan now ran as the CEO. Nate was an outlaw falconer with a Special Forces background who had been a longtime friend of their family, despite his many interactions with federal law enforcement.

"I haven't talked to him yet," Sheridan said. "I didn't think that it was a good idea this early in the game."

"Because he might just start ripping ears off and blasting people all over the county?" April asked.

"Yes."

April said, "Personally, I wouldn't have a problem with that."

"I would," Sheridan said.

"Me too," Lucy agreed.

"Two against one again, as usual," April observed. "But it won't be long before he finds out. The shooting of the local game warden is pretty big news around this valley, I'd guess."

LATER THAT NIGHT, Lucy slipped into the guest room where April slept. Boone was curled up on her bed.

"What?" April asked, bleary-eyed.

"Isn't it weird for the three of us to be in Mom and Dad's house without them? I mean, it's not like we even grew up in this house."

"Yeah, it's weird. You came in here to ask me that?"

"Not really."

"Then what, Lucy?"

"If he makes it, what's he going to be like?"

April sighed. "I don't know. I never saw him. I don't think Mom knows, either."

"What if he doesn't remember us?"

April moaned and lowered her head to her pillow. "Thank you for that morbid thought," she said. "Now I won't be able to sleep."

CHAPTER SEVEN

November 16

EARLY THE NEXT morning, Dorn Peddy and Hillbilly Jimmy D. O'Bryan traversed the sagebrush badlands near Antler Creek Road in the ATV, eventually locating the camper trailer. It was tucked away in an aspen grove three miles from the junction where the ambush had taken place the day before.

Peddy quickly leaned down and turned the headlights off. "See it?"

"I see it," O'Bryan replied. He'd been in a foul mood since Peddy had awakened him at four thirty that morning. Peddy had whispered that they needed to find that hunter who'd called in the incident, and fast.

"Why?" O'Bryan had asked.

"I've been thinking about it all night long," Peddy had explained. "We don't know if that guy saw us. If he did, it could fuck up everything. And, brother, I want to get paid."

O'Bryan had reluctantly gone along with Peddy's argument,

and now they were sweeping across the labyrinth of two-track roads on public land near the junction. They plowed through snowdrifts on the back roads.

Peddy had explained that since the hunter was obviously on foot when they saw him, his camp couldn't be too far away.

"If he has a camp at all," O'Bryan said. But Peddy had ignored him.

O'Bryan wanted to get paid as well, and he wanted to hit the road and never run across Dorn Peddy again for the rest of his life.

Before they located the camper trailer, O'Bryan had been leaning forward in his seat so the heat from the vents would warm him. The ATV was a new-model Polaris Ranger with an overhead cab, but the cold morning still leaked in. O'Bryan couldn't wait until the sun rose over the humpbacked Bighorn Mountains and flooded it with warmth and light. He noticed how the sagebrush that bordered the two-track sparkled with frost from the beams of their headlights. Jackrabbits bolted from the brush and ran ahead of them on the road, but ducked to safety at the last second.

"Why would anybody want to live here?" O'Bryan asked Peddy as they rolled along. "Yesterday, the wind was blowing a million miles an hour. Today, it's colder than hell. What's wrong with these people?"

Peddy had started to answer, when the camp came into view and he stopped the Ranger on the top of a hill.

There was a massive sagebrush swale between the Ranger and the camper trailer. The swale, like the trees that bordered the terrain, was still plunged into shadow. Lone junipers, like sentinels, stood at attention across the plain.

"We better move," Peddy said as he restarted the engine. "I don't want him to see us because we've skylighted ourselves." When he stopped again farther down the hill, he asked O'Bryan for the binoculars.

"They're around your neck."

"Ah."

Peddy rested the binoculars on the top of the steering wheel and leaned into them.

"There's a pickup truck parked in the trees behind the trailer," he said. "It's sidewise, so I can't see license plates."

Then: "It's a hunting camp, for sure. There's no other reason for anyone to be set up out here."

Then: "The trailer is pretty beat-up, and the truck is at least twenty years old. This guy isn't rich, I'd say."

Then: "The trailer is rocking a little. I think someone is walking around inside."

O'Bryan "Hmmm'd" after each report to acknowledge what Peddy said. He noted that there was now a soft yellow glow from interior lighting through the windows of the camper.

"There he is," Peddy said suddenly. "There's our man."

"Are you sure?"

"One hundred percent," Peddy said as he handed over the binoculars.

O'Bryan focused the lenses. It was still too dark to see clearly. What he could make out was the figure of a stout man, a dark form, as he emerged from the trailer door and took a tentative step down into the snow and grass. The man was stocky, but O'Bryan couldn't see his face or make out his clothing. The hunter closed the door of the unit behind him.

The man lumbered the length of the camper to the front, then stood still and bent back a little, his right hand at crotch level. Steam from his urine rose in a small cloud near his feet.

When he was done, he turned and went back into the unit.

"I'm sure as hell not one hundred percent it's him," O'Bryan said. "Could you actually see his face?"

"I can tell by the way he moves," Peddy said, but there was a trace of uncertainty in his tone.

"How do we find out?"

"We go ask him, idiot."

O'Bryan scowled and looked away. Getting the hell away from Dorn of the Mountains couldn't come soon enough.

THEY CHECKED THEIR weapons using a headlamp Peddy had brought along. He choked the beam down to a glow so the light from inside the Ranger wouldn't be discernible from the camper trailer.

Peddy checked the loads in the magazine of a .40 Taurus G2C semiautomatic and racked one into the chamber. He slipped the pistol into a shoulder holster beneath his stiff canvas barn coat. O'Bryan opened the cylinder of a .38 Smith & Wesson short-barreled revolver and snapped it back into place. He dropped the revolver into his right parka pocket. Both weapons had been provided by their employer from a large supply that was kept in an armory. The serial numbers on both pistols had been filed off.

"Let me do all the talking," Peddy said.

"I wouldn't want it any other way."

"There's that fucking attitude again," Peddy said.

O'Bryan shrugged. "So what's our story, anyway?"

"We're ranch hands. We're out here looking for cows that wandered away from the ranch onto public land. I'll ask our guy if he's seen them."

"Okay, and then what?"

Peddy threw back his head and rolled his eyes, as if he'd never heard a dumber question. "By then we'll know if this is our hunter after all. We'll know if he recognizes us. If he does, there will be a tell."

"And if he does?"

"We'll deal with him," Peddy said.

"And if he doesn't?" O'Bryan asked.

Peddy scoffed at the question and shoved the gear lever from park into drive. Then he turned the headlights back on.

THEIR HIGH BEAMS bathed the side of the camper trailer as they approached it. O'Bryan could see the head and shoulders of a man move to the side window of the unit and peer out. He still couldn't see his face clearly.

Peddy parked and shut off the engine, but he kept the beams trained on the unit. As he strode up to the door, it opened.

O'Bryan slipped out of the Ranger through the passenger door. Rather than catch up with Peddy, he stepped to the side so he'd have a clear view of what happened next. From this vantage point, O'Bryan could also see that the pickup had plates on it with a *1* next to a bucking bronco logo. So the hunter was from

Wyoming, but no doubt far enough away from the Bighorns to find it necessary to camp out rather than return home at night.

O'Bryan had learned that license plates in Wyoming all began with the number of the county where the vehicle was registered. He didn't know the counties well enough to know which one had the *1* designation. All he knew was that the license plates he'd noticed in Twelve Sleep County all began with the number *3*.

The stocky hunter pushed the door open and stood in the threshold with a pot of coffee in his hand. O'Bryan could smell bacon cooking from inside.

"Greetings," the man said. "What can I help you with?"

Even though they were closer and the sun was starting to overtake the gloom, O'Bryan still wasn't sure he could identify the hunter as *the hunter*. The man looked to be in his early sixties. He had a full, short-cropped black beard and a wide face with a bulbous nose. He wore long-handled underwear and a cooking apron.

"Good morning," Peddy said. "Sorry to bother you so early."

The hunter nodded and took in Peddy, then O'Bryan behind him. His face crinkled into a smile.

"You two look like dime-store cowboys," he said.

"We're ranch hands," Peddy said.

"And I'm a pirate of the Caribbean," the hunter said with a laugh. "It looks like you two were dressed this morning by Roy Rogers or somebody who watched too many episodes of *Yellowstone*."

O'Bryan felt his neck flush with embarrassment and he looked away for a moment. Peddy, for once, had no words.

"Hey, I didn't mean to insult you," the hunter said. "Do you guys want a cup of coffee? I just made it."

Peddy looked over his shoulder at O'Bryan. O'Bryan said, "I could use a cup."

"Sure," Peddy said to the hunter.

"Let me clear a place for you to sit. Then come on inside and get out of the cold."

IT WAS CRAMPED and close inside the camper trailer. The table in the nose of the unit was propped up by a single aluminum leg and it was the only place to sit down. Peddy squeezed into a bench seat on one side, and O'Bryan slid in next to him. When the hunter joined them on the other side of the table, their knees nearly touched his.

O'Bryan surveyed the interior of the trailer. It was dated and had seen a lot of use. The bed at the foot of the unit was covered by a crumpled sleeping bag, and the single propane lamp above the stove hissed through a brilliantly glowing mantle. It was warm inside and bacon was sizzling in a cast-iron pan on one of the burners. A scoped hunting rifle was leaned against a wall near a closet, and a daypack was on the floor near it. Weathered hunting boots had been tucked away under the bed.

"I'm Budd Betts," the hunter said as he poured two cups of coffee. "What can I do for you fellows this morning?"

O'Bryan sipped from his mug. The coffee was hot and very strong.

Finally, Peddy said, "We're from one of the ranches farther up the road. We're looking for a half dozen lost cows and we were wondering if you've seen them."

"What kind of cows?" Betts asked.

O'Bryan did a side-eye to Peddy, wondering with amusement what he'd say. Peddy had put himself in a spot.

"Black ones," Peddy answered.

Betts smiled. "*Black ones?* Do you mean Angus?"

"Yeah, Angus."

O'Bryan tried not to smirk.

"I'll tell you what," Betts said. "I'll let you know if I've seen any of your *black ones* if you'll tell me if you've run across any big mulie bucks this morning on the way out here."

"We haven't seen any mules," Peddy said.

Betts looked to O'Bryan as if to say, *Who is this idiot?* But instead, he said, "Mule deer. I'm looking for mule deer. We call them mulies."

As he said it, Betts raised his hands to the top of his head and wiggled his fingers to indicate large ears. "What do you call them on your ranch?"

As much as he enjoyed watching Peddy getting humiliated, O'Bryan stepped in and said, "We call them mulies, too. But no, we didn't see any this morning on the way out here."

Betts shook his head. "It's been tough going this season. It's like all the big deer moved out. I've had pretty good luck in this area in the past, but this year, it's been damned frustrating. I saw a bunch of does and fawns yesterday, and a couple of little forked horns. But nothing I couldn't pass up."

Then Betts said, "And I haven't seen your missing cows, either."

"How long have you been hunting?" Peddy asked. O'Bryan noticed that Peddy had yet to drink any coffee. Both of his hands were under the table on his lap, and he leaned forward a little. His manner was deflated, O'Bryan thought. As if Peddy had lost much of his usual swagger.

"This'll be my third day," Betts said.

"You've been hunting on foot?" Peddy asked. "Or have you been driving around?"

"I hunt on foot," Betts said. "That's how my dad taught me to hunt, and that's what I still do. I'm no road hunter and I don't really have any respect for the guys who do that. I want to earn my meat for the freezer. On foot, I can usually get pretty close to a big buck that way and put him down with one shot."

"How long are you here?" Peddy asked.

"I better find one today because I need to head back to Casper tomorrow morning. My daughter's playing in the state volleyball tournament." Then: "I don't know why I'm answering your questions."

Casper was in Natrona County, O'Bryan knew. He'd arrived in Wyoming at the Natrona County Airport. So Natrona County must have the number *1* designation on its license plates, he thought. Interesting.

"If you haven't seen our cows," Peddy asked Betts, "what have you seen? Anything unusual?"

Betts sat back, apparently confused. "What do you mean, unusual?"

"You know, unusual."

"Like what?" he asked again. "To be honest, the only unusual thing I've come across since I've been hunting is two guys obviously not from here dressed up like Hollywood cowboys and not really pulling it off."

Before Peddy could respond, Betts said to Peddy, "You know what, mister? It's been nice meeting you this morning, but I've got a pretty good bullshit detector and all I've heard so far from you is bullshit. I don't know what your game is, but I'm not playing. How about you finish your coffee and get on your way? I want to get out there and get my buck before we burn any more daylight."

The gunshot from under the table was deafening inside the small trailer.

Betts grimaced and clutched his belly, and Peddy fired again. Then Peddy swung his pistol out from beneath the table and pressed the muzzle against Betts's forehead and delivered the kill shot.

Betts flopped back and slumped over out of view on his seat.

"What the fuck? Why did you do that?" O'Bryan yelled at Peddy as he scrambled to get out of the bench seat to separate himself further. The interior of the trailer smelled sharply of gunpowder and his ears were ringing from the concussions of the shots.

"It was him," Peddy said with certainty. "He was lying to us. I could tell by his eyes."

"There was *nothing* in his eyes," O'Bryan said. "He didn't know what the fuck you were asking him."

"I saw it," Peddy said in triumph as he slid out from the table. "There was a tell. I saw it in his eyes. He recognized us, and he didn't want us to know it. Plus, he was an asshole."

"Jesus," O'Bryan said. "You're crazy. What do we do now?"

"We burn this to the ground. The propane tanks will goose it along."

O'Bryan felt his fingertips brush against the heavy revolver in his right parka pocket. He looked at Peddy as the man jostled Betts's body to make sure there was no reaction. The back of Peddy's fat thick neck was three feet away.

It was simple, O'Bryan thought. He'd tell their employer that Peddy was nuts, that he'd got himself killed in an altercation with a local hunter. That he never should have been paired up with a maniac in the first place.

Then Peddy turned suddenly and locked O'Bryan in a glare. He reached out and gripped O'Bryan's shoulders in his huge hands. O'Bryan didn't reach into his pocket to grasp the revolver.

"Snap out of it, dude," Peddy said, misreading the look on O'Bryan's face or what he'd been contemplating. "What did you think was going to happen?"

THEY WERE OUTSIDE of the burning trailer walking toward the Ranger with the heat of the fire on their backs when Peddy dug his burner phone out of his barn coat.

O'Bryan got into the ATV on the passenger side and closed the door. He was still numb from what he'd witnessed. Plus, he didn't want to be outside if the propane tanks on the front of the trailer ignited. He watched Peddy talk on the phone through the windshield and he saw the man gesture with his free hand, then use the same hand to slap himself on the top of his head. Then he did it again.

When Peddy got in his face was bright red.

"What was that?" O'Bryan asked.

"That fucking game warden," Peddy said.

"What about him?" O'Bryan asked with alarm.

"He's still alive. It's impossible, but he's still alive. And the boss is *pissed.* Says we won't get paid until we finish the job."

O'Bryan groaned and leaned against the passenger window. "I told you we should have checked on him to make sure."

Then: "Where is he now?"

CHAPTER EIGHT

AT THE SAME time, Sheridan backed through the double doors of the Twelve Sleep County Sheriff's Department carrying two paper cups of coffee. Clamped under her right arm was a small box of cinnamon rolls. As she turned around in the lobby, the doors wheezed shut behind her.

"Is Sheriff Sondergard in?" she asked Kristy Austin, the receptionist behind the counter. Austin, who was skeletal and severe and wore silver metal-framed glasses, had outlasted the previous three sheriffs. It was well known that she ran the place like her private fiefdom and she knew where the bodies were buried, so no one questioned her. Her weakness, Sheridan knew, was sweet rolls.

"Do you have an appointment?" Austin asked rhetorically as she scanned the master calendar in front of her.

"No," Sheridan said. "But I have coffee and fresh cinnamon rolls from the Burg-O-Pardner."

That got Kristy's attention, Sheridan noted.

Before Austin could reply, Deputy Frank Carroll shot up into view from his desk behind a cubicle wall divider. His sudden emergence struck Sheridan as akin to a prairie dog popping out of its den.

"I can take you back," Carroll offered. "Follow me."

Sheridan left the box of rolls on Kristy's desk and she fell in beside Carroll.

"I'm sure sorry about what happened to your dad," Carroll said. "I was one of the first people on the scene yesterday. Can I ask you how he's doing?"

"He's alive. Thanks for asking."

"Well, thank God for that," Carroll said. "Joe's a good man. I hope we don't lose him. How's your mom doing?"

"She's in Billings," Sheridan said. "She texted us this morning to say that the night went well and that she's waiting to hear more from the surgeon in charge. He's in critical condition in an induced coma."

Carroll whistled. He began, "If you would have seen him yesterday, you wouldn't think . . . ," then he caught himself before he said more. "I'm sorry," he said. "Sometimes I talk too much."

"Sometimes you do," Sheridan said.

They were now outside the sheriff's office, down the hall from the lobby. "Tell me," she said to Carroll, "do you guys have a name on the man who called it in? We'd like to thank him."

"Not that I'm aware of," Carroll said. "Steve might know more."

"Don't you find it odd that the guy reported the shooting, but didn't stick around for the first responders?" Sheridan asked.

"I find everything about this case pretty odd," Carroll said with a shrug.

"Thanks for escorting me through the office," Sheridan said, as a means to move Carroll back to his cubicle. It took a moment before he got it and shuffled away.

The door to the sheriff's office was ajar and she could hear movement inside. Before pushing it all the way open, Sheridan reached down and slid the nameplate for the previous sheriff out of its metal holder.

Sheriff Sondergard was in the process of moving cardboard boxes from the top of the desk to a conference table. When he looked up and saw Sheridan, he smiled and said, "Good morning. Let me clear a place for you to sit."

Sondergard was a striking man, she thought. He was tall and trim, with wavy light brown hair, blue eyes, and an easy smile. The only feature she didn't like about him was his brushy cop mustache, but she figured that came with the territory. He was in his early thirties, so older than Sheridan, and he was divorced, but had no children. According to his campaign materials, he'd served as a U.S. Marine before being hired as undersheriff in the Park County, Wyoming, sheriff's office. He'd run unopposed in Twelve Sleep County and had won the office less than a week before.

Sheridan had met Sondergard at the Stockman's Bar while he was campaigning. He'd asked her politely if he could buy her a drink, and she'd accepted.

She thought he had an easy manner about him, and he wasn't full of himself like so many cops she'd met over the years. He'd asked her about her bird abatement business, and he showed genuine interest in falcons and falconry. He'd also asked her what it had been like growing up in the county as the game warden's oldest daughter, and if her dad's job had made other students at school give her a wide berth. She found herself liking him more than she'd intended to, and had been surprised by it. He'd asked her if she'd be interested in having dinner with him once the election was over, and she'd given him her number.

He hadn't called yet, but it had only been a few days since the polls closed.

She showed him the nameplate, which read **Sheriff Jackson Bishop**, and said, "Do you mind if I throw this in the garbage?"

Sondergard's reaction was puzzled surprise for a moment, which turned into a knowing grin. "That's right," he said. "You didn't get along very well with my predecessor."

"Nope," Sheridan said. "In fact, I held him at gunpoint in my chicken coop for a while last year before he hit the road for parts unknown. I don't miss him at all. Here, I brought you coffee."

"Thank you kindly." He took the cup from her and set it on his desktop, then he removed a box from a chair across from it and motioned for her to sit.

"I'm just moving in, as you can see," he said.

She noted that the room was bare, not even a photo or plaque remained on the walls. Only nails where items had been hung. There was a dead plant on the credenza behind his desk.

Before she sat down, Sheridan dropped Jackson Bishop's nameplate into a garbage can.

"I'll have to ask Kristy to get me a new one, I guess," Sondergard said. "From what I understand, she's done it several times before."

"We do have a problem keeping sheriffs around here," Sheridan said. "And a real hard time keeping *good* ones."

"I hope I'm able to stay out of your chicken coop."

"I do, too," she said.

"So, what brings you here? I assume it's not just to bring me coffee."

"Correct. I was hoping you could brief me on the investigation involving my dad's shooting yesterday."

Sondergard sighed and ran his hand through his hair before speaking.

"We really don't know much at this point," he said finally. "We've got no suspects, no motive, and no evidence. I've got a crime scene tech out there on Antelope Creek Road right now, and I'm hoping he can give us some more information."

"*Antler* Creek Road," Sheridan said, correcting him gently.

"*Antler* Creek Road," Sondergard repeated. "It's going to take me a while to get my bearings, so I apologize for that."

"No apology needed," Sheridan said. "Can I ask you a few questions?"

"Ask away," Sondergard said. "My aim is to be fully transparent with you, or with any citizen in the county. I've worked for bosses who kept everything close to the vest and didn't communicate well with their constituents, and I don't want to be one of them."

"Great, thank you. First of all, do you know how many shooters were out there?"

"Not for certain, but if I'd guess I'd say it was more than one. The bullets seemed to come from different angles, based on the damage done to your dad's pickup. That's an educated guess, though. I hope the tech can confirm it."

Sheridan processed that for a moment, then asked, "Did you determine the location from where the shots were fired? Or the distance?"

"Not yet. We're looking for shell casings and tire tracks. Honestly, it was kind of a clusterfuck yesterday when everyone arrived out there. The priority was getting your dad flown out. The snow is melting and turning the ground into mud, so we can't find tracks. I'm hoping we can figure out more today with people dedicated to do just that."

"Will you let me know what you find?" she asked. "My family would like to be informed."

"I promise you I'll do that," he said.

"Have you interviewed the three ranch families out there in the area to see if they know anything?"

Sondergard nodded his head and said, "I've asked Frank and my new deputy, William Bowkley, to interview them today. If something the ranchers say doesn't jibe, I've asked my deputies to bring them in so I can talk with them as well."

"I don't think I've met Deputy Bowkley."

"He's brand-new here, just like me," Sondergard said. "I just hired him off the street."

"Seriously?"

He chuckled and flushed a little. "I shouldn't have put it that way. Bowkley showed up a few days ago with an impressive résumé. He obviously knew we were short-staffed—everybody does. I called his references in Campbell County, where he used to work, and he checked out completely. So I hired him on the spot. He started here officially this morning."

"Good," Sheridan said. "I know the department has been pretty . . . thin."

She leaned forward. "I'd be very interested to hear what your deputies find out. It makes sense to my sisters and me that one of the ranch families might have been involved in this, since the shooting came from private property, and my dad was obviously headed out there to one of the ranches."

"You might be out a little ahead of your skis on that one," Sondergard said with a note of caution. "But I get what you're saying."

"Is his truck still out there?" Sheridan asked. "I'd like to know exactly how it was positioned, if possible."

"We had it towed last night."

"To where?"

Sondergard jabbed his desktop with his index finger and said, "Here. It's in the county garage next door."

"Can I see it?"

He narrowed his eyes. "Sheridan, I'm not sure you really want to do that."

"Because of the blood?"

"Yes. You know how head wounds can be. Plus, we need our tech to really go over it inside and out. We don't think the shooters accessed the pickup, but we aren't sure. If they did, we might be able to pick up a print or fabric, and maybe even DNA. We wouldn't want any unauthorized people inside of it until we can do a complete forensics analysis."

She said she understood. Then: "Did you recover a notebook? Or my dad's phone?"

Sondergard hesitated for a moment, then said, "Not that I'm aware of. But I'll let you know, like I said."

Before Sheridan could ask about the missing reporting party, Sondergard stiffened in his chair and leaned across his desk.

"Tell me that you're not going to investigate this on your own, Sheridan. I'd be disappointed to hear that's what you plan to do.

We'll do a thorough and professional investigation, and we'll keep you updated every step of the way."

She shifted uncomfortably in her chair. "We'll do the same with you," she said finally. "And we won't interfere in your investigation. But what you need to understand is that those ranch families out there go back generations, and they're used to doing what they want despite who the sheriff is at the moment. All three families are dysfunctional in their own way, and they don't necessarily get along with one another. There are secrets they don't want found out, I can promise you that."

Sondergard eyed her warily. "What exactly are you saying? That you plan to investigate this with your sisters?"

"What I'm saying is that you're new here, and so is your team, for the most part. Frank has been here a couple of years, but both you and Deputy Bowkley are at a real disadvantage when it comes to looking into those ranch families. I think it would be helpful for all of us to get a more local perspective on things as well."

Sondergard didn't respond. Instead, he made eye contact with Sheridan, as if he could dissuade her that way.

"No disrespect meant in regard to you and your team," Sheridan said, "but this is personal for us."

"I see that," Sondergard said. "I also see where it might help to get some local perspectives on the players involved."

Sheridan sat forward in her chair, waiting.

He said, "Please don't make me have to tell you and your sisters to back off. That would be really unhelpful."

"I understand," she said. "We can work together."

Sondergard started to say more, but he apparently caught himself.

"Thank you again for the coffee," he said. "I'd better get back to work unpacking my stuff."

As he said it, Sondergard's manner was cooler toward her than it had been and she felt a sharp pang of guilt. Had she just used his initial attraction to her to manipulate him? Had she derailed their relationship before it even got started?

She rose and reached out to shake his hand. He shook it.

"I've still got your number in my phone," he said.

"And don't hesitate to give me a call," she said, relieved.

Later, she'd describe the conversation she'd had with the new sheriff to her sisters as him granting them "tacit approval" for their investigation.

Sheridan hoped that was the case.

OUTSIDE, SHERIDAN PAUSED for a moment while she reached for the door handle of her SUV. The county garage was right there in front of her and she could see it clearly over the top of her vehicle. The garage was attached to the county building, a large, rambling redbrick structure with high ceilings inside and four roller-track doors facing the street.

She cautiously looked around the parking lot to see if any other employees were about. They weren't. There was a parked police cruiser on the street in front of the Saddlestring Police Department, but no officer inside.

Sheridan shoved her hands into the front pockets of her jeans and ambled across the lot in the general direction of the sheriff's department entry, but as she neared it, she cut a sharp right along the sidewalk and continued on. She didn't want to try to access the garage through the interior of the building and possibly be noticed by Kristy or Deputy Carroll.

She ducked as she passed by Sondergard's office window in case he glanced outside, then she proceeded on the sidewalk in front of the closed garage doors. When she got to the end of the building complex, she turned left. The first door she found on the side of the building was locked, as she suspected it would be. So was another door on the back of the building in the alleyway. There were four garage doors on the back side as well, but they were shut. The building was designed so that vehicles could pull through it without having to back out.

Sheridan was about to give up and go back to her SUV when she heard the hum of an engine and then the crunching of tires on gravel behind her. A car was coming down the alley.

She stepped behind a dumpster next to the exterior garage wall and ducked down in time to see a county road maintenance truck cruise by in the alley. Then it slowed and stopped and the driver positioned it in front of the first garage door. While the truck idled, the driver apparently triggered a remote control device inside his truck and the door in front of him rumbled and rose. When it was fully open, the maintenance truck driver drove it inside.

Sheridan gave it a five count, and before the door started to close again, she jogged from behind the dumpster and entered the cavernous building. She could see the taillights of the truck ahead of her and to her left as it parked in its designated spot. The driver didn't look up and see her in his rearview mirror as she kept to the shadows and advanced through the building.

Spaces within the garage were obviously partitioned for each agency in the main county building. The first slot was for maintenance vehicles, the second for the EMT van, and the third for employees of the county court and the county clerk's offices.

SHE LOCATED THE green Game and Fish pickup parked under fluorescent lighting in a space reserved for the Twelve Sleep County Sheriff's Department. It was backed into the space so that its toothy grille faced outward from the brick wall.

Sheridan held her breath as she took it in. The Ford F-150 was punctured with bullet holes in both front fenders. She counted seven bullet holes in the exterior of the pickup. But it was the three bullet impacts on the windshield that rocked her. Each was an imploded white starburst with a hole in the center. One was directly above the steering wheel, where her dad's head must have been.

She pulled out her phone and took rapid-fire photos of the pickup. April and Lucy, she thought, should see the damage firsthand. She did it quickly because she didn't know how much time she'd have before someone came into the garage either through the alley or from the county building itself.

Then Sheridan pulled on a pair of ultralight gloves from her jacket. She hesitated a few seconds before opening the driver's-side door and leaning inside.

The metallic smell of blood on the fabric of the seat and headrest made her gag. To think that it was her dad's blood was traumatic in itself. Sheridan tried to push a rush of emotions aside.

What affected her in a surprisingly emotional way wasn't just the blood on the seat, or the holes in the windshield. It was looking into the cab of her dad's pickup at the everyday items inside. She'd grown up doing ride-alongs with him, and although he'd gone through a series of vehicles in his career and this was a newer-model pickup, the cab itself was arranged the same as she remembered it. There was his thick bundle of local topo maps stuffed between the seats, and his thermos of coffee was on the passenger floorboard. The Game and Fish Department regulations manual and citation book was clamped beneath the closed sun visor. The passenger seat was fuzzy with dog hair from Biscuit.

The back seat was piled with clothing and gear and items he'd apparently picked up along the way, like shed antlers and a cow skull. A faded photo of the entire Pickett family taken the previous Thanksgiving was taped on the front panel of the glove box. That choked her up.

Joe Pickett's pickup was his office, the place he spent the most hours of every day. Viewing all of the familiar items inside without him there felt like an intimate betrayal to Sheridan, as if she were rooting through his underwear drawer.

Sheridan kept in mind Sondergard's admonitions about fouling the crime scene, so she didn't touch anything. But she did strip off her right glove so she could work her cell phone, and she took more photos inside the cab.

She froze when she heard a door open and close in the garage. Had someone come in? Then she recalled the driver of the maintenance truck, who had probably returned to his office.

Sheridan leaned farther into the cab so she could look into the console between the seats. That was her dad's junk drawer of sorts, and it contained protein bar wrappers, pens, a range finder, worn gloves, sunglasses, a small pair of binoculars . . .

As she leaned in to search for his notebook and cell phone, Sheridan felt a presence behind her.

"Who are you and what in the hell are you doing in there?"

She wheeled around to find a large man in a deputy sheriff's uniform two feet away from her. He had a round Slavic face, close-cropped blond hair, a nose that had obviously been broken long before, and a wide, rubbery-lipped mouth. His small eyes were fierce.

His hand gripped his weapon in its holster. He was so close she couldn't run away. Then he moved even closer. She could see that he wore a temporary name badge with hand-lettering that read *Bowkley*.

BOWKLEY WAS STRONG and quick as he pulled her away from the pickup by her collar and flung her face-first into the brick wall. As he did so, he kicked the pickup door closed behind them.

The deputy used the weight of his upper torso to pin her to the wall so hard that she had a difficult time getting breath.

"Let me explain," she wheezed.

"You shouldn't be here," he growled into her ear. She felt him pry her feet apart with his knee between her legs until they were spread, and then he jerked her right arm behind her back and then her left. The cuffs went on with a ratcheting sound and he cinched them tight.

He said, "What's your name?"

She spat out, "Sheridan Pickett, Officer. This is my dad's truck."

"Well, Sheridan Pickett," Bowkley said, "you are under arrest for tampering with a crime scene, interfering with a law enforcement officer, resisting arrest, and both breaking and entering *and* trespassing in a government building. And I might think of some more charges before we go inside."

"What?"

"You have the right to remain silent. Anything you say can and will be used against you . . ."

CHAPTER NINE

AT THE SAME time, in room 497 of the critical care unit at St. John's Hospital, Marybeth stood at the window. The room afforded an unattractive view of the roof of another wing. The rimrocks of Billings were in the distance.

Dr. Ralston entered the room with a clipboard. Ralston's expression was stoic when she asked Marybeth to please sit down.

Fearing the worst, Marybeth felt her legs go weak for a moment. Then she gathered her composure and sat down opposite Dr. Ralston.

"I've studied the results of the CT scan and consulted with my colleagues here," Ralston said. "We think we've come up with the best plan of care for your husband, but it involves risks you need to be aware of before we proceed with anything."

Marybeth nodded for the doctor to go on. She'd spent the last several hours seated next to Joe. The left half of his head was heavily bandaged, and all she could see of his face was his closed right eye, cheek, and mouth. He appeared to be sleeping the whole time and his breath was steady and gentle. She'd reached under the sheets to hold his limp hand, and at one point she'd leaned over him. He smelled of adhesive tape and disinfectant.

She'd whispered, "I love you, Joe. You know that."

Of course, there had been no response of any kind. She wondered if he'd heard her. She hoped so.

Was he dreaming in there?

DR. RALSTON PLACED the clipboard on the table between them. The top sheet was a printout of a generic face and head. She pulled a black felt-tip pen from her smock and drew an X about an inch and a half above the right eyebrow.

"This is approximately where the bullet entered," she said. "It came in from the front and it penetrated his skull right here. It didn't exit the skull, however. It's still in there."

"What exactly does that mean?" Marybeth asked with a dry mouth.

Dr. Ralston removed the top sheet to show a second figure of a head in profile. Inside the profile was an oblong outline of a human brain. She drew a series of dashes from the entry going up through the top front part of the brain, and she made another X on the underside of the skull.

"The bullet went through part of the frontal lobe in an upward trajectory until it stopped here," she said. "It is lodged within the meninx as we suspected. There doesn't look to be any damage to the top of the skull. This might be quite a lucky break, Mrs. Pickett."

"How so?"

Dr. Ralston tapped on the line of the bullet path. "If the

trajectory of the bullet had been going down instead of up, it would have likely plowed through several more lobes of the brain. Meaning it would have been instantly fatal.

"But in this instance, whether the bullet itself was deflected by the windshield or your husband was looking up when the impact came—or both—the trajectory went upward. I'm guessing it was the windshield. The glass retarded the velocity of the bullet and possibly deflected it, but we'll never know for sure. And because the velocity of the bullet was decreased, it didn't go through the brain and create an exit wound outside his skull. That might have been fatal as well because of the internal and external hemorrhaging."

"This almost sounds like good news, Doctor."

Dr. Ralston held up her palm. "That might be overstating things. What it means is that we might have a better percentage chance that he survives than we thought when he was brought in. But I can't guarantee it. I need you to understand that."

Marybeth nodded that she did. Then she glanced over at Joe in his bed. "Can he hear us?"

"No."

"Are you sure?"

"No. But it's unlikely."

Dr. Ralston went on to detail the surgery required to remove the bullet by going through the top of the skull into the meninx. She went on to say how many things could still go wrong, and that there was no way to definitively say how much damage had been done to the brain by the path of the bullet.

"Removing the bullet could start massive hemorrhaging in itself," she said. "Sometimes when you disturb the status quo, it's like a house of cards suddenly falling down. The bullet itself might be plugging the rupture of important blood vessels and removing it could cause them to hemorrhage severely. We won't know until we go in."

Marybeth absorbed that, then asked, "I know you doctors like to go by percentages in surgery. Knowing what you know, what odds would you give for a successful operation?"

"Fifty-five percent," Dr. Ralston responded.

"That's all?"

"I might be a touch conservative, but that's what I'll go with."

"Why so low?" Marybeth asked.

"Because there are just so many variables—some we know, and some we won't know until they happen. Although his vital signs are stable right now, this is brain surgery, after all. We could do a successful surgery and remove the bullet, but a relapse could occur when we slowly bring him out of the coma. Mental activity and increased blood flow could wreak havoc in the damaged areas. We'll have to monitor that very carefully."

"What part of the brain might be damaged?" Marybeth asked.

Dr. Ralston touched the top of her forehead just below her hairline. "The top of the frontal lobe. We didn't find any additional damage beyond that."

Marybeth asked what injury to the frontal lobe could mean.

"As you probably know," Dr. Ralston said, "every part of the brain has distinctive functions. The frontal lobe is in charge of thinking, planning, decision-making, and maintaining an attention span. Other lobes control movement, speech, smell, memory, and everything else. So again, it's fortunate that the bullet only nicked the frontal lobe."

"But that sounds terrible," Marybeth said. "How could the damage affect him if he comes out of this?"

Dr. Ralston sat back and sighed. She said, "It's impossible to say at this point. There have been a lot of advances in brain science, but we aren't far enough along to make any kind of prediction about how your husband will be affected by this—if everything goes well.

"Let me give you a couple of examples I'm very familiar with," the doctor said. "There's the case of Juan Martinez, who was a twenty-two-year-old gang member here in Billings. They brought him in six or seven years ago with a gunshot wound to the head similar to what we're talking about here. The bullet passed through the frontal lobe and exited through the top of his skull. I was on the surgery team, and we were able to patch him up the best we could.

"I didn't know Juan before he was shot, but from what we learned of him, he was known to be a pretty bad customer, with a long rap sheet even at his young age, including an arrest for attempted murder. He was covered in gang tattoos. But when you have a patient like that, you can't make judgments. Our job was to save his life and provide the best care possible, which we did.

"He recovered well," Dr. Ralston said. "He was young and strong, and he was talking a mile a minute the last few days he was in the hospital. He told us how grateful he was that we saved his life. But when his friends—mostly other gang members—came to visit him, they told us Juan was like a different person, that his personality had changed. Later, we found out he'd enrolled in community college and had learned to play the piano. Imagine that."

"So he went from a being a bad person to a good person?" Marybeth asked.

"Apparently," Dr. Ralston said. "But it didn't work out for him in the end. The gang didn't like it that he left them, and apparently there were a bunch of old grievances. Juan was killed in a drive-by shooting a year after he was released from the hospital. He was on his way to college when they got him.

"Then there's the case of Phil Gage," Dr. Ralston said. "He was a thirty-two-year-old husband and father of two little ones, and he worked construction over in Red Lodge. One day, he was going up a ladder when another worker was coming down. This other worker was holding a nail gun at his side and Phil climbed right up into it and it discharged. The nail gun shot a sixteen-penny nail through Phil's skull into his frontal lobe. When they brought him to the emergency room, the point of the nail was sticking out of his face right here," she said, indicating a spot just below her left eye.

"We put Mr. Gage into an induced coma, just like we did for your husband, and we removed the nail. Phil recovered nicely. He had such a wonderful family, and they were a delight when they came to visit him. His two little daughters were dolls, and they gave us hand-drawn thank-you notes. Mrs. Gage told us that Phil was the best husband and father in the world, and that they were very devout Mormons who didn't drink, smoke, or party. Phil's employer told us he was grateful that he hadn't lost the best worker he'd ever had."

Marybeth felt her stomach tighten. She was dreading what would come next.

"A year after he was released from here, Phil Gage beat his wife almost to death and he went on the run with a seventeen-year-old runaway he'd met at a bar in Red Lodge. We later learned that he'd been fired from his construction job because he'd become belligerent and insubordinate, and he kept getting into fistfights with other employees.

"When the police finally located him at a bar in Hardin, Phil shot one of the officers and they shot Phil a half dozen times. They brought him here for emergency care, and I recognized him right away. It was Phil Gage on that operating table, but everything about him was different. He was surly, profane, and vicious. He's divorced now, and he's serving time at the state prison in Deer Lodge."

When Dr. Ralston read the look on Marybeth's face, she said, "Oh, I'm sorry. I might have said too much. What you need to keep in mind is that it's possible your husband may have no changes at all, or *some* changes in his personality. It can go either way. There is no way to know at this point."

She went on to brief Marybeth on the next steps: reducing his medication slightly to stimulate brain function, keeping his blood pressure stable, and preparing for surgery when his GCS level was adequate.

Marybeth half heard what the doctor was saying. Mostly, she wondered what her life would be like after the surgery, provided that Joe recovered.

Would he start playing the piano?

Or would he chase her through their house with a baseball bat?

With those questions in mind, Marybeth signed the paperwork authorizing surgery. Dr. Ralston rose, patted Marybeth gently on her shoulder, and left the room.

As SHE DID, a call came through on Marybeth's phone from her mother, Missy. Marybeth stared at the screen for a moment, weighing whether or not she wanted to answer it. She sighed, punched the icon, and said, "Yes?"

"Marybeth, I just heard," Missy said.

"Thank you for calling."

"Sweetie, I've been thinking about it. You can look at this as a tragedy or an opportunity to start a new life."

"*What?*"

"That's what I've always done, you know. I look past a bad situation and move on. It's worked for me, Marybeth."

Marybeth held the phone out and stared at it for a moment, trying to imagine the monster on the other end. She pictured Missy sitting on her love seat in her home in Jackson Hole with a martini in front of her. The woman could barely contain her glee.

"Mom, Joe is not dead," Marybeth said.

"He isn't? I heard he got shot in the head."

"He did, but we're in the hospital. He's very much alive, and they're going to do surgery."

There was a pause before Missy said, "Oh."

"Do *not* call me again," Marybeth said before angrily terminating the connection.

BECAUSE THERE HAD been so many texts and calls in regard to Joe's condition from so many people—Governor Rulon, Sheriff Sondergard, the new director of the Game and Fish Department, and what seemed like half of Twelve Sleep County—Marybeth decided to write a social media post that would address Joe's status. The idea went against her instincts because she was not a Facebook person and she disliked the idea of offering up their privacy like that. But she couldn't think of any other way of providing an update to so many people, many of whom were close friends.

Marybeth decided to leave out everything Dr. Ralston had told her about the condition of the other patients who'd had similar injuries.

But when she activated her phone, she saw the text from Lucy:

> Sheridan has been arrested and she's in the county jail.
>
> We're headed there now to try and spring her.

CHAPTER TEN

Three Weeks Before

WITH BISCUIT SNORING on the seat beside him, Joe hummed down Antler Creek Road in his pickup, leaving a long wash of dust that looked like the rooster tail of a speedboat. It was midmorning and the sky was leaden and close and snow flurries obscured the summits of the mountains that rose to his left.

When he reached the junction, Joe took the middle fork of the road and passed under an ancient wrought-iron arch that read **BUCHOLZ CATTLE COMPANY**. Soon, there was a series of old tires hung on fence posts with **PRIVATE–NO TRESPASSING** spray-painted in white along the sidewalls.

Joe scrolled through contacts on his cell phone and punched up the name Shelby Bucholz. The call was routed through the truck's interior speakers via Bluetooth, and after five rings she answered. He'd learned not to call John Bucholz because the rancher never picked up.

"Hey there, Shelby," he said. "It's game warden Joe Pickett."

"I can see that. What's up?"

Shelby Bucholz had a high, grating voice that cut through fog, or in this case, a poor connection.

"I'm headed out your way. Are you at home?"

"Today?" Shelby asked in alarm. Then: "We're sorting cattle out in the corrals."

"Yeah, I need to talk with you today. Just a few minutes of your time. Is John there with you?"

"He is, but we're pretty busy."

"Great—I'll be there in fifteen minutes."

"What's this about?" she asked.

"It's about a moose," Joe said.

"Oh, that," Shelby said with obvious disdain.

"We can talk about it when I get there," Joe said before disconnecting the call. He didn't want to give her the opening to delay his visit or try to reschedule it. There wasn't enough time for that.

HE'D RECEIVED THE call through dispatch in Cheyenne an hour before. The reporting party, a hunter from Wisconsin, said that he'd wounded a bull moose in the willows near Antler Creek, but that the animal had broken into a run before he could finish it off. The bull had loped from the public land through a barbed-wire fence onto private land, dragging yards of wire with it. Eventually, the animal had disappeared into a thick stand of pine forest.

According to the RP, the geomapping app on his phone had said the private land belonged to John and Shelby Bucholz. When the hunter called the Bucholzes to ask if he could pursue the wounded game, the woman he spoke to—no doubt Shelby, Joe thought—had allegedly told him to "fuck off."

The moose hunter was distraught, and said he was at a loss at what to do.

Legally, as Joe knew, the Bucholzes had every right to deny permission to the moose hunter to cross over onto their property. They even had the right to deny access to their ranch to Joe unless he could show probable cause or arrive with a warrant.

Ethically, though, Joe hated the idea of letting a magnificent creature slowly suffer and die while wrapped in barbed wire. There weren't *that* many moose in his district since the wolves had moved in, and standing by while the meat from a twelve-hundred-pound bull rotted simply disgusted him. He hoped the ranchers would be reasonable with him.

THE BUCHOLZ RANCH wasn't the largest landholding in the valley by a long shot, but it was geographically diverse. Mountains occupied the western half of it, and the steepest slopes held elk, bighorn sheep, mountain lions, black bears, and ptarmigan. Preceding the foothills were rough badlands, a labyrinth of deeply cut and multihued draws and arroyos. The valley floor, where the ranch headquarters was located, was lush with good grass and irrigated hay.

As Joe skirted the foot of the mountain on the way to the headquarters, something caught his eye through the passenger window. He slowed down. There was an aircraft of some kind flying low in the distance, passing over the contours of the badlands. It was noticeable because of its low altitude and bright colors against the dark sky. A helicopter.

Joe stopped his pickup and plucked a pair of binoculars from the console. Biscuit noticed the lack of movement, yawned loudly, and stretched.

The helicopter was painted red and yellow, and there was an anomaly about its shape, he noticed. Instead of a rounded-off nose, there was a long pole of some kind sticking out from beneath the craft, like the stinger of a wasp. At the tip of the pole was an oblong protuberance in the shape of a football.

The craft completed a long sweep of the badlands, then banked and continued on in the same direction from which it had come. Joe was too far away to see the markings on the side, or to see who was piloting the helicopter. Eventually, it flew too far to the south to see it clearly. Joe knew that Lorne Trumley's Crazy Z-Bar Ranch bordered the Bucholz property in that direction, and he wondered if Trumley was aware of the helicopter flight so near to his land.

He lowered the glasses and thought about it. Some ranchers used aircraft to keep track of their cattle, but as far as he knew the Bucholzes didn't have a plane or a helicopter. Owning and flying an aircraft was expensive. The rumor around Saddlestring was that the couple was in financial straits, and that they had outstanding debts everywhere from the feedstore to the large-animal veterinarian. Joe recalled Sheridan telling him that they'd stiffed her as well.

Hunters sometimes illegally scouted game from the air, but using a helicopter out in the open like that seemed risky and unnecessary.

Joe jotted, "Copter, Bucholz Ranch, 10:03 a.m." and the date in his notebook. It was to remind himself to ask the manager of the county airport about the aircraft. If there were reports of poaching or cattle rustling in the area, he might be able to provide a clue as to who was responsible.

He'd also ask Lorne Trumley. Joe enjoyed having coffee with the old rancher from time to time, and simply checking up on him. Since Trumley was in his eighties and lived alone on his ranch, Joe worried about him.

The ranch headquarters was a smattering of old buildings on the valley floor. A massive barn dominated the collection, and like all of the structures it was painted white with a red roof. The main ranch house was three stories without a large footprint, and it looked to be over a hundred years old, like the barn. As he got closer, Joe noted that the landscaping had been overlooked for quite some time and that most of the buildings could use fresh paint.

A dust cloud hung over the corrals behind the barn, and Joe could see that the pens were packed with writhing cattle. It was that time of year, he knew, for cattle to be sorted and shipped to other pastures in warmer climates or to meat-processing facilities.

Four figures on horseback stood out as Joe neared the corrals. The riders were within the pens, waving their arms or slapping their thighs with coiled rope to sort cattle. John Bucholz was there, as well as Shelby. Two hands Joe recognized were with them. Both men were longtime tweakers who hung out in the parking lot of the Wet Fly Bar on the outskirts of town, haranguing patrons to throw a few dollars their way or buy them a drink. They weren't cowboys, although they'd obviously been convinced to help out with the gathering of cattle. Apparently, Joe thought, the Bucholzes were desperate for temporary hired hands. The mounted tweakers, who were dressed in baggy hoodies and sneakers, were visibly sweating, despite the chill. Their riding style suggested they weren't comfortable in the saddle. They looked like they couldn't wait to dismount and score a hit with whatever cash they were making that day.

Joe told Biscuit to stay inside the cab when he got out. He approached the corrals on foot. He rested his arms on the top rail. The cacophony of frenzied bleating and calling from the cattle was almost mind-numbing.

Shelby acknowledged him with a wave of her coiled rope, indicating that she'd be there soon. John did a quick tip of his hat brim, but turned back to the cattle.

While Joe waited, he surveyed the ranch from his vantage point. Beyond the ranch house and two small structures that looked like they might have once been used by employees, the other outbuildings were weathered and in poor shape. What had once been a proud ranch headquarters now looked to be in steep decline. Windows were missing, roofs sagged, and brick chimneys were crumbling.

On the edge of the compound was a long line of vehicles parked next to each other. It was like an automotive history of the Bucholz place, with pickups, sedans, and SUVs dating back to the 1920s. The most recent auto was an International Harvester Scout from the 1970s.

Beyond the grounds itself, he noted several small log cabins tucked away in an ancient aspen grove about three hundred yards from the main ranch house. He wondered if the cabins had once been used by visitors or guests, or perhaps hunters.

That's when he noted a movement through the window of the nearest cabin. A form passed from right to left and Joe caught a glimpse of a round white face. Then it was gone.

"So what can we do for you, game warden?" shouted John Bucholz over the noise from his animals.

Joe gestured toward his pickup while covering his ears with his hands. *Someplace we can talk*, he mouthed.

Bucholz nodded in agreement, then turned in his saddle and hollered, "Shelby, take a break." When his wife turned her horse to join him, John pointed at his two temporary ranch hands.

"You two, keep sorting."

Joe opened the side gate so John and Shelby could ride out of the pen, then followed them across the ranch yard to his pickup. He noted that they'd engaged in a very animated conversation as they rode side by side, but that they were keeping their voices low so he couldn't overhear them.

John was swarthy, with a heavy brow and deep-set eyes. His four-day growth of beard made him look vaguely sinister, Joe thought. Shelby was thin and wiry, with gray-streaked red hair. She had a hawklike nose and pale blue eyes. She wore a brace on her right hand, but the injury didn't prevent her from waving it around emphatically as she made a point to John.

Joe was used to locals sometimes acting strangely uncomfortable when he arrived. It came with the territory. Even completely innocent citizens sometimes acted guilty while in the presence of law enforcement. But in Joe's experience, the Bucholzes hadn't reacted to him that way when he'd met them previously in town.

After both riders had dismounted, Joe said, "Thanks for taking a break. I won't take much of your time." Then, to Shelby: "What did you do to your hand?"

"Broke it."

There was no more explanation.

John and Shelby exchanged a quick glance. To Joe, it appeared to be the kind of look violators shared with each other when he entered their hunting camp.

He quickly outlined his reason for showing up, and he pointed toward the mountainside.

"If you let that hunter go up there and get his moose, I'd really appreciate it. I'll even go help him so he can get it moved off your property back onto public land. I'll give you a call and let you know how much damage was done to your fence."

"Is he gonna pay for the damage?" John asked. "Them moose walk through fences like they was tissue paper. That's why I don't like them on our ranch."

"I'll float the question about payment," Joe said. "But he's under no obligation to pay for the damage made by a moose. I suppose you'll just have to go over there and fix it yourself. I'll volunteer to help you out with that as well."

"No," Shelby said with finality.

"No, what?" Joe asked.

"We're not allowing that guy to trespass. Not today."

Joe was confused. He said, "Are you saying he could follow that moose another day?"

Again something passed between John and Shelby. It was as if neither wanted to speak next.

"Look," Joe said. "I'd be happy to go find the bull myself and put it down so it won't suffer any longer. I could donate the meat to the Wyoming Hunger Initiative in your name, if you want."

Finally, John shook his head. "I'll do it when we're done sorting cows."

"You'll take care of the bull?" Joe asked.

"I'll shoot the son of a bitch."

"I was kind of hoping for a different outcome," Joe said.

"Not today," John said. "As you can see, we're busy. The shipper is coming tomorrow." As he spoke, he placed his hand on Shelby's shoulder to indicate they were done talking. She got the message and turned toward her horse.

Joe was flummoxed. He couldn't explain the behavior or attitude of the Bucholzes. But there was little he could do about either.

John had his left boot in the stirrup and was starting to swing his right leg over the saddle when Joe asked, "What's with the helicopter out in the badlands?"

John froze for a second. Shelby did the same thing. It was a tell of some kind, Joe thought. Then the rancher mounted himself in the saddle. When he was up there, he refused to make eye contact with Joe. Shelby also looked away.

"Don't know what you're talking about," John said.

"Really?" Joe asked. "It's kind of hard to miss. It's flying low on some kind of grid pattern, it looked like to me. You really don't know that it's been flying over your ranch?"

"Probably over Trumley," John said.

"No, I'm pretty sure it was over your land."

"Don't know nothin' about it," John said. Shelby had already spurred her horse to return to the corrals. Her back was to Joe.

"Another thing I was wondering," Joe said. "Who is it that looked at me from one of your old cabins? Is he a ranch hand, or a boarder, or what?"

John Bucholz turned his head and glared at Joe. His eyes were mean. He said, "You've had your five minutes, game warden. Now I gotta get back to my cows."

"You're sure about putting that bull out of its misery?" Joe asked. "I thought you were too busy."

"I said I would, didn't I?"

"What about the meat?" Joe asked.

"Coyotes gotta eat, too," he said.

FRUSTRATED, JOE LEFT the ranch and drove toward Antler Creek Junction. He told Biscuit, "That was one of the strangest experiences I've had in a while." He felt like he'd just had a long exchange with people using English as a second language.

Biscuit looked back with empathy.

The helicopter was no longer flying over the badlands, he noted. But before he reached the junction, he had to pull over to allow a high-tech drilling truck to pass by. Inside was a driver and a passenger, and the lettering on the driver's-side door read **GLOBAL EXPLORATION**. The license plates were from Texas.

Under his previous note about the helicopter sighting, Joe wrote down the name of the company so he could look it up later.

As he did, his phone lit up with a text. It was from Shelby Bucholz.

> John's on his way to take care of that moose, like he said. You'll keep that helicopter stuff just between us or you'll be sorry.

Joe thought, *What* is going on out here?

And: Was Shelby threatening him?

CHAPTER ELEVEN

November 16

An hour later, April pushed through the double doors into the lobby of the sheriff's department and made a beeline to Kristy Austin behind the counter. The receptionist looked up as April flashed her PI license card and said, "We're here for Sheridan Pickett."

Lucy was a few steps behind her sister, and she was visibly uncomfortable with the situation. April's typical "ready-aim-fire" way of dealing with the problem didn't jibe with Lucy's preference for more reasonable persuasion. Lucy had her hands thrust deep into the pockets of her parka and she studied the ceiling as April made her demand.

"I'm sorry," Austin said. "But no one is here who can help you right now."

"What do you mean?"

"Deputies Carroll and Bowkley are in the field investigating the shooting incident that happened yesterday. You know, the one that involved your *father*," Austin said with emphasis.

"We're glad they're actually doing something," April said. Then: "So where is this Sheriff Sondergard?"

"He's not in the office at the moment."

April put her hands on her hips and glared at Austin. "We need to get our sister out."

"I can't help you with that," Austin said. "You'll just need to take a seat and wait for one of the officers to come back."

April said, "We don't have time for that. Is she under arrest right now?"

"I'm not privy to the details."

"You have no right to hold her if she isn't," April said.

Lucy attempted to intervene by touching April on the arm and gesturing toward the door. April ignored her.

"Where is the sheriff right now?" April asked Austin.

"I'm not at liberty to say."

April sighed loudly and rolled her eyes in frustration.

"Showing me a private investigator credential from Montana won't get you anywhere here in this office, by the way," Austin said. "But it was a nice try."

"I told you that wouldn't work," Lucy whispered to her sister as they retreated.

"This is a small town," April said to Lucy in a huff. "We'll just go out and find him."

WITHIN FIVE MINUTES, April and Lucy located a sheriff's department SUV parked in front of the Burg-O-Pardner restaurant. The lot was filled with other vehicles.

"He's joining the good old boys right off the bat," April said to Lucy. "We probably should have come here first."

The "Main Street Mafia," as they were known around Saddlestring, convened every day for midmorning coffee at a round table in a side room of the Burg-O-Pardner. The Mafia consisted of the mayor, several town councilmen, a county commissioner or two, the man who owned the grocery and liquor store up on the hill, the superintendent of the school district, and Hugh Williamson, who owned the largest construction company in the valley.

The group convened to discuss matters of the town and the county, and it was well known that the Burg-O-Pardner was where the real decisions were made.

Lucy once again reluctantly trailed April as her sister strode into the room and pointed at a tall, uniformed man who had to be the new county sheriff.

The men at the table all turned their heads toward April and Lucy, and the discussion they were having about the shooting of Joe Pickett went immediately quiet.

Lucy heard one of the men whisper, "*They're two of the Pickett girls*" to another.

"How's your dad doing?" the mayor asked. "We're all real worried about him."

"It's touch and go," April said. Then: "Sheriff Sondergard, could I please get a minute of your time?"

Lucy added, "He's *maybe* a little better than that."

"Tell your mom we're praying for him," the mayor said.

"Thank you."

Sondergard looked quizzically at the back-and-forth, then excused himself, saying, "I should be right back."

"THANKS FOR GETTING me out of there," Sondergard said as he joined April and Lucy and they moved into the main dining area away from the Mafia. "I was told this is the 'room where it happens' here in Twelve Sleep County and I thought I better come see what it's all about. Now, what can I do for you two?"

"Our sister Sheridan is in your jail," April said. "We need to get her out."

"*What?*"

"You heard me. She called us about an hour ago and said one of your guys roughed her up and threw her into the county jail."

Sondergard stepped back, genuinely surprised. "One of my guys? You mean, one of my deputies?"

"That's what she said."

Sondergard's eyes got big and he raked his fingers through his hair. "I just saw her this morning in my office. I don't know anything about this. What was she arrested for?"

"You'll have to ask her," April said. "She told us she was looking into our dad's shooting."

"Look," Sondergard said, fitting his cowboy hat on his head, "we need to sort this out. I'll meet you two at the department in five minutes. I'll take my cruiser and I'll call my deputies to find out what happened. Did she say who arrested her?"

"Deputy Bowkley," Lucy responded. "I think that's his name."

"He's new on the team," Sondergard said. "There's probably some kind of misunderstanding."

"We'll meet you there in five," April said.

When they had shut the doors of April's vehicle, Lucy said, "Sheridan's right. He's kind of hot. And he seems nice, too."

"Never trust a cop on first impression," April said as she started the engine. "That's one thing I've learned in Montana."

"That's Montana," Lucy countered.

"It's the same everywhere."

"Well, I like him."

"You like everybody."

Sheridan followed Sondergard through the hallway that led to the lobby from the cell she'd shared for an hour with a sixty-year-old vagrant named Marta, who had been arrested the day before for soliciting customers at the Stockman's Bar. Marta had told her that she was from Hot Springs, South Dakota, and she was just trying to get enough money to get someplace warm, like Los Angeles. She had an ex who had a tent on a street there, she'd said.

Sheridan was grateful Sondergard had released her, and she tried to read his mood, but it was difficult. He'd barely said a word when he let her out, and his manner was all business.

She got a glimpse of her sisters waiting in the lobby, but Sondergard ushered her into his office before they got there. "I need to talk with you," he said brusquely.

Sheridan sat down in the chair she'd used earlier, and Sondergard swung behind the desk into his. "I talked to Deputy Bowkley on the way over," he said. "He didn't know who you were and he thought you were trying to screw up our crime scene and maybe even steal some objects from inside. He's a by-the-book kind of guy and he was probably trying to impress me."

"It was a misunderstanding," Sheridan said. "I never would have taken anything from inside my dad's truck."

"I believe you," Sondergard said. "But that doesn't change the fact that you were caught inside the county garage potentially contaminating a crime scene."

"I was careful not to do that," Sheridan said. "I didn't disturb a thing."

"That better be the case," Sondergard said. "If we find anything different, I'll have to charge you."

"You won't."

"I told you to stay away."

"I know you did," Sheridan said. "And I told you my sisters and I planned to look into the case on our own."

Sondergard rubbed his face with his hands, clearly frustrated.

Sheridan looked away so he couldn't see tears in her eyes. "I had to see it. Seeing my dad's pickup brought it all home to me in a way I didn't expect. Seeing those bullet holes in the windshield . . . I can't believe he survived. And I definitely agree with you that there was more than one shooter. The bullet holes in the front fenders came at different angles. Even I could see that."

Sondergard sat back in his chair and studied the ceiling tiles for a moment. "I'm sorry. Still," he said, "you're making this difficult for me."

"That's not my intention. I think if we're going to solve this crime, we all have to work together, like I said earlier. You and your team have the tools, and we have local knowledge. It's a good combination if we keep each other informed of what we find."

"I'm going to let you go, Sheridan," Sondergard said. "It may be against my better judgment, but that's what I'm going to do. But this can't happen again."

"It won't—I don't think," Sheridan said with a smile.

Sondergard told her that he'd sent both of his deputies out to interview suspects on Antler Creek Road.

"That's good," she replied. "I'd suggest you go take a look inside my dad's pickup as well. His phone has to still be in the cab somewhere. And there's a notebook you need to find. The information from the phone and the notebook could help lead to who did this."

Sondergard raised his eyebrows when he heard that.

"The password to his phone is 1-2-3-4," she said. "I told him to change it a dozen times to something better, but as far as I know, he never did."

OUTSIDE, THE THREE sisters gathered inside April's battered Toyota Tundra pickup with Montana plates. April sat behind the wheel and Lucy took the passenger seat. Both turned toward Sheridan as she briefed them on what she'd found in their father's pickup, and what Sheriff Sondergard had told her about the investigation thus far.

Sheridan opened the photo app and handed the device over the front seat so they could scroll through them.

"Be careful," she said. "Some of them are *really* hard to look at." Then she waited for the reaction.

Lucy gasped when she saw the bullet holes and the amount of blood inside the cab.

"I can't look at this," she said as she handed the phone to April. April scrolled through the photos with a grimace.

"It's a miracle he survived," she said.

"Deputy Bowkley arrested me before I could find Dad's phone or notebook," Sheridan said. "But they have to be in the cab somewhere. When I talked to Mom earlier, she confirmed that he didn't have them on him when he was flown to Billings."

"We need to know who he talked to that morning," April said. "And what he wrote down."

The sisters talked for a half hour about possible ways of finding out what their dad had done the morning he was shot.

Lucy asked if the sheriff's department had the capability to use cell tower records to identify the location of the last incoming calls to their dad.

"Possibly," April said. "We've worked with law enforcement in Montana to track lowlifes that way before. But it all depends on the circumstances. If someone is calling from a landline or a phone booth, that won't help us. But I suppose," April said with an evil grin, "Sheridan can use her feminine wiles to ask Sondergard to run that check."

"No, I can't," Sheridan said. "I'm on really thin ice with him right now. I'm not sure he trusts me since I broke into the county garage, and I really don't blame him."

"Maybe he'll figure to do that on his own," April said. "If he's competent, he might be sending a request to the phone companies as we speak."

"He's competent," Sheridan said defensively.

"We'll see," April countered. "After all, he just let you go . . ."

Lucy said, "Even if there's nothing helpful on Dad's phone, we really need to see his notebook. He probably jotted down his destination that morning, and even if he didn't, there might be something in there that could steer us in the right direction."

Finally, April said, "We're just throwing shit at the wall now to see if it sticks. This is getting us nowhere."

Although they knew that Deputies Carroll and Bowkley were in the process of interviewing the three ranch families, Sheridan said they needed to follow up in their own way. April and Lucy concurred.

"Do the three of us just show up at each ranch?" Lucy asked. "That might seem kind of overwhelming."

"I agree," Sheridan said. "I've been thinking about this while I was in jail. I think we interview them individually and then compare notes."

"Who talks to who?" April asked.

Sheridan said she thought April should interview the people at the McElwee Ranch and Lucy should go to the Double D. She'd take the Bucholz Ranch.

"What's your thinking?" Lucy asked.

"The McElwee Ranch is full of rough-and-tumble rowdies," Sheridan said. "April would fit right in with them."

April snorted at that.

Sheridan said, "The Double D owners are high-class individuals, or so they think. They'd welcome a young woman who just came back from Europe. They won't feel threatened by someone young and sweet."

"Makes sense," April said. "Plus Lucy is closest in age to Brandy than the two of us."

"Good point," Sheridan said.

"I guess," Lucy offered with an eye roll.

"Besides," Sheridan said, "I can't go to the Double D. Things are a little weird between Clay Junior's dad and me since Clay was killed. He kind of thinks of me as the daughter-in-law he never had, and I don't think he'd be very forthcoming.

"I'll go back to the Bucholz place. Maybe I'll use the pretense of trying to collect my fee. I think they'd buy that."

"When do we start?" April asked.

"Tomorrow."

Sheridan drove her SUV toward their parents' house on the river, with April following behind in her Toyota Tundra. Lucy had opted to join Sheridan and she sat in the passenger seat. She said she didn't like traveling with April. "April drives like a madwoman," she said.

They were discussing the questions Lucy should ask Clay Hutmacher when Sheridan's phone lit up. It was from the Twelve Sleep County Sheriff's Department.

"Ah," Sheridan said with a smile. "He kept my number."

"Of course he did," Lucy said.

"This is Sheriff Sondergard," he said through the Bluetooth speaker in Sheridan's car. Not Steve, or even Steve Sondergard. *Sheriff.* His tone was official, and both sisters exchanged a glance.

"I need you to bring the items back that you took," he said. "And I mean right now."

"What are you talking about?" Sheridan asked.

Sondergard's voice rose as he spoke. "Don't bullshit me, Sheridan. I need them back, and I mean immediately."

"You need what back?"

"The notebook and the phone. I need them back."

Sheridan said, "Steve, I didn't take anything. I swear to God. I got arrested before I could find them."

"Then why aren't they there?"

"I honestly don't know. Are you sure they're gone?"

"One hundred percent," Sondergard said. "Don't play more games with me."

"I'm not playing games, I swear it."

"They aren't there now," Sondergard said. "How do you explain that?"

"I can't. But tell me this, Steve. I had to surrender everything in my pockets when I was booked this morning. I even had to leave my own phone after I called my sisters. There wasn't another phone or a notebook taken from me. Check your records."

There was a long pause. Finally, Sondergard said, "Then who took them?"

"I don't know. But it wasn't me."

Again, Sheridan and Lucy exchanged a long look. They could hear a muffled exchange from Sondergard's side, and Sheridan guessed he'd covered the mouthpiece with his hand. When he came back, he said, "I'll have to call you back."

"Why? What's going on?"

"We got a report that there's been an incident near Antler

Creek Road. Something about a camper trailer. There may be a fatality."

"Is it related to what happened to my dad?" Sheridan asked.

"I don't know until I get out there," Sondergard said. "But in the meantime, keep your phone close."

With that, he terminated the call.

"You've got my number," Sheridan said to the dead line.

"What's *that* all about?" Lucy asked her.

"Your guess is as good as mine. Something about an incident."

"What about Dad's notebook and phone?"

"I just don't know," Sheridan said as she dialed April, who was still behind her, and filled her in.

"I've got to say it," April said after a beat. "How much do you trust your man 'Steve'?"

ON THE COUNTY road that led to the game warden station and state-owned home, Sheridan frowned when she looked into the rearview mirror. April was back there, all right. But a quarter of a mile behind April was a dark-colored GMC pickup.

Sheridan punched up April's number.

April answered by saying, "It's been with me since town."

"Do you know who it is?"

"No, but there are two men inside."

CHAPTER TWELVE

SHERIDAN SLOWED DOWN as she approached the sign that read **Game Warden Station / Saddlestring District** and took a left off the main county road and entered the dense lodgepole forest.

"Are they still back there?" she asked Lucy, who was turned around in the passenger seat looking out the back window.

"There's April," Lucy reported. Then, with her voice rising in alarm: "Yes, those guys are still behind her."

Sheridan called April and said, "Remember the trick we pulled on those dudes who followed us home from the Stockman's Bar last Thanksgiving?"

"I was just thinking the same thing," April responded.

"What trick are you talking about?" Lucy asked Sheridan.

"You'll see." Then to April: "Let's do it. I want to find out who these guys are."

The pines were dense on either side of the road the entire mile and a half from the county road to the Pickett home, which also served as the game warden station. So dense, in fact, that it was difficult to see the resident moose that often lurked in the timber and then suddenly stepped out onto the road in the evening and blocked traffic until it finally ambled off. But there were two old crossroads once used by lumber crews that weren't entirely reclaimed by the forest.

Sheridan increased her speed and built a cushion between her and April.

"Hold on," she said to Lucy.

"What are we doing?"

Sheridan hit the brakes and backed up onto one of the ancient roads to the left side. She reversed far enough that a driver on the road couldn't see her until they were upon her.

"We're trapping them," Sheridan said. "Hand me my shotgun."

"Shotgun?" Lucy asked, alarmed.

The weapon was on the back seat in a leather case. Rather than explaining herself due to the time crunch, Sheridan reached through the console opening and got it herself. She quickly shed the case and tucked the shotgun muzzle down between the driver's-side and passenger bench seat cushions. It wasn't lost on her that she'd learned the procedure from her dad while doing ride-alongs over the years.

As she checked the loads in the 20-gauge pump-action shotgun, April cruised by and greeted them with a friendly wave.

"Now what?" Lucy asked.

Before Sheridan could respond, the dark GMC pickup passed by them. Sheridan got a glimpse of the driver—he was wearing a stiff straw cowboy hat—but she couldn't see the passenger. She didn't recognize the driver.

"He didn't even look over," Sheridan said as she put her SUV into gear and roared out onto the road, where she stopped but kept her engine running.

April had also stopped, and her brake lights flashed as she reversed her momentum and shot backward. The GMC lurched to a halt, then backed up to avoid being hit by April's vehicle. It stopped moving fifteen feet from Sheridan's SUV.

"Trapped him," Sheridan announced.

"That's good, I guess," Lucy said with despair.

Both Sheridan and April emerged from their vehicles at the same time. Sheridan left the shotgun inside hers, but kept the door open for easy retrieval. April didn't display the same caution. She held a semiautomatic pistol down by her side as she walked toward the GMC.

"And here I am—the only one without a gun," Lucy lamented.

"There's a pistol in the glove compartment," Sheridan responded over her shoulder.

"Oh, great. Of course there is. Like I know how to use it."

Sheridan ignored her younger sister as she approached the GMC's driver's-side window. April went to the passenger side.

Sheridan rapped on the window and it whirred down. The driver was a big man in his late thirties or early forties with scarred cheeks and light-colored hair. He turned his head to her as his cheeks flushed pink with humiliation.

He's a hothead, Sheridan said to herself.

"What in the hell are you girls doing?" he growled.

"Seeing who is following us," Sheridan said.

"You blocked our progress."

"That was the idea."

The driver took a deep breath and turned so he was looking straight ahead. Sheridan stepped forward so she could get an angle on the passenger. He was roughly the same age, but dark and feral-looking. He wore a straw hat like the driver's. The passenger tried to ignore April, who was now right outside his window. He looked supremely annoyed.

"Who are you, anyway?" Sheridan asked. "What are you doing on this road?"

"It's a public road, isn't it?" the driver asked. "Isn't this the road to the game warden station?"

"It is," Sheridan said. "So what do you want with him?"

"This is fucking ridiculous," the driver said, whacking the steering wheel with the palm of his hand. "You two need to clear the road so we can get on our way."

"Again," Sheridan said, "who are you? I see you've got local plates, but I know most of the people around here. I've never seen either one of you before."

"You've got names, I'm sure," April said from the other side of the pickup.

"I'm Jason Witten," the driver said. "My buddy here is Marion Barber."

"Have you ever heard of these guys?" April asked Sheridan.

"Can't say I have."

"Your dad knows us," the man named Witten said.

"Probably poachers," April said.

Witten ignored her. He was quietly seething, Sheridan thought. She didn't want her sister to goad him any further.

"Mr. Witten," Sheridan said, "we were wondering why you were following us."

"I wasn't following you," Witten responded. "We were just all going to the same place."

"We live there. At least for the time being. What is it you wanted from my dad?"

Witten flinched, and Sheridan caught it.

"Your dad? Your dad is the game warden?"

"That's right," Sheridan said. "I'm Sheridan Pickett and the nasty one on the other side of your truck is April. The one in my car with the pistol aimed at you is Lucy."

Witten seemed tongue-tied all of a sudden. She was grateful he didn't look behind him to see that Lucy was unarmed. But that's when the passenger spoke up.

"How is your dad, anyway?" Barber asked. "We heard he got hurt."

Sheridan nodded. She wasn't sure she wanted to tell them anything. It was too painful to talk about at the moment.

In her peripheral vision, she noticed that Lucy had opened her door and was approaching them. She'd left the revolver behind. Lucy now stood shoulder to shoulder with Sheridan. She leaned into her older sister out of the men's earshot and whispered, "*Bad vibes.*"

April said, "He got hurt, but he's recovering nicely. He'll be back on his feet in no time at all."

"Well, that's good," Barber said. "I'm glad to hear it."

She said, "Do you really expect us to believe that you drove all the way out here to find out how our dad is doing?"

"It's true," Barber said with a grin. "We'd like to know where we can visit him. Or at least send a card."

"Are you friends with our dad?" Sheridan asked.

"Isn't everybody?" Barber said.

"*Real bad vibes,*" Lucy whispered. Then: "*Do you want me to get your shotgun?*"

Sheridan shook her head.

"Where did you two dudes get your new cowboy duds?" April asked with a chuckle. "It looks like you're dressed up for your first junior rodeo or something. Don't you know that you wear straw hats in the summer and black hats in the fall and winter?"

April's observation simply sounded like an insult, Sheridan thought. There was no way Witten or Barber could know that April used to work in a retail western-wear store. But at least April had distracted them from asking about where their dad was hospitalized for a moment.

"Your story is full of holes," Sheridan said to Witten and Barber. "I think it's time the two of you beat it."

"I'd be happy to do that," Witten said through gritted teeth. "But you've got us trapped here on this road."

"I'll back up," Sheridan said to Witten. "That way you can get out of here."

Witten nodded his head.

"Give me a minute," Sheridan said.

Lucy followed her and got into the passenger side again. Sheridan saw that April was returning to her own vehicle.

"There's something really off about those two," Lucy said. "I'm glad you didn't tell them about Billings."

"Me too," Sheridan said as she backed up onto the logging road.

The GMC fishtailed so fast in reverse toward the main road that both sisters waited to hear the sound of a crash. Which came less than a minute later.

Sheridan and Lucy exchanged a glance before Sheridan eased out onto the road to follow the vehicle to report the accident.

"I didn't like them at all, but I hope they didn't kill themselves," Lucy said.

But Witten hadn't smashed into a tree trunk, as they had first thought. The cow moose lay across the road with two broken legs and blood streaming out of its mouth. Broken glass from the GMC's smashed taillights sparkled on the road. But Witten and Barber were gone.

"Well, shit," Sheridan said. "Give me that pistol."

"Poor old girl," Lucy said with her eyes full of tears. "We're all going to miss her."

IN THE HOUSE, as Lucy rooted through the chest freezer for something other than pronghorn antelope or elk meat for dinner, and April scrolled through emails on her phone that she'd need to find time to answer, Sheridan's phone lit up with an incoming call from Sheriff Sondergard.

"It's Steve," she announced. "I need to take this."

"*Oh, Steve,*" April said, clutching her hands over her breasts and swooning to mock her sister. "Now it's '*Steve.*'" Which made Lucy laugh in the other room.

After listening for less than a minute, Sheridan disconnected and lowered her phone.

"So what does 'Steve' have to say?" April asked.

Sheridan's demeanor was grave. She said, "The sheriff's department was investigating a fire at a camper trailer today."

"So?"

"A man approached them and said he was the guy who called in the shooting. He said he saw everything."

"You're kidding," April asked, suddenly interested. "Who is this guy?"

"I don't know," Sheridan said. "But he's giving a statement now at the sheriff's office. Steve asked me if I'd like to sit in."

"What are you waiting for?" Lucy asked. "*Go.*"

"I'm gone," Sheridan said as she gathered up her jacket and key fob. "Call Mom for an update."

"I was just going to do that," Lucy said.

CHAPTER THIRTEEN

Sheridan found Sheriff Sondergard in the break room pouring coffee into two paper cups. His uniform was discolored from soot, and his eyes were red from exhaustion. "It's bad coffee," he said. "Do you want a cup?"

"That's okay, I'll pass."

She entered the room and then backed quickly away.

"I know," he said wearily. "I reek. I just spent the whole afternoon at the scene of a camper trailer fire in the middle of nowhere. It was amazing how fast that thing burned down to nothing. And then our tech guy showed up and found a body inside. Do you know what a human body smells like that's been burned to a crisp?"

Sheridan shook her head.

"It smells like roast pig," he said. "You know, when they take the whole pig out of the pit?"

"I get the idea."

"Anyway, it's been a rough day."

"Do you know what happened?"

"It's too early to say," he said. "The tech guy thinks accelerant might have been used to start it. We won't know until more testing is done. It could be suicide or an accident, but it could be murder. Man—a shooting one day and a possible arson and murder the next. What's going on in this county?"

"Nothing good," Sheridan said. "Is the trailer fire related in any way to what happened to my dad?"

"I thought about that, of course," Sondergard said. "If they're related, I can't offer a plausible connection. But it's still early. The tech wouldn't have been there so quickly, but he was just a couple of miles away at the junction where the shooting took place. So it's all in basically the same area."

"Do you know who it was?"

Sondergard nodded. "We're pretty sure. A guy from Casper named Budd Betts. We ran his plates. But please keep that confidential until we can notify the next of kin. That's another thing I'm not looking forward to."

"What about the guy who called in the shooting?" Sheridan asked.

"He's in the witness room. I know I probably shouldn't do this—asking you to sit in. But since we're sort of working together, I made that decision. I haven't started with him yet. He said he'd like a cup of coffee."

Sondergard pointed at the second cup and said, "After he tastes this, he might not want to talk to us."

Sheridan followed Sondergard into the small room off the lobby that was used for staff meetings, witness statements, and interrogations. It was bare-bones except for a faded photo of the Tetons on the east wall. There was no one-way mirror, although there was a video camera mounted in the top south corner and a digital recorder on the tabletop.

The witness thanked Sondergard for the coffee, then winced when he sipped it.

"Sorry," Sondergard said. He sat down in a hardback chair across from the man and motioned for Sheridan to take the other one.

"This is Sheridan Pickett," Sondergard said. "I asked her to sit in."

The witness nodded as he studied her closely. He was not as dirty as Sondergard, but it was close, Sheridan thought. He was in his midthirties, with a long unkempt beard. His eyes were startlingly blue, and he had an axe-like nose and thin lips partially obscured by facial hair. He wore buckskin trousers that were shiny from use, and a rough cotton tunic decorated with tiny colored beads. The skin of his hands was darkly tanned. He looked like someone who had just stepped out of a tipi at a mountain man rendezvous in 1829, Sheridan thought. Except for the cell phone that was facedown on the table in front of him.

Sondergard reached out and pressed the RECORD button on the machine.

"It's eight forty-two p.m. on Wednesday, November 16. I'm speaking to Earl Wright of Yoder, Wyoming. With me is Sheridan Pickett, the daughter of the game warden who was shot yesterday morning."

Wright frowned. "He was your dad?"

"Yes."

"Damn, I'm sorry for your loss."

"He's not dead."

Wright's eyes enlarged. "He's not?"

"No, he's hanging in there."

"He sure as hell *looked* dead to me."

"Well, he isn't. Nevertheless, we're hoping that what you tell us can help identify and catch the shooters."

"That's a lot of pressure on me, isn't it?" Wright asked rhetorically.

"Excuse me," Sondergard said, shooting Sheridan a *Cool it* look. "Can we start this at the beginning? Mr. Wright, you told me earlier that you were hunting by yourself yesterday morning around ten o'clock. Let's start there with just the facts."

"Yup, I can do that. How detailed do you want me to be?"

"As detailed as possible, Mr. Wright."

Wright sat back and stared at the ceiling for at least a minute. Sheridan presumed he was gathering his thoughts.

Sondergard flipped to a fresh page on a legal pad and poised his pen over it. Sheridan was impressed that the sheriff planned to take his own notes, even though the interview was being taped and filmed. It showed professionalism, she thought. It had been a long time since "professionalism" and the Twelve Sleep County Sheriff's Department had been considered together in her mind.

"Okay," Wright said, "I got up about an hour before the sun rose. It was damned cold with all that snow on the ground, and my fire had gone out during the night. So I spent about forty-five minutes getting a new one going. Are you familiar with a bow drill?"

Sondergard looked at Sheridan for clarification.

"It's a primitive fire starter," she said. "You wrap a stick with string or twine and rotate it quickly to create enough friction at the base that sparks make a fire."

"Exactly right, little lady," Wright said. "On TV it looks pretty easy. But in the dark without perfectly dry kindling and your muscles trembling because it's so damn cold—well, it takes a while. But it finally worked and I got my fire started."

"Why not use a match?" Sondergard asked.

Wright grinned. "Then that wouldn't be pure hunting now, would it?"

"Pure hunting?"

"Some folks call it primitive hunting, some call it traditional hunting. It's a thing I'm into. I head out into the field with the least amount of gear possible. In my case, it's the recurve bow I made myself, and my homemade arrows, and nothing to sleep under except an elk hide that I tanned myself. No matches, no optics, no ATV, no tent. It's basic survival hunting. It's Zen hunting."

"I've never heard of it," Sondergard said.

"Like I said, it's as close to nature as you can get," Wright explained. "I'm not one of those idiots with a custom rifle who bangs away at game animals from a thousand yards away, or sleeps in a lodge on fresh sheets. I do it my way. And when I'm blessed enough to harvest an animal, I process it myself and use every bit of it."

"Yet you have a cell phone," Sheridan said.

"My wife insists on it," Wright moaned. "It's my only concession to the modern world. I hate having it, and I wish I didn't. But she wouldn't let me go out unless I promised her I'd take it."

"Anyway," Sondergard said, "you started a fire. Go on."

"Once the fire burned down to coals, I roasted half of a rabbit for breakfast. I'd eaten part of it the night before. It sure was good."

Sheridan had been around her father enough over the years that she wondered if Wright had a small-game license with him for the rabbit. But for the sake of getting on with the story, she held her tongue.

Wright slowly recounted how he'd left his camp on foot with his bow and arrows. He found a small herd of mule deer in an arroyo, but after a half-hour crawl, he was unable to get close enough to get a shot at the buck. He stayed within the network of draws and arroyos in pursuit of the deer, trying not to make a sound.

Around eight thirty, he guessed, he heard the sound of a motorized vehicle ahead of him. The wind picked up and drowned it out, so he presumed whoever was driving it had left the area.

But as he topped a sagebrush-covered hill, he saw that he'd been wrong. The ATV he'd heard was parked about a mile away on a slope opposite him, and Wright watched as two men worked their way down to the bottom of the swale on foot. They both had rifles slung over their shoulders as they walked, and they were dressed in camo.

"I couldn't figure out what their game was," Wright said. "I thought they must be hunters, but I couldn't figure out their strategy. They were walking from their ATV toward the road. I mean, that area is a known migration route for game, but that's not how you'd hunt them."

Wright said he hid behind a six-foot lone juniper bush and he watched the two men through the branches. When they reached the bottom of the swale, he said, they split up. The bigger one hunkered down behind a large sagebrush on one side of the road, and the shorter man stretched out in a slight depression twenty yards from Antler Creek Road. They both set up facing east toward the road before it split off into three directions.

"That's when I saw the pickup," Wright said. "It was coming from the south. A green Ford, I think."

"My dad's truck," Sheridan said.

"It wasn't until that minute that I knew what was going on," Wright said. "It was an *ambush*. They were waiting for him like they knew he'd be coming, and when. There was nothing I could do to stop it. The truck was too far away, and the wind was blowing so that even if I started shouting no one would hear me.

"Then I saw those two fellows raise their rifles and *pop-pop-pop-pop*! They both just kept blasting away until the pickup stopped not far in front of them. I could see holes all over the truck and bullet holes in the windshield. It was a hell of a thing. Then them guys got up and started walking back to their ATV. It looked like they was arguing about something."

Sheridan asked, "Could you tell which road my dad was planning to take at the junction?"

"No. He never got close enough to take one."

"Can you describe the men?" Sondergard asked.

"Well, like I said, one was pretty big. Kind of fat. Maybe two hundred twenty to two hundred forty pounds. He had light hair, maybe red. He looked like a blustery kind of guy. The other one was more my size, and darker. He moved in a real deliberate way."

"My God," Sheridan said suddenly.

"What?" Sondergard asked.

"He just described two men who followed us home tonight. I can't be positive they were the same men, but it sounds like it."

WRIGHT DESCRIBED APPROACHING the pickup after the shooters had left. He said he did it cautiously. When he saw the holes in the windshield and all of the blood inside the cab, he powered up his phone and called 911.

"But why didn't you identify yourself when you called it in?" Sondergard asked. "And why did you leave the scene?"

"Well, it turns out those two shooters hadn't completely left the area," he said. "In fact, they took a couple of shots at *me* and missed. So I hightailed it out of there."

"Did you see what direction the shooters went when they finally left the area?" Sheridan asked.

"I didn't stick around that long," Wright said. "I boogied straight for my camp and didn't look back."

"You could have come back when all the emergency vehicles showed up," Sondergard said. "Surely you saw them."

"I did. But I was so bummed out by the whole experience that I didn't want to get further involved. I hiked back to my little camp."

"Why were you bummed out, as you put it?" the sheriff asked.

"Well, it goes back to what I was telling you earlier," Wright said. "This is supposed to be a purifying experience. Just me and nature harmonizing. It's not supposed to be about ATVs, or shooters, or emergency vehicles. That's too much reality crashing in on me. It's like when one of those animatronic figures at Disneyland stops working right in front of you and you're reminded it's just a damned robot, not Abraham Lincoln. It just really spoiled my mood."

"So what changed your mind?" Sondergard asked. "Why come forward this afternoon?"

"Because of the damned spacecraft that nearly landed on me last night, that's why."

Sheridan and Sondergard shared a puzzled glance.

"Spacecraft?" Sondergard asked.

"Great big huge fucker," Wright said. "Lights all over it, coming right down like it was going to land on my camp. It filled the damned sky, and the exhaust from it kicked dirt up everywhere. I really did think it was going to land on me, or scoop me up, or some damned thing.

"I got up this morning and I just said to myself, 'To hell with this.' So I gathered my stuff and started walking out."

"That's when you showed up at the burned-up trailer?" Sondergard asked.

"Yup," Wright said. "I figured that spacecraft decided to leave me alone and go burn down some guy's camper instead. It probably used some kind of laser to do it.

"I'm lucky I survived," he said. "And I'm damned happy I decided to get out of there when I did. UFOs or UAPs—whatever they call 'em now—is a bridge too far in my primitive hunting experience, you know? I mean, I came here to commune with nature—not wind up getting poked and prodded by aliens like a piece of meat."

Sondergard sat back without responding. Sheridan noticed that he'd stopped taking notes.

"So WHAT DO you think?" Sheridan asked Sondergard out in the hallway after Wright had left the building.

The sheriff sighed. "I don't know what to think. I was right there along with him until he told us about the flying saucer. Now I wonder about his entire story."

"Me too," Sheridan said. "But he might have helped us identify the shooters after all."

"Tell me more about the two guys who followed you," Sondergard said.

Sheridan described them. "They introduced themselves, even. The driver said his name was Jason Witten and that the passenger was named Marion Barber."

"Those are the names they gave you?"

"Yes."

Sondergard eyed her and said, "Those two guys used to play pro football for the Dallas Cowboys."

"Ugh," Sheridan said, feeling her face flush. "I wouldn't possibly know that, but I guess I'm not that surprised."

"Probably two names they thought up on the spot. Did you get a plate number?"

"No, but it was local." She felt stupid for not thinking of writing down the license plate. "I'll ask my sisters if they thought to jot it down."

"Do that," Sondergard said. Then, after a long pause, he said, "We did a thorough search of your dad's truck. There was no cell phone or notebook. I've questioned everybody who had access to it as well. No one saw the items."

"Damn," Sheridan said. "It's a mystery."

"Yes, it is," he said. Then: "I'd love to ask you out for a nightcap tonight. But I stink so bad and I'm about ready to fall asleep standing up right here."

"I'll take a rain check."

"That's good news. Now go home. I know I will."

There was an awkward moment where she thought he might try to kiss her. But he apparently talked himself out of it.

"Keep an eye out for UFOs on your drive back," he said. "And Dallas Cowboys."

CHAPTER FOURTEEN

SHERIDAN ONCE AGAIN felt a wave of sadness wash over her when her headlights swept over the body of the dead cow moose as she neared the Pickett house in the dark. Ravens had already found it, and they took off en masse through the trees. She knew they'd need to fire up her dad's tractor to move the carcass farther into the forest off the road. She couldn't stand the idea of watching the moose be eaten away on a day-to-day progression by predators.

Seeing the moose again gave her another reason to find "Jason Witten" and "Marion Barber" as soon as possible. Those bastards.

As she arrived at the house, she was surprised to see Nate Romanowski's battered Jeep parked out front next to April's pickup. She pulled in beside it and turned off her lights and engine.

Sheridan glanced inside the Jeep when she walked past it, to note that Kestrel's black plastic car seat was buckled in the back. It looked incongruous in Nate's vehicle, which was usually filled with rifles, shotguns, climbing gear, animal parts, and hooded falcons perching on the headrests.

In fact, Sheridan nearly decked Kestrel when she opened the side door to the mudroom. April was chasing the little girl, who whooped at the close call. Kestrel managed to avoid the door as she ran athletically through the obstacle course of boots and shoes on the floor. She escaped by ducking under April's Frankenstein-like extended arms. After being eluded, April waved a quick hello to Sheridan, and then resumed her role as the monster-like pursuer of children.

Sheridan kicked off her shoes and she joined Lucy and Nate at the table in the dining room. There were several à la carte boxes of fried and rotisserie chicken on the table, with several pieces of each left. She grabbed a fried breast and bit a large hunk out of it.

"It was the best we could do," Lucy said. Then: "What did you find out in town from . . . Steve?"

Sheridan ignored the "Steve" jibe. "It turned out to be mostly a bust. The hunter was the guy who called in the ambush, we think. But he had credibility issues."

"Well, crap."

"Yeah. But we might have learned some things. I'll tell you all about them."

Nate said nothing.

Sheridan eyed Nate closely as she ate. He was tall and rangy, with a long blond ponytail secured by a falcon's jess. As always, there was an almost surreal stillness about him. She couldn't tell from looking at him how much he knew about the ambush, or about the actions the Pickett sisters planned to take to find the shooters.

"I talked to Mom for a long time," Lucy told Sheridan. She had to raise her voice because April was roaring in the hallway as she chased Kestrel. Sheridan could hear the furious pitty-pat of Kestrel's stocking feet on the hardwood as she ran to avoid capture.

"What did she say?"

Lucy got her phone out and opened a notes app. "I wrote some of it down because I didn't want to mess up the terminology," she said. "This is all pretty complicated."

Sheridan looked up at Nate. "So you know."

"I do now," Nate said in his whispery voice.

"Well, it's not like we can just call you," Sheridan said a little defensively.

It was true. Since Nate had returned from hunting Axel Soledad and was reunited with his daughter, he'd deliberately chosen to resume the ways he'd adopted for years before. He stayed off the grid the best he could, meaning no cell phones, no social media, no computer even. His presence on the internet stopped two years before, back when he was attempting to go legit as a husband, a small businessman, and then a father of a little girl.

Nate was still the primary owner of Yarak, Inc., the bird abatement company Sheridan managed. She delivered monthly profit and loss reports to his mailbox herself, and she went to his house on his distant compound in person if she needed to talk anything over with him. He seemed pleased with the way she was running the business, and he showed no inclination at all to step back in.

He was making up for lost time, he'd explained to Sheridan. Joe and Marybeth had taken Kestrel in while he was gone. Marybeth made no secret of the fact that she relished having a little one around her house again. So had her dad, although he wasn't as ready to admit it.

But as far as Sheridan could tell, Nate was doing a surprisingly good job as a single father to Kestrel since Liv had been killed and Nate had returned. He was singularly attentive to the little girl. He read to her, kept her away from screens, and cooked her meals. He also took her along with him everywhere he went. When Nate needed someone to look after Kestrel, he relied on Joe and Marybeth primarily and Sheridan on occasion.

Kestrel seemed amazingly well-adjusted, Sheridan thought, even though the four-year-old had rarely interacted with children her age. If she recalled the circumstances of her mother's murder, it didn't show. And if she'd rather be playing at home instead of helping her father field dress and skin out a pronghorn antelope or elk, or feed a mews of falcons fresh chunks of meat, she didn't protest that, either. Yet.

Kestrel was rambunctious, intelligent, and exceedingly verbal. She never stopped chattering, and Sheridan often wondered where she'd obtained her vocabulary living with the notoriously taciturn and at times obtuse Nate Romanowski.

Sheridan wasn't yet comfortable having the conversation with Nate that she assumed her mother had brought up with him: *What will you do when she gets older?*

"Mom said the neurosurgeon had an important talk with her today," April said. "They're doing a hemicraniectomy."

"What does that mean?"

"They're cutting a hole in the side of his skull," Lucy said.

"My God," Sheridan said, lowering the piece of chicken. "He

goes into the hospital with a bullet wound to his head and their way of treating it is to cut *another* hole into his head?"

"It's normal, I guess. Opening a hole in the skull allows the brain to sort of ooze out. It's a way of dealing with swelling."

Sheridan interrupted again. "I thought that's why they induced a coma in the first place—to reduce the swelling."

"And it's worked to a degree, Mom said. But this is the next step."

"I think we need a second opinion. How many holes are they going to drill in his skull?"

Lucy shook her head. "It's not like the brain shoots out or anything like that. Instead, it kind of swells out through the new hole like the top of a muffin."

"A *muffin*?"

"That's exactly the word she used. Think of a muffin top."

"I'd rather not," Sheridan said.

"Again, Mom stressed that the surgeon said it was standard operating procedure. The hole might remain open for a while, even when the brain stops swelling and it recedes back inside the skull."

"What about the piece of skull they remove?" Sheridan asked. "What happens to that?"

"I asked the same question," Lucy said. "I had this image of Dad walking around with a hole in his head. Well, apparently they can either fit the piece of skull right back into the hole, or they can make a new one with a 3D printer. Can you believe that?"

"It's hard to imagine," Sheridan said. "Do they know how bad the damage is yet?"

"Mom refuses to give us too much hope," Lucy said. "I think she's protecting us, like we're still little kids. She doesn't want us to think that he'll definitely survive this, and if he does, she doesn't want us to think he'll be back to his old self. I guess it all depends on where the bullet is lodged and how much damage it did on the way in. It also depends on how much damage is done when they take it out.

"But I got a vibe from her," Lucy said. "I got a vibe that maybe things aren't as bad as they could be. That if it all goes well, he might come through okay. She didn't say that, but I read it in her voice."

"Does she want us there?" Sheridan asked.

"She didn't say that."

Sheridan and Lucy looked at each other for a few seconds, each with their own thoughts. They came to the same conclusion at the same time.

"If she thought he was going to die, she'd want us there," Sheridan said.

"Exactly," Lucy said.

"He'll be fine," Nate said, weighing in. "Joe has never really used all of his brain before, anyway."

"Thanks for that," Sheridan said with a sigh.

"I've known him a long time," Nate said.

"So have we," Lucy said. "*All of our lives, in fact.*"

"DID YOU TELL her what we're doing?" Sheridan asked Lucy.

"Not really. If I did, I think she'd want to get too involved," Lucy said. "Or she'd insist that we stick tight and not take any chances. Either way, I made the executive decision that her time is best spent being up in Billings with Dad and not trying to run everything here."

"Which she'd do," Sheridan agreed.

"Can I say something that isn't sarcastic?" Nate asked.

"Go ahead," Sheridan said.

"Don't underestimate your mother. You may want to bring her in if things get hairy. In fact, you may want to bring *me* in."

"You can't just start ripping the ears off of three ranch families in Twelve Sleep County," Lucy said.

"That's too bad," Nate said. "They probably deserve it."

AT THAT MOMENT, Kestrel zoomed into the dining room and buried herself in Sheridan's arms. April appeared from the hallway and grinned.

"Is that monster after you?" Sheridan asked Kestrel.

"She is," Kestrel said, breathing hard.

"April is very scary," Sheridan said.

"She's diabolical," Kestrel said with emphasis.

"Where did she learn that word?" Sheridan asked, looking at Nate. He shrugged.

Back to Kestrel, Sheridan asked, "What do you think? Should Lucy and I go *get* her for you?"

Kestrel looked up, her eyes gleaming. "Yes, go *get* her."

Sheridan looked over at Lucy, who was already placing her phone on the table. Lucy was game.

The two sisters tore out from their chairs and April turned and ran down the hallway. Their footsteps thundered through the house. Sheridan and Lucy pinned April to the bed in the guest room and held her down until Kestrel could catch up with them.

"Tickle her!" Lucy said. "Get the monster."

Kestrel hesitated a second, then tickled April gently in her ribs with a single tiny finger. April knew to overreact. "Please, Kestrel, that's enough! Stop it, Kestrel!"

So Kestrel did it again. And again. Until April gave up.

When they were through and untangling, April looked at her two sisters and said, "You know I can take you both, don't you?"

"Yeah, we know," Sheridan confessed.

"Speak for yourself," Lucy said. "I've gotten stronger."

"Ha!" April snorted.

It felt good, Sheridan thought. It had been years since the three of them had wrestled like that. It had been years since they'd all been together for a meaningful length of time. Usually in the past, when they tangled, April would do something underhanded to break up the scrum, like give Sheridan a wet willy or elbow Lucy in the throat. But she'd restrained herself this time.

As soon as they were all up off the bed and standing, Kestrel called out, "Monster, come get me!"

She ran from the bedroom looking over her shoulder at April, beckoning her to follow.

"She's wearing me out," April confided before once again giving chase.

BACK AT THE table, with Kestrel watching *Bluey* in the family room, Sheridan briefed Nate on everything they knew thus far. Lucy and April added context and embellishments.

As they talked, Nate narrowed his eyes in anger twice. Once when Sheridan described her interaction with Deputy Bowkley and again when the sisters described their brief entrapment of Jason Witten and Marion Barber.

When they'd caught him up, Nate placed his hands flat on the table and looked from Sheridan to April to Lucy.

"Let's go over your plan again," he said.

CHAPTER FIFTEEN

Two Weeks Before

JOE ALWAYS DREADED making the journey to McElwee Land and Cattle. He never knew what to expect, and more often than not his experience there went pear-shaped.

Sisters Lisa and Lainie McElwee were notorious well beyond Twelve Sleep County, and their names bubbled up anytime there was a criminal conspiracy anywhere in northern Wyoming and southern Montana. Since he'd arrived to take over the Saddlestring District, the McElwee sisters' names had been linked to a large car theft ring, a big-game poaching scheme, a cattle-and-horse-rustling operation, and the disappearance of several undocumented transient workers in the area.

Recently, Joe had heard through the grapevine—which meant Marybeth overhearing what her morning library patrons talked about each day—that the McElwees had been associated with a scandalous scheme involving a Wyoming state trooper. The trooper, who'd been based in the neighboring town of Winchester, had been arrested and accused of pulling over suspicious-looking cars on the east-to-west Interstate 90 and confiscating large quantities of drugs and cash—without apprehending the drivers. The charges suggested that the trooper had been doing it for several years and that he'd come up with his methodology while stationed in Elk Mountain in the southern part of the state. There, he'd preyed on miscreants driving on I-80. The trooper operated under the assumption that the drug mules he stopped would be unlikely to report him for the thefts.

It worked for years. His scheme hadn't been exposed until he was caught on a remote Wyoming Department of Transportation webcam that was used to monitor the condition of the highway. In the video, the trooper could be seen throwing duffel bags of drugs or cash into the trunk of his cruiser while the driver and passenger were detained within his vehicle. After the transfer was made, the out-of-state travelers were kicked out of the cruiser and left gesticulating on the side of the road.

Although the trooper didn't overtly implicate the sisters in his crimes, there was no doubting that nearby I-90 bordered the northern edge of McElwee Land and Cattle, and that very little of the contraband was ever recovered. The rumor was that, after the trooper made a score on the interstate, he quickly laundered it via the McElwees and got it out of his hands.

The sisters weren't arrested, however. In fact, the trooper never got the *chance* to implicate Lisa and Lainie. On the day of his arraignment in Cheyenne, the trooper and his lawyer were the victims of a deadly car crash on I-90 when the lawyer's SUV plunged though the guardrail into the maw of a steep canyon below, killing both of them. There were no witnesses to the incident, although paint scrapings and broken glass found on the pavement above suggested that they'd been forced off the highway by another vehicle.

The canyon itself was located on the McElwee Land and Cattle Ranch. The McElwee sisters charged the county a trespass fee to access the smashed vehicle and to recover the two bodies.

Joe knew a little about the history of the ranch, and how unusual the sisters were when it came to fitting into the tapestry of the local ranching community. Unlike neighboring ranches, where the owners helped each other out when it came to fixing fences, gathering cattle, pulling pickups free of mud or snow, or lending equipment, no one had anything good to say about the McElwee sisters after the patriarch, Buck McElwee, died in the 2010s.

Joe knew that the vast majority of local ranchers were hardworking, community-minded, and stalwart guardians of the land. Lisa and Lainie stood out from them. And although the two sisters had created mayhem in Saddlestring and Winchester when they came to town and started drinking, the troubles hadn't really started until they'd inherited the ranch from their father. Apparently, Buck had been able to keep them under control.

Buck himself had been known as a tough negotiator and a hothead who sometimes stole water from his neighbors when he had the opportunity, but he'd generally gotten along with his fellow landowners—and the local game warden, whom he treated like a somewhat necessary but irrelevant "pain in the ass," as he'd referred to Joe.

When Buck was still around, the McElwee Trophy Hunting

operation, which was run by Buck, had had sometimes questionable clientele with Italian surnames from Chicago and Rhode Island. Although ninety-five percent of the hunters Joe had checked over the years were legal and law-abiding, it was the five percent who were the problem, and some of Joe's thorniest cases over the years had involved clients of Buck McElwee's.

In addition to killing the wrong species, like taking a trophy mule deer during elk season, or a bull elk during cow/calf season, some of Buck's hunters had performed remarkable feats of malfeasance. There was the "accountant" from Providence who'd shot Lorne Trumley's best mule, thinking it was a moose. And the "management consultant" from Chicago who'd sprayed a herd of cow and calf elk with bullets from a Thompson submachine gun and posted the video to social media.

Somehow, Buck was always able to make the case that he hadn't been present during the infraction, and Joe could never prove that he was.

But dealing with Buck McElwee was one thing. His daughters were something else entirely.

When Joe had departed the house that morning and left Biscuit at home for her own safety, Marybeth asked where he was going.

"McElwee Land and Cattle," Joe replied.

"God be with you," Marybeth said. "And please come home in one piece."

The issue this time was a fairly outlandish report from an archery hunter who'd said he'd been after mule deer on public land that bordered the McElwee Ranch. The hunter said he had climbed into the timber on the side of a mountain that overlooked the property and the ranch headquarters. From his stand near a game trail, he'd focused his binoculars on the corrals that adjoined the main house.

According to the archery hunter, he could see a magnificent six-by-six bull elk inside of one of the horse corrals. He said there was a short rope around its neck tethering it to a snubbing post in the center of the corral so it couldn't jump out. As he watched, the RP said a man emerged from one of the cabins behind the main house and approached the corral. Soon after, two other men joined him to watch the first man pull a semiautomatic pistol out of a shoulder holster and start firing. It took ten shots to bring the bull down.

"They didn't exactly look like hunters," the RP said.

What exactly that meant, Joe didn't know. The comment had been relayed to him from dispatch in Cheyenne.

"One other thing," the dispatcher told Joe. "The RP said the bull elk was staggering around."

"Staggering around?"

"Like it was drunk or something."

WHAT JOE *did* know was that it was highly illegal to forcibly restrain a big-game animal, or to hunt with a weapon of small caliber incapable of dispatching the elk in a humane fashion. And if the antlers were sawn off and the carcass left to rot, like the RP suggested, it was a case of wanton destruction for which Joe would happily charge the perpetrators—and the ranch owners who set it up and allowed it to happen.

Out-of-state hunters often joked with landowners that they'd appreciate it if a trophy animal was roped and tied to a tree so they'd be assured of success. Joe had never heard of it actually happening. Or *alleged* to have happened, in this case.

THE McELWEE LAND and Cattle headquarters was located on the other side of Eagle Mountain from the Bucholz Ranch, with the dividing line somewhere near the summit. The road in was rough; it hadn't been graded for years. Water-filled potholes made it slow going. Football-sized rocks migrated from beneath the surface into the road itself, making it even more hazardous.

Two miles from the headquarters, Joe flinched as a bald eagle nearly grazed his windshield, and he followed it as it flew away toward the mountain. As the eagle gained altitude, its talons folded up below it like landing gear. Then it suddenly veered to the north above a copse of aspen trees. The tree stand was a quarter way up the mountain slope. It was as if the bird didn't want to fly through the airspace above it.

Upon closer examination, Joe saw flashes of white among the aspen trunks and he brought his pickup to a stop. Something was in the trees that he'd never noticed before.

He fitted a spotting scope to his quarter-open driver's-side window and focused in on the aspen. When he did, he saw there was a two-track road through the sagebrush to the trees, and what looked like a camper trailer hidden inside. He thought that in the summer, when the trees were leafed out, it would be impossible to see the unit. But the lack of leaves exposed it.

"Hmmm," he said as he unfastened the spotting scope. "Why would they need a trailer all the way up there?"

THE TWO-STORY MCELWEE home was built of logs and it sprawled across the eastern side of the headquarters compound. There was a rough gravel lot in front of the home, with a series of open lean-to garages on the west side. To the north was an ancient barn also made of logs, and several large corrals behind it. Old and new vehicles filled the garages, as well as haying and stacking equipment.

Before entering the compound yard, Joe searched the distant mountain to the south. It was timbered, and he could see a border fence stitched up the slope until it disappeared in the pines. On the other side of that fence, he knew, was where a section of public land was located. He guessed that to be the location where the archery hunter had set up, and where he had reported seeing the elk in the corral.

Before Joe parked, he made a loop around the ranch yard so he could take a quick look at the corral. He was looking for an elk carcass, or possibly a gut pile or large bloodstain on the packed ground. He saw neither, although it did look like someone had raked over fresh dirt near the snubbing post, possibly trying to conceal the crime scene.

He pulled into the yard and parked out in the open within sight of the main house. When he cracked open the door to his pickup, a sudden outcry of manic barking broke the silence of the morning. Ranch dogs that were hybrid wolf mixes boiled out from beneath the porch of the log house and rushed the truck.

The pack of dogs snapped their jaws and barked at him and completely surrounded his vehicle. Joe waited, grateful that he'd made the decision to leave Biscuit back at home.

After about five minutes, he saw Lisa McElwee open the front door of the main house and shout at her dogs. When they didn't retreat, she slapped at her thighs and called them a bunch of "butt-holes."

Finally, the lead alpha male backed down and trotted to the house. The others followed.

When Joe swung out of his pickup, he had his right hand on his large canister of bear spray, just in case he needed to pull it out if the dogs attacked.

"You better not spray my babies," Lisa called out cheerfully.

"I hope I don't have to," Joe replied.

"You won't," she said, as equally cheerful. "Unless I decide to sic 'em on you."

LISA WAS A sight, all right, Joe thought. In her late forties, she wore a flowing floral caftan of some kind and Muck boots. Her dyed rust-colored hair was unkempt and it stuck out from her head in points like a starburst. She was fleshy and solidly built, but surprisingly fluid in her movements. Her eyes were dark and heavily mascaraed, which made her look like a raccoon emerging from a flower bed.

"Do you mind if I check out your corral?" Joe asked.

Lisa narrowed her eyes. "Why would you want to do that?"

"Oh," Joe said, intending to downplay it, "we got a report that there might have been some shenanigans involving a bull elk over there this morning."

"Shenanigans?"

He nodded.

"Ah, to hell with that," she said with a dismissive wave of her hand. "Why don't you come in and have a cup of coffee first? I just made it."

Joe hesitated. He'd never been invited inside the ranch house before. Usually when he arrived, either Lisa or Lainie met him on the porch. They kept a close eye out for visitors.

"Aren't you game wardens supposed to be big on landowner relations?" Lisa asked with a mischievous grin. The way she said "landowner relations" made it sound salacious.

"Yup."

"Then come on in. Whatever you want to look at ain't going anywhere."

From what Joe understood, Lisa and Lainie shared the house. Lisa occupied one side of the home and Lainie lived in the other. In the middle were the common rooms, including the kitchen, great room, and a pair of small business offices.

Joe glanced over his shoulder at the corral. He thought he saw some items glinting in the cheatgrass on the approach. Shell casings?

Whatever they were, he thought, they'd still be there after he had a cup of coffee inside. Plus, he was naturally curious to see what their house was actually like. Because he'd heard things.

"Sure," he said. "Thank you kindly."

"You don't need to take off your boots," Lisa said when Joe stepped across the threshold. "Unless, of course, you're planning to stay here awhile."

Joe stayed mum as he scraped the mud off his soles on a mat in the mudroom. He wasn't sure how to respond to that.

"This way," she said as she turned. He followed her flowing robes through the great room toward a small nook off the kitchen. The interior of the home was spacious but dark, with ancient hardwood floors and an unlit elk-antler chandelier hanging from the ceiling. All of the furniture was overstuffed and musty, and European mounts of elk, deer, bighorn sheep, and pronghorn antelope were affixed to the walls. Cobwebs stretched between the tines of most of the antlers, and dust motes floated across the floor as they walked.

A massive painting of a nude woman sprawled across a cowskin rug dominated one of the walls. In the painting, the woman lay on her belly looking up at the artist with a come-hither look. Her buttocks were in full view and illuminated with light from a source to the side, and her large breasts ballooned below her onto the cowhide.

It made Joe pause in his tracks. The painting was one of the things he'd heard about, but he hadn't been sure it was true until that moment.

"Yes, that's me," Lisa said. "Twenty years and thirty pounds ago."

"It's . . . nice," Joe said.

"That rug gave me lice."

"I'm sorry to hear that."

"I've got other ones up in my bedroom, but they're definitely not rated PG-13 like that one."

Was she inviting him to see them? Joe wasn't sure.

"My second husband, Eduardo, was a painter," Lisa said. "He was an asswipe, also. When I kicked him out, he wanted the paintings, but I wouldn't let him have them. You can guess why he wanted to keep them, but I didn't want him to have the pleasure, if you know what I mean. He called the artwork his 'wanker collection,' after all.

"I don't know where he is now, young Eduardo, but I'd guess he's found another older woman with a lot of money. But if someone ever broke into this house and either vandalized the painting or stole it off the wall, I know who I'd blame."

Joe followed her into the breakfast nook, which was more brightly lit due to a big east-facing window that looked out at the grounds.

"Between my sister and me," Lisa said as she poured coffee into a mug for Joe, "we've had a six-pack of rotten husbands over the years. Lainie has four exes and I have two. None of them have been worth a damn."

Joe cleared his throat and asked, "Do you mind if I ask you a couple of questions?"

Lisa cocked her head and pouted her lips. "I thought we could have a nice little visit first."

Joe conceded and sat back in his chair. He sipped at his coffee.

"I could warm up a cinnamon roll if you'd like," she offered.

"Thanks, but I already had breakfast."

"Then I hope you don't mind if I eat one in front of you."

"Feel free," Joe said.

After Lisa heated up a softball-sized roll in the microwave and sat down across from Joe, she studied him for a moment while she pulled it apart and ate it. She chewed her food in a slow, sultry way. She finished by licking her lips in a deliberate rotation of her tongue, and finished by licking her fingers. Her eyes never left his, and Joe felt the back of his neck flush.

"Has anyone ever told you that you have soulful eyes, Joe? Sensitive eyes. Even kind of sensuous?"

"Nope," he said.

"Well, you do. I mentioned that to Lainie once and she agreed."

Joe focused on a spot over her head to avoid her gaze. It felt to him that it was getting a little warm in the room.

"Marybeth winds up with the soulful-eyed game warden," Lisa said wistfully. "Lainie and I end up with the assholes of the world. Life just isn't very fair sometimes, wouldn't you agree?"

"I would agree that life isn't fair," Joe said. "This isn't a conversation I thought I'd be having today."

It was then that he contemplated the situation he was suddenly in, and what it might *actually* be about. Not Lisa flirting with him, not the painting of Lisa in the great room. Not his soulful game warden eyes.

It was about drawing him into the house and away from the corral.

Joe stood up and walked around the table to the large window. From there, by leaning far to the right, he could look to the south, which had been out of his view from where he'd sat at the table.

"What are you *doing*?" Lisa asked, obviously annoyed.

"Watching your sister collecting the shell casings by the corral," Joe said.

LAINIE MCELWEE WAS younger than Lisa by a few years, with long blond hair and delicate birdlike features—except for her eyes, which were hard and remorseless. She looked as though she'd been poured into her Wranglers. Lainie was a looker, Joe conceded. Hence the four husbands thus far.

Lainie was semi-famous in Saddlestring for mounting the bar at the Stockman's and swanning down the length of it kicking over every glass, then choosing a young cowboy to fall into the arms of. Joe had seen the performance once, and he'd had the wherewithal to grab his bourbon and water from the counter and retreat before she could vanquish it.

Lainie's hands were in the pockets of her Carhartt barn coat as she walked from the corral toward the house. Joe stepped outside and she froze when she saw him.

"What do you have in your pocket, Lainie?" he asked.

She didn't flinch or show any guilt. "Why do you ask, Joe? What business is it of yours?"

"It's my business if you picked up all of the shell casings," he said.

"What shell casings?" Lainie asked.

When Lisa shouldered her way past Joe on the porch to join her sister, Lainie asked her, "What in the fuck is he talking about?"

"Beats me," Lisa said. "He's pretty piss-poor at landowner relations, I've found."

JOE SQUARED OFF across from the McElwees, who stood shoulder to shoulder, confronting him. Their backs were to the corral, and it was as if they were daring him to get through them to reach it.

"I'm responding to a call we got this morning," Joe said. "An archery hunter up on the public section said he saw three guys shoot up a bull elk that was tied in place in your corral. If it's true, that's breaking a bunch of laws. And if it's true, it makes me pretty mad. I hate things like that."

Lainie rolled her eyes and said, "That's why they call him 'Dudley Do-Right' in town behind his back."

Lisa guffawed at that.

"They call me that to my face," Joe said, instantly regretting it. Then, to change the subject, he said: "Something else. The guy who called said the bull elk was staggering around like it was drunk. Do you have any idea why the elk would act that way?"

"You're the expert on elk," Lainie said. "Not us. Isn't that part of your job to know?"

Joe had given it a little thought on the way out. Chronic wasting disease was spreading in mule deer in pockets across the state. The natural disease caused deer to lose weight rapidly, and to walk around as if disoriented. There had been a few cases of CWD reported in elk, but none thus far in the Bighorn Mountains.

"If it was CWD," Joe said, "you'd be required to submit a blood sample for analysis. And if you didn't, that would be one more violation to add to your growing list."

"Maybe you ought to climb into your truck and get off our

private property," Lisa said. "We don't exactly remember inviting you on our ranch."

"I've got probable cause to be here. Lainie has a whole pocketful of probable cause. What are they, Lainie? Nines? Why don't you show them to me?"

Lainie didn't move, and she didn't take her hands out of her coat pockets. He'd heard the McElwees were rarely without concealed weapons on their persons. Did Lainie have a weapon on her? Joe wondered. And there was certainly enough room beneath Lisa's flowing caftan for a gun.

The McElwee sisters weren't backing down, which was another trait they were known for. He chose to de-escalate the situation. There was no need for a western gunfight. Even for a bull elk.

"So tell me," Joe said. "Do you two have hunters staying on your ranch right now? If they did this, and it sounds like they did, I'll cite them and let you two off the hook. Unless you want to confess that you roped a bull, poured whiskey down it, and tied it to your snubbing post."

The sisters exchanged a quick glance. Lisa said, "We don't have any hunters."

"So who were the three guys the archery hunter reported?"

Another look. And maybe a crack in their facade.

"Maybe our ranch hands," Lisa said.

"You've got three ranch hands?"

"Yes," Lisa said. "Our Mexicans, we call 'em. You can't hire good American dudes these days. They don't want to work."

Joe recalled that the reporting party said the shooters "didn't look like cowboys."

"Where are your men now?"

"Out," Lisa said.

"Do you know where?"

"No. Could be anywhere. It's a big ranch."

Joe sighed. He said, "I'm going to go check out your corral and bring my necropsy kit. I'll be able to determine if there's elk blood in the dirt where you raked it over. If so, I'll be back to talk to your ranch hands."

"They don't speak much English," Lainie said.

"I'll figure it out somehow," Joe said. "Are they legal?"

Neither sister responded, which told Joe all he needed to know.

"I'd hate to involve ICE in this, too," he said. "But that's your call."

It was an empty threat. The closest ICE agents were in Casper and they'd rarely respond unless the miscreant was incarcerated already. But he hoped the McElwees didn't know that.

"Now please step aside so I can get to work."

Reluctantly at first, the sisters parted so Joe could walk between them to his pickup. As he brushed by Lainie he heard the tinkle of what were likely shell casings in her pocket. Joe looked over his shoulder at her and said, "Gotcha."

"Fuck you," Lainie spat.

DEPARTING THE RANCH with several soil samples from around the snubbing post, Joe looked into his rearview mirror. Lisa and Lainie were still outside, still watching him. They'd observed him crawling around on his hands and knees in the corral, and they said nothing to him as he collected the evidence and climbed into his pickup to leave.

He'd send the samples to the Game and Fish lab in Laramie, and he'd likely know results within the next week. He kept an eye out for any vehicles that might contain the three Mexican ranch hands.

If they were actually ranch hands.

JOE CHECKED IN with dispatch on his way out toward Antler Creek Junction to ask for the contact details of the archery hunter who had made the report. He said he'd like to question the RP further about the cowboys who didn't look like cowboys, and especially the drunk elk. The dispatcher said she'd text him the RP's details.

As he disconnected, he realized that he was once again perpendicular to the trailer on the hillside he'd seen on the way in. He also saw that there was a fresh pair of tire tracks from the main road up to the trailer. Because the aspen grove was a few hundred feet higher in elevation than the main road, there was a dusting of snow from the night before on the ground that hadn't yet melted. The tracks became more pronounced as they rose toward the trees. He knew whoever had gone up there had done so between the time he arrived at the ranch headquarters and the time he was leaving.

Joe slowed, and turned right on the two-track. He could see no vehicles parked near the trailer, but the unit itself blocked him from seeing if a car or truck was hidden directly behind it. He was aware that he had no probable cause to enter the camper, although it was, *almost*, a couple of miles away from the public land where the archery hunter had called in. He could make a (poor) case that he wanted to look at the ranch from the vantage point of the RP, he thought. But he hoped it wouldn't come to that.

As he neared the unit, Joe noticed signs of life. A wisp of smoke or exhaust emerged from a pipe that poked through the metal skin of the roof. He slowed his pickup to a crawl and drove around the left side of the trailer.

It was an ancient single-wide, more of a house trailer than a camping unit. The sheet metal exterior was dented and rust was creeping up its sides. Old tires had been thrown on the roof to keep it from blowing away in the wind. He noted that the twin propane tanks on the front of the unit were commercial rentals that could be acquired at a half dozen locations in Saddlestring. That meant the trailer was being maintained by someone.

There was no vehicle parked there, but the tire tracks showed that one recently had been. There was also a flurry of boot tracks around the front door of the trailer. Apparently, whoever had come up there had left the trailer quickly.

He parked and swung out. Large prints of pointy cowboy boots were in the snow headed toward the front door, which was accessible by a set of stairs constructed of two-by-fours.

As he started for the door he heard a barely discernible *click* behind him and he froze. The sound was familiar, and he backed away and turned. In a thick juniper bush, he noted the double lenses of a game trail camera partially hidden within the branches of the bush. It was aimed at the front door of the trailer.

Joe circled around the juniper and approached the camera from the side. He reached in and plucked it out. He was familiar with the brand and model, and he opened the door on the back and plucked out the memory card.

Had it captured him near the trailer? Probably. But standing near a trailer was perfectly okay. He wished he could insert the card into a computer to look at the contents, and perhaps see the owner of the pointy boots. Instead, he dropped the card into his side vest pocket.

Joe looked around, then checked the main road, to make sure no one was watching him up there. Then he mounted the stairs and pounded on the door.

"Wyoming Game and Fish Department," he announced. "Is anyone home?"

There was no response from inside, so he grasped the handle of the door. It was locked.

He backed down the stairs, thinking that was that. He was almost grateful the door was locked, so he wouldn't compromise his job even further.

Then Joe squinted at the chimney pipe again. Someone had *just* been there. The furnace was obviously on. Someone had been concerned enough about visitors that they'd placed a trail cam in the junipers. Since the Mexican ranch hands the McElwee sisters had described presumably bunked in the outbuildings at the central compound, who was using the trailer and for what?

Against his better judgment, Joe climbed the stairs again, grasped the door handle, and pulled hard. Maybe because the hardware was as old as the trailer itself and the metal was fatigued, it swung open. He was glad he'd left Biscuit at home, because he wouldn't have wanted his young dog to witness him breaking and entering.

Rather than wandering through the single-wide and leaving boot prints and fingerprints, Joe simply leaned inside and looked around. To his left was a bedroom with a bare mattress on a frame. To his right was a built-in table packed with bottles, plastic containers, and a half dozen empty bottles of Corona.

Joe drew out his phone and thumbed open the camera app. He stuck his arm inside the trailer and took photos of everything inside, then did a quick panoramic video from the left to the right.

As he did so he noted that the containers on the table were labeled with names he wasn't familiar with: sodium hydroxide, phenethyl bromide, tert-butoxycarbonyl, acetone, xylazine, propionyl chloride.

There were saucepans on the propane stove, as well as two stockpots. An immersion blender was propped up on its stand on the counter. Next to it was a container of blue food coloring.

On hooks attached to the outside of the small bathroom were white hazmat suits. The bench seats on either side of the table were strewn with gas masks, buffs, and oversized gloves.

While he was sweeping the camera from side to side, Joe suddenly felt dizzy. It hit hard and fast, and he stumbled backward and slammed the door shut behind him.

Outside, he bent forward with his hands on his knees and sucked in cold mountain air. Still, he felt like swooning and it was difficult to keep his balance.

Ten minutes later, he felt steady enough to stand up. His vision was still blurred, and it was difficult to concentrate enough to return the memory card into the trail cam and back away. His head remained foggy as he drove down the mountain until he reached the main road and turned toward Antler Creek Junction.

CHAPTER SIXTEEN

November 16

LATER THAT NIGHT, after being humiliated by the Pickett girls on the road to the game warden station, Dorn Peddy and Hillbilly Jimmy D. O'Bryan sat in their borrowed pickup on a remote county road fifteen miles outside of Saddlestring. Peddy ran the heater inside the cab and O'Bryan silently fumed in the passenger seat.

"I hope this is where we're supposed to meet him," Peddy said after looking at his wristwatch. It was ten forty-five and they'd been told to be there at ten thirty. "He said County Road 131, Skull Ridge Road. This is Skull Ridge Road."

When O'Bryan didn't respond, Peddy said, "Look on your phone and make sure we're on Skull Ridge Road."

"Look on your own damned phone," O'Bryan said finally. Then: "Marion Barber and Jason Witten? What in the hell were you thinking?"

"They were the first two names that came to mind," Peddy said.

"I used to be a huge Cowboys fan when I was growing up in New Mexico. Since we don't have a team of our own and the Lobos are lame, the state is divided up kind of weird. There are a few Arizona Cardinals fans in the western part of the state, and there are Bronco fans in the north. The eastern part that's closest to Texas is all Cowboys fans. Where I grew up in Albuquerque, we were all Cowboys fans. Santa Fe, Roswell, Clovis—all Cowboys."

"That's a lot of information I don't need," O'Bryan said.

"Those girls didn't know," Peddy said. "They didn't have a clue I was bluffing them."

O'Bryan looked out the passenger window and sighed. He couldn't make himself look at Peddy behind the wheel.

What he could see, far below the mountain where Skull Ridge Road was located, were the few city lights of Winchester. Beyond that smattering of streetlights laid out in a pattern that best resembled a tic-tac-toe blank, there was total darkness in every direction. Most of the stars were obscured by a horizontal blanket of clouds that had moved across the sky in the last half hour.

O'Bryan stared into the mirror on his side of the truck. The ground was covered by pine needles tinged pink by the single taillight that remained functional on the pickup. The other light had been smashed when they backed up too fast and hit the moose. So was the tailgate, which was buckled in the middle by the force of the impact. The rear bumper was holding on by a single bracket, and the tailpipe was collapsed like an exhausted accordion.

The journey from the valley floor to Skull Ridge Road had been harrowing, O'Bryan thought. It consisted of switchbacks and hairpin turns up the mountain and there'd been no guardrails. O'Bryan didn't trust Peddy's driving skills, even though the man bragged about the mountain driving he'd done in New Mexico while growing up there. And it didn't help O'Bryan's mood that Peddy sipped on a pint flask of Jim Beam while he drove.

Peddy fished his phone out of his coat and stared at the screen. "He hasn't tried to call me since we've been up here. So we must be at the right place."

"Why don't you call him?" O'Bryan asked.

"Because he told me not to," Peddy said. "He don't want us calling *him*. That's not how it works. He calls me. Got that?"

"Whatever."

It continually annoyed O'Bryan that Peddy always made sure to mention that their employers had hired him first and provided the initial brief, and that O'Bryan had been brought in as a backup. Peddy liked to lord it over O'Bryan that *he* was the conduit to their employers, and that O'Bryan needed to know his place in the scheme.

It would be different, O'Bryan thought, if he trusted Peddy. But the man had screwed up time after time, and he'd proven his judgment to be skewed and mistaken. O'Bryan didn't like it that his life—and his eventual payout—were in Peddy's hands.

TEN MINUTES LATER, O'Bryan saw a flash of headlights below them on the mountain road. Someone was coming after all.

As the vehicle made the final turn on the switchback and came toward them, Peddy screwed the cap on his bottle and quickly deposited it under his seat. That way, O'Bryan guessed, Peddy wouldn't be caught drinking when the headlights of the oncoming car flooded their pickup cab.

O'Bryan squinted and raised his hand to shadow his eyes from the lights, as did Peddy. The vehicle pulled within twenty feet and stopped. Then the driver doused his headlights. O'Bryan was surprised to see that the SUV in front of them had a light bar on top and a fortified grille guard on the front for pushing stalled vehicles out of the way. No doubt, it was a law enforcement vehicle.

He looked over to Peddy with alarm, but Peddy waved him off.

"Relax. This is our guy," Peddy said.

"Are we supposed to go to him?" O'Bryan asked.

"I don't know. I can't see a damned thing after being blinded by those lights."

A moment later, the Yukon's back door opened and the cab lights blinked on. O'Bryan could see that the man entering their truck was in a brown and beige uniform, and that he was wearing a badge over his left breast pocket. He was a big man with a squarish block of a head topped by a brimmed cap that read **Twelve Sleep County Sheriff's Department.**

"This is Deputy Bowkley," Peddy said to O'Bryan. "He's on our side. He recommended us to do this."

O'Bryan nodded to the deputy as the man crawled into the back seat and closed the door. Bowkley didn't return the gesture.

"I spent the whole fucking day at the scene of a camper trailer fire," Bowkley said. "I don't suppose you boys know anything about that?"

O'Bryan held his tongue.

But Peddy said, "It had to be done. The guy inside could have ID'd us and blown our cover. We had to keep him quiet."

Bowkley said nothing for thirty seconds, and O'Bryan felt the tension rise. Peddy seemed oblivious to it.

"Is that what you think?" Bowkley asked Peddy. "How did you know it was the right guy?"

"He gave himself away. I've got a nose for those kinds of things."

"So you killed him and burned his trailer down," Bowkley said. It wasn't a question.

"We handled things," Peddy said. "There's no reason to get worked up about it."

Again, there was a long pause from the back. Then Bowkley said, "You got the wrong guy."

"What?"

"He was just a random hunter from Casper," Bowkley said. "We confirmed that today. He wasn't the guy who called the sheriff's department."

"How do you know that?" Peddy asked. O'Bryan noted a hint of panic in his tone.

Bowkley said, "Because the guy who actually called it in was in the sheriff's office earlier tonight. He gave a long statement, and I heard the gist of it. His name is Earl Wright."

"You've got to be shitting me."

"No, Dorn. I'm not shitting you. And Wright described you and your partner to a T. Now you're on the sheriff's radar, and you might have just fucked everything up."

For once, Peddy didn't respond.

"And not only that," Bowkley said, "you didn't finish the job yesterday like you bragged to our boss."

"What do you mean?"

Peddy was on the verge of panic, O'Bryan thought. He had no compunction to intervene and bail the man out.

Bowkley leaned forward so he spoke almost directly into Peddy's ear. O'Bryan observed that as Bowkley leaned forward he'd dropped his hands down between his knees.

"Joe Pickett is still alive as of this evening. He was airlifted to a hospital in Billings."

"That's not possible," Peddy said.

"Did you check him?" Bowkley asked. "Did you make sure?"

"Of course."

Bowkley turned to O'Bryan. "Let me ask you a question and you better not lie to me like your partner. Did you check on Pickett after the ambush?"

"No," O'Bryan said. "I tried to persuade him, but he wouldn't listen." O'Bryan could feel the white-hot glare of Peddy's eyes on him as he said it. Then Peddy turned his head and stared out the windshield. He apparently didn't want to look into Bowkley's eyes.

"So in two days," Bowkley said, "you geniuses fucked up the ambush, then you killed a random hunter and burned down his trailer. Then you drive up this mountain to meet me with your breath smelling of booze. This isn't exactly going according to plan."

"There's no way Pickett made it," Peddy said defiantly. "I saw the bullet holes in the windshield. I know where I aimed."

"Our employers know everything," Bowkley said. "Because I told them."

"Why did you have to go and do *that*?" Peddy whined. O'Bryan could see that there were tears forming in the man's eyes. For the first time since they'd been together, O'Bryan was grateful that it wasn't him making the decisions. This was all on Peddy.

It was at that moment that O'Bryan realized why Bowkley had leaned forward. It was so he could hike up his pant leg and retrieve a pistol from an ankle holster.

O'Bryan reflexively burrowed into the passenger door as Bowkley raised the small-caliber revolver and held the snub-nosed muzzle an inch behind Peddy's right ear.

Pop-pop-pop-pop.

The rapid gunshots were loud within the cab. Peddy's head rocked with the first round and bounced with each subsequent shot. Then he slumped forward until his forehead pressed against the top of the steering wheel. His face, a mask of surprise and terror, was frozen in place and aimed at O'Bryan. There was a final, rattling breath and then he was still. The cab smelled sharply of gunpowder.

O'Bryan inched his right hand to his side, where his handgun was located in his coat pocket. He didn't want to be next. But Bowkley didn't swing the revolver in his direction. Instead, he withdrew it entirely.

Through the ringing in his ears, he heard Bowkley say, "Four pops with .22 Shorts. The rounds bounce around inside the skull and they don't make an ugly exit wound. But they do the trick, don't they?"

"Yes," O'Bryan said. His mouth was dry.

"Should you be next?"

"I hope not."

Bowkley chuckled. "The word came down that we couldn't let him do any more damage. I'm taking over, even though I wanted to stay arm's length from the whole operation. But your buddy gave us no choice. Are you on board with that?"

O'Bryan nodded. "He wasn't my buddy. He was an asshole."

"Good to hear. So here's what we're going to do next," Bowkley said as he removed the black nitrile gloves from his hands and stuffed them into his trouser pocket. "You push him out of the way and get behind the wheel. Then you'll follow my car to the top of this mountain a ways down the other side to a place called Savage Run Canyon. It's a hell of a steep canyon, believe me.

"You'll drive to the rim and leave the transmission in neutral and get the hell out. I'll push this truck over the edge. That canyon is so remote it could be years before anyone finds the wreck.

"Then you can hitch a ride back into Winchester with me, where we'll check you into the Wagon Wheel Motel. I don't want anyone to see you around Saddlestring, especially the sheriff. The Wagon Wheel is a dump, but it's a place the cops use to stash drunks and dopers for the night. They don't ask questions there. Got all that?"

O'Bryan said he did.

"I'll get rid of this peashooter up there, too. I borrowed it from the evidence room and I don't think they'll miss it."

"Okay," O'Bryan said. "Then what? Am I still gonna get paid?"

"Is the job done?" Bowkley asked.

"Not exactly."

"That's right, buddy. You'll get paid when the job is done."

"What's that mean?"

Bowkley again leaned forward in his seat, and O'Bryan flinched a little.

"I've got some time off to move the rest of my shit from Gillette to Saddlestring," Bowkley said. "Are you up for a little trip north to Billings, Montana?"

CHAPTER SEVENTEEN

November 17

LUCY AWOKE HOURS before the sun came up. She'd slept fitfully through the night, and every hour or so she'd check the time on her iPhone next to the bed. Finally, when she heard stirring in the kitchen, she sat up, wrapped a robe around her, and padded down the hall.

April was there glaring at the coffee maker, as if willing it to brew faster. She was wearing baggy sweats and cowboy boots, and her hair was a bird's nest.

"I couldn't sleep," Lucy said. "I wish I could still blame jet lag, but I know that's not the reason why."

"You're not the only one," April said. "You'd think I might be used to this sort of thing, but I guess I'm not. This all feels . . . different."

"Because it's Dad," Lucy said.

April nodded, and resumed glaring at the coffee machine.

"I've never done anything like this before," Lucy said. "I'm scared. I'm nervous about interviewing people on my own."

"It has to be this way, baby sis," April said. "We have to do all three investigations at the same time, and this is the only way to do it. It's possible that two, or even three, of the ranches were involved. If the three of us traipsed from one to the other they could tip each other off to what we're doing. So you have to do your part."

"Can I have a cup of coffee first?" Lucy said.

"That's why I'm making it. But don't expect any of that fine-ass French crap. This is cowboy coffee, the kind us true Americans make in the morning."

Lucy smiled while she found three mugs in the cupboard.

"Do you have a weapon?" April asked Lucy when they were seated at the table.

Lucy held up her phone. "Only this. I plan to record everything."

"I'm gonna lend you a handgun," April said.

"I don't know what I'd do with it. I'm just planning to ask questions, not start shooting people."

April dug into her large handbag and came out with a small can of pepper spray. "Will you at least take this? You just never know what might happen. I'd feel better if you took this along."

Lucy sighed and took the can. Then April retrieved a snub-nosed revolver from a drawer in the kitchen. "This is Mom's gun," April said as she opened the cylinder and confirmed that it was loaded with five rounds. "It's a .38 Smith & Wesson Ladysmith. No safety to remember, and no hammer to snag on your clothes. It's idiotproof. You just point and pull the trigger."

"I won't be needing that," Lucy said.

April rolled her eyes and returned the weapon to the drawer. "Don't forget where it is, okay? In case you change your mind?"

"All right, but I won't."

"Listen," April said. "Remember what we talked about last night. Our job is to gather information, to get these ranchers on the record. It's not to accuse them of anything, or arrest them. When we've all done our jobs, we'll meet back here and compare notes. That's all."

"That's right," Sheridan said as she entered the kitchen. Unlike her two sisters, she'd already showered and dressed. "When we've all compared notes, we need to share what we found with the sheriff. That was my deal with him. And he promised to do the same with us."

"Oh, yes," April said with a roll of her eyes. "We must be true to *Steve*."

Sheridan ignored the dig. She said to Lucy, "If you feel threatened in any way, you just get the hell out of there. Even if you feel suspicious, you leave."

"Or if you get one of your famous vibes," April chimed in.

"Don't be a hero," Sheridan said.

"I don't plan to be."

"Here," Sheridan said, tapping quickly on the screen of her phone. "This is Nate's number. If something bad happens, whatever that is, you have to promise to call him. I made him promise to keep his phone with him for once, and to keep it on."

Lucy heard her phone chime.

"Sheridan won't be far away, either," April said. "And I'll be at the next ranch down the road. If you need some help ass-kicking, you call one or both of us. Promise?"

"I promise," Lucy said.

"Of course," April said, "Sheridan is kind of a physical weakling, as we know. If you need some heads knocked together, call me."

That made Lucy smile. As Sheridan walked past them to get a mug of coffee, she cuffed April on the top of her head.

As SHE LACED on her boots and gathered up her coat in the mudroom, Lucy asked, "Any word from Mom during the night?"

Sheridan and April both checked their phones and said there was no news.

"I take that as a positive," Lucy said.

"Either that, or she's too gutted by what might have happened over the last few hours to even talk to us," April said.

"And on that happy April-like note," Sheridan said sarcastically, "we've got work to do today. Let's get going and let's keep in touch with one another."

LUCY HAD SPENT over two hours the night before sitting in bed with her laptop, researching Michael Thompson. She'd wished she had access to the law enforcement databases that her mother was privy to, but what she found on her own was intriguing enough.

Michael Thompson was the former CEO of a southeastern telecom company that he'd sold to a conglomerate for hundreds of millions of dollars in the late 1990s. He'd used his profits to found a hedge fund based in New York and Atlanta, and within ten years he was celebrated in the business and local press as a self-made billionaire. He owned properties in Atlanta, Hawaii, South Carolina, Switzerland, and of course his ranch in Wyoming.

Thompson had divorced his second wife of twenty-nine years in a high-profile proceeding that was covered in depth by the *Atlanta Constitution.* His ex-wife claimed that he'd not only cheated on her in serial fashion but that he'd hidden most of his assets in offshore accounts. Although the terms of the divorce were sealed, it was assumed by court watchers that the settlement to her amounted to well over five hundred million dollars, plus the compounds in Hawaii, South Carolina, and Europe.

They apparently had no children.

Brandy Thompson, aka Brandy Schwartzkopf, was thirty-two years younger than Michael. She'd been a cheerleader at South Carolina University before being named runner-up at the Miss South Carolina pageant while still in college. Michael Thompson was listed as one of the judges of the competition, and that's apparently where they'd met.

Lucy found a photo of them following the marriage ceremony at the Buckhead Club in Atlanta. Michael was beaming in a tuxedo, his arm wrapped around Brandy, who had chestnut hair at the time. She was slim and gorgeous in a full-length white wedding dress sparkling with sequins. Lucy thought he looked like Brandy's father.

Since their marriage six years before, Brandy's name could be found primarily in society items and at prestigious fundraisers on both coasts of the country. Three years before, she'd launched a cosmetics and yoga clothing line called "Brandy" with a heart replacing the *a.* Lucy had never heard of the lifestyle brand before, so it must not have been popular with her college friends. Lucy assumed it wasn't doing very well, although the photos in the marketing materials made Brandy look very good indeed.

In the last year and a half, Michael Thompson had been implicated in two scandals that made the news. The first was a series of #MeToo accusations from former female employees of his companies, who claimed he'd said provocative things to them in the past, and that the atmosphere within Thompson Holdings was toxic. Several ex-employees claimed Thompson had retaliated against them for not accompanying him on business trips or visiting him at home on weekends. The accusations had vanished into the ether the year before when, it was speculated, large-scale settlements had been paid to the accusers.

Lucy developed a crude timeline from the articles, and determined that the majority of the accusations had occurred in the last few years of Thompson's second marriage, and several years after he'd divorced. Then, apparently, he'd met Brandy.

So, Lucy concluded: Michael Thompson was a dog.

The most recent scandal seemed more serious, if harder to understand completely. A U.S. senator from Arkansas had accused Thompson's hedge fund company of working hand in glove with several large corporations owned and operated by the Chinese Communist Party. The CCP-owned companies were attempting to secretly buy telecommunications firms in the U.S. that had access to the personal data of millions of Americans. Thompson, with his background and connections, was accused of being the secret conduit between the CCP-owned entities and the U.S. firms.

Although he vehemently denied the charges, Thompson was slated to appear before Congress in the coming months. His lawyers had been able to postpone the hearings several times, but the senator was relentless. He was quoted as saying that if the charges against Thompson were proven, the man's hedge fund company could "collapse like a house of cards."

The U.S. Department of Justice had opened a probe, and a federal judge had ordered that Thompson Holdings' assets were to be frozen until the matter was fully adjudicated.

Although Lucy had trouble grasping all of the details of the scandal, it appeared that Michael Thompson was a man in serious trouble.

Which, to Lucy, cast the man in an entirely different light. Was he desperate? And if so, how desperate?

LUCY HAD SWITCHED out her little car with her mom's SUV to navigate the gravel surface of Antler Creek Road. She liked the height of the SUV and it certainly blended in better in and around Twelve Sleep County than her little red Camry.

She slowed down as she approached Antler Creek Junction, and got a knot in her stomach when she realized that she was at the location where her dad had been ambushed two days before. Although his pickup had been removed, there was a white panel van parked on the shoulder. A large square was marked off in the sagebrush and yellow crime scene tape had been secured to lengths of wooden laths driven into the ground. A man wearing coveralls was carefully walking through the sagebrush outside the marked location. He was studying the ground, it seemed.

Lucy slowed to a stop, but kept the engine running. The man in the field saw her and waved. She waved back, then motioned for him to come over. As he did, she rolled her window down.

In addition to the coveralls, the man in his midforties also wore latex gloves. A camera with a long lens hung from his neck and the top of a digital recorder stuck out from his breast pocket. She recognized him as the county forensics tech, but Lucy couldn't recall his name.

"I thought you were Marybeth Pickett," the man said. "Isn't this her ride?"

"Yes, it is."

"Can I help you?" he asked. "I'd ask that you please stay clear of the crime scene."

"I will. Can you please tell me which road ahead goes out to the Double Diamond Ranch?"

He gestured toward the road on the left that curved to the west. "That one," he said. Then he stuck out his hand. "I'm Gary Norwood."

"Lucy Pickett. I borrowed my mom's car."

"I *thought* I recognized you. You used to star in plays and stuff at the high school."

"That was me," she said. "But I didn't star in *every* play. So what are you doing out here?"

"Walking the crime scene," he said. "I'm the evidence tech. I prefer to do this when there aren't a bunch of law enforcement guys running around trampling everything. This way, I can concentrate. But honestly, I'm not finding much. The shooters cleaned up after themselves pretty well. They didn't leave any cartridge casings, or items that we could use . . ."

Norwood suddenly stopped talking before he could finish his thought. His face flushed pink and he said, "I'm sorry. Sometimes I forget how crime can affect people who don't do this all the time. This is your dad we're talking about. I apologize."

"It's okay."

"Can I ask how he's doing?"

"We're waiting to hear today," Lucy said. "I think they're doing the surgery this afternoon or tonight. Then we'll know more."

Norwood shook his head. "It makes me sick," he said. "Usually, when I'm at a scene like this, I don't know the victim. But I worked closely with your dad. I admire the hell out of him."

"Thank you."

"Has he been able to talk? To tell anyone who might have done this?"

"Not yet," Lucy said. "They put him in a medically induced coma. It's procedure, I guess."

"Well, damn. If he comes out of it, I hope he can identify the shooters and tell us how this happened. Right now, we're flying blind."

"I hope so, too. We're all praying for him to recover."

"Give my best to your mom and dad, please."

"I will."

Lucy saw her opportunity. She said, "We heard it was probably two shooters. Have you found anything that would suggest more, or maybe just one?"

"Nope." Norwood gestured to the field of sagebrush to the north. "I found where the snow and grass was pressed down in two places. That's where they set up the ambush."

"Do you have any idea which way the shooters went afterward?" she asked.

He shook his head. "We found some ATV tracks up there on

the hill. Unfortunately, the terrain is too rocky to follow where they went."

"If you were to guess?" she asked, and accompanied the question with a smile.

"If I were to guess," Norwood said with a dawning realization, "I would guess that I might lose my job for starting rumors and sending you on a wild-goose chase. I'm here to gather evidence, not to speculate to the victim's daughter."

"I get it. Thank you."

Norwood arched his eyebrows. "Are you sure you want to drive out to the Double D? Thompson and his ranch foreman like to prosecute folks for trespassing."

"I'm sure," Lucy said. "It's just a social call."

THE ROAD IMPROVED just a mile from the junction, and the SUV hummed along its surface. **NO TRESPASSING** signs were posted every mile or so. Before passing below a magnificent elk-antler arch made up of hundreds of sheds and a wrought-iron sign announcing **DOUBLE DIAMOND RANCH**, Lucy pulled over. The arch framed a distant and very elaborate home built into the side of a mountain. On the flat plateau above the estate was a gleaming white corporate jet, meaning Michael Thompson was there.

She pulled out her phone and started a new text thread to her sisters.

> I made it to the Double D. Gary Norwood is at the junction. Drive right past him and look away so he doesn't suspect what we're doing.

Both April and Sheridan responded with thumbs-up emojis. They were both just minutes behind her.

As Lucy neared the spectacular home, she saw a pickup shoot out of the massive garage like a rocket being launched. It was a light gray Ford Raptor, and it turned onto the road and came straight at her to head her off.

Lucy pulled over to the right shoulder as the Raptor screeched to a stop next to her SUV. The window rolled down to reveal a bright red face crowned by a black cowboy hat.

"What in the hell do you want?" he asked. "Can't you read the signs? Don't you know you're trespassing on private property?"

"Mr. Hutmacher?" Lucy said as innocently as she could manage. "How are you doing? I'm Lucy. Lucy Pickett."

With that, Clay Hutmacher's scowl instantly softened. "Oh, Lucy, I didn't recognize you," he said. "You're all grown up."

"It happens," she said with a smile. "I was hoping I could speak with Mr. Thompson. That's why I came out here this morning."

Clay was obviously conflicted. He said, "Do you have an appointment with him? People don't just show up, you know. Mr. Thompson is a busy, busy man."

"I realize that, Mr. Hutmacher. But I'm sure you know that my dad was shot a couple of days ago. I was hoping Mr. Thompson might have some thoughts about who might have been involved. I'd really appreciate speaking to him."

"Hold on," Clay said. "Give me one second. Don't move."

Before Lucy could reply, Clay's window rolled up. She watched as he raised his cell phone to his face. The conversation he had seemed animated.

While Clay Hutmacher talked with his boss, Lucy narrowed her eyes. The foreman had once been a very good friend of her dad's, but he was also Thompson's main man. From Sheridan, she'd heard that Clay had been deeply wounded by the death of his son, and that his entire personality had changed for the worse since then. Sheridan described Hutmacher as petty, bitter, and increasingly erratic. Lucy recognized that she should be wary of him, and also had a feeling that he might know more about what happened with her dad than he let on.

Finally, the window rolled back down.

"Mr. Thompson says he'll give you five minutes of his time, but only because he feels sorry for you."

Lucy bristled at the condescension, but smiled and said, "I appreciate that."

"Follow me," Clay said. "And remember: five minutes."

"Wait here," Clay Hutmacher told Lucy after they entered the Thompson home. Then he backed away down a hallway and left her there.

She stood in the middle of a massive great room. Floor-to-ceiling windows showcased a stunning view of the spine of the Bighorn Mountains in the distance. The decor was almost painfully white: floors, walls, ceiling, and furniture. So much white, Lucy thought, seemed like a direct challenge to the county and community itself, which was filled with dirt roads, muddy pickups, and wind packed with grit.

The only thing to break up the whiteness inside were several huge multihued cowskin rugs on the floor, and a wall of mounted elk, bighorn sheep, mule deer, and pronghorn antelope heads, no doubt taken on the ranch. An eight-foot-tall full-mount grizzly bear stood in the corner looking angry.

Lucy glanced at her phone. It was 8:35 a.m. Five minutes, she'd been told.

Then she felt a presence behind her and looked over her shoulder.

Brandy Thompson stood quietly in the threshold of a doorway. She wore all-black, skin-hugging yoga clothes. Even her fingernails and toenails were painted black. She seemed slightly flushed and out of breath, and Lucy guessed she had just completed her morning workout.

"You're Joe Pickett's daughter?" Brandy asked.

"One of three," Lucy responded.

Brandy's eyes took in Lucy from the top of her head to her boots. It was a clinical assessment, Lucy thought, and it wasn't very admiring. Lucy had studied many photos of Brandy in social settings. She was always the youngest, blondest, fittest, and most attractive woman in the room.

Now here stood Lucy, supplanting her. And she didn't like it.

Lucy broke the icy moment. "Are you wearing Br♥ndy?" she asked. "I love those clothes."

Something registered in Brandy Thompson's eyes. A hint of dominance, after all.

"It's my clothing line," she said. "But we're really launching an entire lifestyle brand."

"That is so cool. I love Br♥ndy, although I can barely afford them."

"Thank you," Mrs. Thompson said. Then: "Tell your friends."

"I will," Lucy said, thinking, she was right. Br♥ndy wasn't selling.

"Maybe I can arrange for you to get a discount."

"Gosh," Lucy gushed. "I would love that."

"But I'm sure that's not why you're here," Brandy said.

"It isn't. We're trying to figure out what happened to my dad a couple of days ago. We were hoping either you or Mr. Thompson might be able to help us."

Brandy asked, "Who's we?"

"My sisters and me."

"What do you want to know?" Brandy asked in a distant, flat tone.

"Well, do you know when he was here last?"

Brandy raised her hand to her chin, obviously showing that she was thinking. "A few weeks ago," she said. "I was working out on the third level and I saw him drive up. He was talking with Clay, and then my husband took him on a tour of the ranch."

"Do you know why?"

"You know Michael. He likes to show the place off."

"So, ARE YOU two getting acquainted?" asked a male voice from behind Lucy. She spun around to see Michael Thompson emerging from what looked like an office or a study. He wore faded jeans, a pressed white dress shirt, and slippers. Lucy thought his face looked haggard compared to the photos she'd seen, and his eyes had dark circles around them. He looked like a man under stress.

"This is Lucy Pickett," Brandy said to him. "She's asking if we know anything about what happened to her dad."

Michael paused and shook his head sadly. "It's a terrible tragedy what happened. May he rest in peace."

"He's not dead," Lucy said sharply.

"Oh, I'm sorry," Thompson said. "I'd heard differently."

"He's fighting for his life," Lucy added.

Brandy then punched the air with her tiny fists in a rhythmic way, and said, "*Fight-fight-fight,*" as if she were cheering on the South Carolina Gamecocks from the sidelines.

Lucy ignored her. So did Michael Thompson, although his lips pursed in annoyance at the display.

"I know I only have a few minutes," Lucy said. "So I'll get right down to it. Was my dad coming out here to see you the other day?"

"No," Thompson said quickly. Then he paused and said, "I don't think so. Maybe he was. I gave him permission to trespass on my ranch anytime. In fact, I encouraged it."

"Really?" Lucy asked. "What does that mean?"

Thompson waved away the implication. "He needed to sign off on a little project I was working on. I wanted to make sure he was comfortable doing so and I welcomed him to visit whenever he could spare the time."

"Did you call him and ask him to come out here two days ago?" Lucy asked. "Did Mr. Hutmacher?"

Thompson went still and he glared at Lucy. The man could be intimidating. She felt a chill race down her spine.

"Why are you asking me these questions?"

"We're trying to determine his movements that day," Lucy said. "That's all."

"I've already explained this to the local sheriff's office," Thompson said with impatience. "I don't want to keep repeating myself."

"If you don't mind, what did you tell them?"

"I told them I'm a very, very busy man right now. I'm in the middle of some very large transactions, and I really can't waste my time going back and forth with local Keystone Kops. The fact is I didn't call your dad and ask him to come out here at any specific time. Like I said, I'd already granted him carte blanche to enter my property There was no need to offer him a special invitation."

"What about Mr. Hutmacher?"

"You'll have to ask him, but I doubt it," Thompson said. "I don't speak for my ranch foreman."

"I will, thanks."

Lucy pressed on. "Do you know of anyone who would want to hurt my dad? Anyone at all?"

Thompson glanced at his wristwatch and looked up. Without saying it, he indicated that the five minutes were just about up. His wife got the message. Lucy turned to see her retreating down the hallway, the fabric of her Br♥ndy yoga pants swishing like a willow branch whipping through the air.

"Look, Lucy Pickett," Thompson said. "You're very cute and sweet, but we're out of time and I think you're more than a little out of your league here. Your dad was . . ." Then he corrected himself and said, "*Is* a nice guy and all. He's very humble and down-to-earth, and he's developed quite the reputation among the locals. I'm sure some of that was earned. But he was . . ." Again he corrected himself, "*Is* basically a state bureaucrat with outsized powers.

"I don't want to bad-mouth him in front of his own daughter," Thompson continued, "but he, like you, was out of his league when it comes to matters of great importance. And frankly, he could be a pain in the ass. I'm sure I'm not the only rancher or the only person in this county to say that. The state needs to work *with* landowners and major donors to the governor's campaign—not against them."

"You're speaking of him in the past tense again," Lucy said in a whisper.

"Sorry," Thompson said, "I must be distracted. And I'm late for a conference call as it is." Then he barked, "Clay!"

Hutmacher dutifully appeared from the hallway, where he'd earlier vanished.

"Can you show Miss Lucy Pickett out?" Thompson asked.

"Yes, sir," Hutmacher said.

Before joining him, Lucy looked hard at Michael Thompson. He looked back in a defiant way, she thought.

"My sisters always say I can read people pretty well," Lucy said.

"And what can you read about me?" Thompson asked.

She thought, *That you're scrambling to stay out of prison at the moment. It might be federal prison, or it might be our jail in town or the Wyoming State Penitentiary in Rawlins. But I have no doubt you'll end up in one of them. I can feel it.*

But instead she said, "I haven't come to any conclusions yet, but I think you may be more impressed with yourself than I am."

Thompson flushed. "Clay, get her the hell out of here."

Lucy felt the grip on her arm. She didn't resist.

On the way out of the house, Clay Hutmacher leaned in close to Lucy and said, "You shouldn't have done that. You shouldn't have pissed him off like that."

"What's he going to do?" Lucy asked. "Get a couple of guys to ambush me as well?"

"I'm sure he had nothing to do with that," Hutmacher said as he opened the SUV's door for her and guided her inside.

"Are you sure?" Lucy asked him.

"I told your dad not to cross him," Hutmacher said, almost apologetically. "And I'm telling you that now."

"Mr. Hutmacher, did you call my dad to come out here the other day? The day he got shot?"

At that, Clay slammed the door shut.

As Lucy drove away from the Thompson home, she glanced in her rearview mirror. Clay was still in the driveway, his body language showing that he was in turmoil. His hands were on his hips and his head was down, and he was frantically walking in a circle.

Directly above him, at a second-story window, Brandy watched her go as well. She had her hands on her hips, too, and her head was tilted to the side. Lucy knew she was too far away to conclude what Brandy's facial expression was at the moment.

But Lucy imagined she was smirking.

Two miles away from the Thompson home, but still on the Double D, Lucy pulled over on the side of the road. She was seething from how Michael and Brandy Thompson had spoken to her, and she had nothing but disappointment and contempt for Clay Hutmacher, whom she'd previously thought was her dad's friend.

She pulled out her iPhone from her coat pocket and stopped the recording. It went on for eight and a half minutes—three and a half minutes longer than she'd been allotted. Lucy looked forward to listening to it again and sharing it with her sisters.

She thought:

What was Brandy's involvement, if any at all?

What did Clay Hutmacher know that he wouldn't tell her?

How desperate was Michael Thompson to get his "little project" approved before his wealth dried up or he was indicted? Desperate enough to order an ambush?

That's when she saw movement in her rearview mirror. Clay Hutmacher's gray pickup was following her, no doubt making sure she left the ranch as ordered.

She quickly added to the sisters' group text.

> Heading home. There's a LOT to talk about.

Then she engaged the transmission and pulled out onto the road toward Antler Creek Junction.

CHAPTER EIGHTEEN

GIVEN THE STORIES she'd heard over the years and her limited interaction with a character named Pablo back in high school, April Pickett wasn't sure what to expect from the owners of McElwee Land and Cattle. She knew they were wild sisters named Lisa and Lainie McElwee, who had outsized legends wrapped around them. And she'd heard Pablo refer to his "crazy-ass stepmother" and her "crazy-ass sister" a few times.

What she didn't expect to witness, after taking the right-hand road at the crossroads at Antler Creek Junction and passing over the ranch boundary, was three men who looked like gangbangers chasing stray cattle away from a salt lick while screeching Spanish phrases and waving their arms like lunatics and firing their handguns into the air.

She could hear the *pop-pop-pop* of their pistols up on the side of the mountain that she skirted en route to the ranch headquarters. The half dozen cows finally got the message, it seemed, and they rumbled down the slope toward the road she was on.

April slowed down, but didn't stop. She watched as the three men finally stopped chasing the cows. Two of them paused and looked visibly exhausted, and they leaned forward with their hands on their knees as if to gulp the thin mountain air.

They did *not* look like any cowboys she'd ever seen, although it wasn't unusual for local ranchers to hire employees from other parts of the world, especially South and Central America.

It was an odd scenario, she thought. Cattle on the high desert were usually encouraged to spend time at salt licks, which were dusty bowls trampled into the sides of mountains. Salt blocks helped sustain the animals.

The three men appeared to have come from a battered travel trailer that was barely visible in a copse of trees halfway up the slope. A two-track road cut across the sagebrush and climbed there, and she could see the back end of an old pickup parked on the other side of the trailer. A wisp of smoke floated from a stovepipe on the top of the trailer before being whisked away by the wind.

What were the men doing up there? she wondered. And why were they so agitated about wandering cattle nearing a salt lick a hundred yards from their trailer?

The third man, the one who wasn't doubled over, appeared to have noticed April's car on the road below him. He was dark and he wore a red bandana on his head. The morning sun glinted off the weapon in his hand, but he held it down and low at the moment. He watched her and said something emphatic to his companions, who both raised their heads.

So as not to give him a reason to aim the weapon or attempt to intercept her on the ranch road, April sped up. The spooked cattle crossed the road in front of her, panicked enough that they threw up small clods of mud behind them that landed with thuds on the hood of her car and the windshield.

Before encountering the strange scenario, April had speed-dialed Cassie Dewell in Montana via Bluetooth in her Toyota Tundra. The call found Cassie sitting in her SUV on surveillance of the bad husband and father they'd been tailing. Cassie said she was parked outside a low-rent motel west of Billings. The subject's car was in the lot and she'd followed him there from a strip club in Billings the night before. She was waiting for him to come out with the two women he'd driven there. She had her camera with the long lens ready on the seat beside her, ready to snap photos when the trio eventually emerged.

"I hope you nail the puke," April said.

"Oh, I will. And I'll be glad to put this case behind us. What's up with you?" Cassie asked her.

"I'm going out to one of the three ranches we talked about," April said. "This is the one my mom suspects the most."

"Are you alone?"

"Yes, but I can get backup if I need it."

"Well, good," Cassie said. "But I hope you'll be careful and diligent. And promise me you'll back out of there for your own safety if the situation isn't good."

"Of course I will," April said, grateful that Cassie couldn't see her rolling her eyes. Then: "I haven't done this a lot, you know. You've hardly ever let me interrogate a potential suspect."

"There's a reason for that," Cassie said. "We're not law enforcement. We don't have the power of the state behind us and we can't call in reinforcements if the deck is stacked against us. Not only that, but no one is obligated to answer our questions, and we can't just cuff suspects and take them to the station for questioning. We've got to always play it very cool, and you aren't exactly known for that, April."

"So how should I play this?" April asked. She quickly detailed what she knew about the McElwee sisters.

"Goodness," Cassie said. "They sound like . . . colorful people."

"That's one word for it."

Cassie said, "Just talk with them, not *to* them, and be friendly about it. Ask them about their lives and their interests. Don't judge them overtly. But most of all, keep them talking. If you keep them talking long enough, they'll let something slip. But if you're dominating the conversation or challenging them, they'll either clam up or get belligerent. That helps no one, and you may only get one bite of the apple.

"Take their side if you can," Cassie continued. "Lend a sympathetic ear to their grievances. If they think of you as an antagonist, that won't help you learn anything. If they think of you as their friend or ally, they might reveal things that surprise you and help you along."

"You're good at that, aren't you?" April said.

"I am, if I do say so myself. Plus, there are very few suspects I can physically subdue if it came to that. So I don't throw my weight around, or my private investigator credentials."

"I'll try to keep that in mind," April said. "I'll try to dial things back, but one thing you said bothers me. How can I try and be on their side? If they had something to do with hurting my dad, I swear I'll mess them up."

"April . . ."

"I mean, I'll try to do what you say. But it might be tough."

"Good. How is your dad doing?"

"We think the surgery will be later today. Until that, we don't know."

"I'll keep my fingers crossed and pray for him," Cassie said.

Until that moment, April wasn't aware that Cassie prayed. And while she might have smirked at it before, she didn't do so now.

"Thank you," April said.

"Keep me updated," Cassie said. "Not only about your dad, but about you. I need you to come back in one piece."

"Aw, *really*?"

"Really. But don't let that go to your head."

Then April said: "Oh, fuck me. You won't believe what I just drove up on."

"*What?*"

"Three gangbangers in the middle of nowhere chasing around some cows on the side of a mountain. They're on foot and they look demented. They're shooting pistols in the air."

After a beat, Cassie chuckled. "That's *such* a Wyoming thing to say."

PABLO WAS A six-foot-three sophomore when April had met him in high school. Until Pablo, she'd not heard the phrase "gender fluidity" before, but Pablo was a walking, talking demonstration of it. Pablo wore flowing scarves, painted his nails black and his mouth bright red. He had scored twenty points in his first high school basketball game, but then promptly quit the sport. Instead, he organized the first-ever Saddlestring High School cheer club to cheer on his ex-teammates. Pablo was smart, popular, quirky, well-liked, and generally the funniest person in the room.

She recalled Pablo talking about moving to Saddlestring from Northern California, and what a shock it was to his system. Pablo's father was a semi-famous artist named Eduardo who didn't use his last name. Likewise, Pablo was simply *Pablo.* Eduardo had married either Lisa or Lainie McElwee. April couldn't recall which one. According to Pablo, his stepmother and step-aunt were "modern-day Wild West outlaws, like Calamity Jane and Annie Oakley."

"Annie Oakly wasn't an outlaw," April had told Pablo.

"Whatever—you know what I mean," Pablo had said with a dismissive wave of his long fingers.

Pablo went on to say that he'd never lived on an isolated ranch before, much less one as unusual as McElwee Land and Cattle. People of all kinds—he described them as "desperadoes"—showed up at any time of the day or night. All of them seemed to have some kind of business with the sisters that had nothing to do with livestock. But it wasn't only sketchy types. There were also cops, politicians, and artists who worked "the fringes."

"I never know who will show up or why they're there," Pablo said. "But the living room in the lodge often reminds me of the bar scenes in *Star Wars.*"

Pablo vanished abruptly when his father was kicked off the ranch by either Lisa or Lainie, or both. April hadn't thought of Pablo for years, but now she hoped he'd landed well. She was a little surprised he wasn't yet famous in one way or another.

THE CROSSROADS

April rolled into the ranch yard and kept alert. She scanned the outbuildings for movement, and the main log house for anyone peering out the windows. A pack of hounds appeared from under the front porch and surrounded her Toyota. While the dogs leapt and snarled at her, she stayed in her vehicle and hiked her jacket with her left hand and tucked a 9mm Glock into the back of her tooled western belt with her right.

A middle-aged blond woman with an exaggerated helmet of hair backed out through the screen door on the porch and turned slowly around to face April. The woman held a combat shotgun at the ready, and she squinted to see who had just arrived. She wore a huge flowing robe with vintage buckaroos printed on it. She looked to April like a human tipi.

April sat forward in her seat and tucked her jacket over the grip of the Glock in her belt. She waited for the dogs to be called off before reaching for the door handle. She could feel her heart race, but she didn't want to betray her anxiety. She also didn't want to be overly assertive, which was her default mechanism that often caused problems.

As the dogs padded back to the porch at the command of the woman with the shotgun, April turned off her engine and slipped out of the Tundra. She kept the door open in case she needed to dive back inside.

"What in the hell do you want?" the woman asked.

Before April could reply, the woman's face reddened and she shouted, "You do *not* come here to pick up product. That is *not* how we do business. Who in the fuck sent you down here, anyway?"

At first, April was confused. Then she realized that the woman on the porch had taken the measure of April's unfamiliar vehicle, the Montana plates, and her unconventional appearance—and assumed she was someone else.

"Who do you think I am?" April asked.

"Whoever you are, you need to get back inside your vehicle and get the hell off our property. This isn't the way we do things. We set up meets outside of our property. I don't know who told you otherwise."

"Forget about the Montana tags," April said. "I'm April Pickett."

The woman's eyes narrowed. "Pickett? As in . . . ?"

"My dad's the game warden here." Then, remembering Cassie's advice, April softened her tone. "He was ambushed a couple of days ago up the road. I'm sure you heard about it. I'm wondering if you could help me out, since you know the people out here on these ranches better than I do."

The woman seemed confused, but she lowered the muzzle of the shotgun. She was thinking.

"I'm not accusing you of anything," April said. "We're trying to find out who might have wanted to hurt him."

"So he's still alive? I heard that, but I wasn't sure it was true."

"He's in a coma. But we're all hoping he pulls out of it."

"Well, son of a bitch," the woman said. "I hope if he pulls through, he won't be such a do-gooder around here. That guy needs to lighten up."

April nodded her head. Not agreeing, but not arguing, either.

"I'm Lisa McElwee," the woman said. "I own this place with my sister. I was kind of expecting someone else . . ."

"I get that," April said. "I'm just glad I'm not the person you were expecting."

Lisa chuckled at that. She obviously didn't want to talk about the misunderstanding anymore. April thought back to the word Lisa had used: "product." She had a pretty good idea what that meant. Lisa had assumed April was a dealer from Montana. And Lisa was selling, not buying. But selling what?

"Your dad was out here a few weeks ago," Lisa said. "I haven't seen him since. I'm not sure I can help you out much. All I know is that you're barking up the wrong tree."

"Why was he here?"

"Something about a hunter who claimed he saw a drunk elk on our ranch. It didn't make any sense. And he didn't cite us for anything."

"A drunk elk?"

"That's what he claimed. But we set him straight and he went on his way. There weren't any problems or fireworks. I even offered him a cinnamon roll."

"I'm glad there weren't any issues," April said, again remembering Cassie's advice, even though it pained her inside. She knew when she was being told half a story.

April said, "I was wondering what you can tell me about your neighbors. Did any of them have a problem with my dad that you're aware of?"

Lisa snorted. "They all did, I would guess. They're not exactly neighbors in, like, a neighborly way. We don't exactly get along with any of 'em. It goes back generations."

"See, that's why I'm glad I met you," April said, swallowing something bitter. "I knew you'd be able to shed some light on the situation."

"The sheriff's already been out here," Lisa said. "He's a good-looking dude, but he's absolutely clueless. Just like all our county sheriffs."

April nodded her head in agreement. She didn't have to misrepresent her own feelings this time.

Lisa McElwee said, "If that new sheriff would have asked me, which he didn't, I would have told him to concentrate on the shitheads that surround our place, not on us. But he just didn't get it. All he asked about was where we were that day, and if we owned identical rifles. Lainie and I told him we had been meeting with our banker in Winchester that morning, which we were. The banker confirmed that."

"I see," April said.

"He never asked about our shithead neighbors, as I call them," Lisa said.

"Would you tell me about your shithead neighbors?"

"Would you like a warm cinnamon roll?"

"Sure."

Still a little stunned by Eduardo's painting of a much younger Lisa in the great room, April absently peeled off a strip of the cinnamon roll at the table in the breakfast nook. Meanwhile, Lisa held court.

"It's a damned shame that you can't pick your neighbors," she said. "We've had difficulties with them for generations. They steal our water, knock down our fences, and call us in the middle of the night to come get the cows that wander across our property line. And they're always poking their noses into our business."

"Who are you talking about?" April asked.

Lisa chinned toward the north. "The Bucholz clan. Don't let them fool you. John is a diabolical man, and his wife is even worse. They'll smile while they screw you out of a nickel, then act all innocent when you call them on it.

"John plays like he's a big shot, but he isn't. Him and Shelby connived their way into owning that ranch by screwing all of their relatives. I hear they owe everybody in town money these days, but John acts like he's about to win the lottery. He's got something going on over there, I tell you."

"Like what?" April asked.

"Some kind of big secret, is all I know," Lisa said. "There's been heavy machinery over there, and we've seen small airplanes and helicopters flying over their ranch. I have no idea how the guy can afford all that activity based on what I've heard."

"Did my dad know what was going on?"

Lisa shrugged. "I have no idea, but your dad likes to keep things close to his vest when it comes to dealing with us landowners. I wouldn't be surprised if he knew what was going on over there. And maybe," Lisa said while leaning across the table, "it got him shot up."

"Then you've got the Double D Ranch," Lisa said while gesturing to the north again. "We call it the 'Double Douchebag' because that's what he is. Him and his trophy wife. You've never met such a pompous windbag in your life, I tell you."

Lisa pressed an index finger against the tip of her nose and pushed it up. "He looks at my sister and me like we're low-rent scum of the earth. Like we're second-class citizens. That guy thinks he can buy and sell everything in the county, and he's got too many people convinced that he can. Did you know he called the feds on us?"

"I hadn't heard that," April said.

"Well, he did. He went to the U.S. attorney and claimed we were dealing narcotics from our ranch. DEA agents showed up in SWAT gear, pointing guns in every direction, and tearing up the house looking for drugs. But they didn't find any, did they?"

"I guess not?" April said.

"You bet your ass they didn't," Lisa said. Then: "Thompson may own a fancy ranch here, but he doesn't understand this state at all. He doesn't realize we all know each other, but we mind our own business. He doesn't get it that we're all connected."

It took a moment for April to realize what Lisa was telling her. "Are you saying someone tipped you off about the raid?"

Lisa grinned coquettishly. "I'm just saying Thompson is just another rich out-of-stater who thinks he's got it all figured out. But he doesn't, and he never will. And neither will his brain-dead plastic Botox Barbie of a wife."

April said, "I know my dad went out to the Double D on occasion. Are you aware of any issues he might have had with Mr. Thompson? Or the other way around?"

"Not particularly," Lisa said. "But here's something to think about: Thompson doesn't like it when he can't own people. He thinks it's his right. He owns cops, politicians, regulators, and anyone he thinks he needs to get his way. I could see Thompson butting heads with your dad the do-gooder. Can't you?"

"My dad can be stubborn," April said. "He takes his job very seriously."

"So there you go," Lisa said. "Maybe Thompson asked your dad to do something he didn't want to do? Or to look the other way while Thompson launched another one of his little schemes?"

"I hadn't thought of that," April conceded.

"Thompson is used to getting what he wants," Lisa McElwee declared. "He's not used to dealing with men like Joe Pickett who can't be bought."

April sensed a presence behind her in the kitchen, then heard a shrill "*Lisa, what in the hell are you going on about?*"

"Meet April Pickett," Lisa said. Then she rolled her eyes. "And this is my sister, Lainie."

April turned around in her chair to find Lainie standing in the threshold. Lainie was a younger, slimmer, and flintier version of her older sister. April hadn't heard her coming down the hall.

Lainie looked over April's head as if she wasn't there and said, "Lisa, I think you need to quit talking. You never seem to know when to shut up." And to April, "You need to leave our place now."

"She's trying to figure out what happened to her dad," Lisa said. "I was just filling her in on our shithead neighbors."

"We've got projects to get done this morning," Lainie said to Lisa. "Things that can't wait. And you're just in here gossiping the day away."

"I'm trying to help," Lisa said.

April glanced from sister to sister. They glared at each other and there was tension in the air. There was obviously an understanding between them that *something*—probably their "projects"—should be left unsaid.

April wasn't sure what she should do.

"Get up," Lainie said to April. "I'll show you out."

"Lisa has been a big help."

"I'm sure she has," Lainie said, reaching out and grasping April's upper arm. "We're done here. Let's go."

"I still have questions," April said while jerking her arm away. She didn't like to be touched without an invitation—by anyone.

"Lisa's done talking for now," Lainie said with finality.

April rose and glanced back at Lisa, hoping the sister would come to her rescue. Instead, Lisa glowered and looked away.

As she ushered April through the great room toward the door, Lainie said, "One of my sister's big-ass flaws is that she talks too much."

"She was just filling me in on the Bucholzes and the Thompsons."

"How do we know you're not working with them?" Lainie asked.

"I'm not. Why the hell would I be?"

"So you say."

Lainie pushed open the door with one hand and guided April outside firmly with her other hand on her back. April bristled, and the polite veneer she'd adopted upon meeting Lisa melted away.

Once outside, April wheeled around and faced Lainie. "Did you have anything to do with my dad getting shot?"

"Maybe he deserved it," Lainie said with a shrug. "Did you ever think of that? He has a habit of poking his nose in places it doesn't belong."

April felt her cheeks flush hot. "What are you hiding out here, anyway?" she asked. "What is it you didn't want him to know about?"

Lainie's face set in a mask.

"Is it the 'product' you two sell to dealers? Or does it have to do with the three gangbangers I saw who look real out of place? Clearly they're doing something on your ranch that has nothing to do with beef."

Lainie's eyes flared. A second later, Lisa pushed through the door behind her. Lisa once again held the shotgun. She stood shoulder to shoulder with her sister, facing April down.

Lisa had chosen Lainie over April. April knew she would have done the same thing when it came to her own sisters.

"I know when it's time to leave," April said as she backed away.

Several pickup doors slammed shut behind her and she turned around. The three men she'd seen on the mountain had entered the ranch yard and they now stood near April's Tundra. All three were obviously still armed.

"You're dead meat," Lainie said.

April didn't dare reach for her weapon. She was trapped on both sides.

Instead, she brushed a strand of hair out of her eyes and said, "My sisters know exactly where I am today. So does my mom, and so does the sheriff. If I don't come back, they'll know where to come and who to come for. And this time, you might not have time to hide all of your *product* before the cops show up."

Lisa and Lainie exchanged a glance. Then Lainie said, "Fuck off, April Pickett. Now get in your truck and drive away. And don't look back."

The three men stepped aside so she could climb into the cab of her Tundra. One of them, the one who had stared at her earlier, now leered to reveal a mouthful of gold teeth.

April was halfway to Antler Creek Junction before her heart stopped whumping in her chest.

She used the dictation feature on her phone to send her sisters a text. I had a close call, but I'm out of there. Then: I think the McElwees are people of interest. They def know more than they let on.

CHAPTER NINETEEN

SHERIDAN READ THE texts from her sisters one after the other as she drove toward the Bucholz Cattle Company headquarters, and she replied by sending thumbs-up emojis. She was grateful they were both safe, and extremely interested in what they'd have to say later. Sheridan also breathed a small sigh of relief that April hadn't shot anyone.

Working daily with the falcons of Yarak, Inc., Sheridan had noticed that her visual perception had improved when she was out in the field. Although not even close to the ability of the raptors she flew, she found that she could spot subtle items on the landscape and in the air that had previously eluded her, like prey birds and small animals. Sheridan could look out over familiar vistas and note small aberrations that she would have previously missed. Nate attributed her newfound ability as a beginning stage of *yarak* itelf. She wasn't so sure of that, but she welcomed a higher sense of natural awareness.

Which is why she noticed an almost imperceptible column of dust rising into the morning sky far in front of her on the road.

She could not yet see the vehicle or vehicles that made it, but the haziness above the sagebrush terrain and below the massive blue sky indicated that someone was coming her way from the ranch.

Since they'd all decided to arrive at their respective ranch targets around the same time and without a heads-up to the owners, for a moment Sheridan wasn't sure what to do. Encountering John and Shelby Bucholz on the road would be less than optimal. The Bucholzes could rightly send her back on her way, or even call the sheriff and report her for trespassing.

And even if they did neither one, any exchange she had with them while they parked side by side on the road would be truncated and incomplete.

She could perform a three-point turn on the road and beat it toward the junction, but that would defeat the purpose of their whole strategy that morning.

Sheridan chose to eliminate those choices altogether.

Instead, she engaged the four-wheel drive and turned sharply left off of the ranch road. She kept one set of tires in a meandering cowpath and bounced over sagebrush with the other. She drove up a small hill, topped it, and fled down the other side out of view from the road or the oncoming autos.

Sheridan killed the engine of her SUV and snatched a pair of powerful Zeiss binoculars she used for falconry spotting from her console. She piled out of her SUV and jogged back up to the top of the rise and ducked down.

She poked the lenses of the binoculars through a thick sagebrush and focused on the road. Within a few minutes, Sheridan watched as three identical white pickups in a convoy appeared.

Road dust rose like a wake behind them. None of the pickups resembled any of the ranch models she'd seen the previous summer. That meant the Bucholzes were likely still at home and once the vehicles passed she could resume her journey. Or she hoped so.

As they got closer, she could see that each of the trucks had a logo of some sort on the driver's-side door. The middle truck had a bed filled with brightly painted metal gear with an arm of some kind extending the length of the bed.

The convoy didn't drive as far as where Sheridan had set up, but instead slowed down and took a new-looking two-track to the east. As the trucks made the turn, she focused in on the graphics on their front doors.

Each read: **GLOBAL EXPLORATION.**

She'd never heard of the company before, but she noted that all three pickups had Texas plates.

SHERIDAN WATCHED THE convoy as it proceeded southeast. She could make out the boundary fence of the ranch ahead of them, and she wondered how far they would go. She knew that Lorne Trumley's Crazy Z-Bar Ranch was just beyond the fence line they were approaching.

That's when the first vehicle stopped. The second and third pickups nosed in behind it and people started getting out.

The driver of the first vehicle was a big man wearing a blue long-sleeved shirt, jeans, and a baseball cap. He was big and dark-haired, and effusive in his movements.

John Bucholz climbed out of the passenger side and stood next to him. Shelby opened the door from the back and joined them. For a moment, Sheridan was flummoxed. She hadn't expected the Bucholzes to be there.

The driver gestured across the landscape, and both John and Shelby looked on in rapt attention. The man pointed, and gestured, and waved his hands to explain something to them. The Bucholzes both nodded along.

After a few minutes of explanation, the burly driver stepped aside and let the other men who'd followed him hold court for a few minutes, pointing out things Sheridan couldn't see across the swale. It seemed like some kind of on-site presentation. As before, the Bucholzes seemed to listen carefully and asked a few questions.

Sheridan wished she could lip-read what was going on, and what was being discussed.

Whatever it was, she decided, John and Shelby were excited about it.

Then, instead of climbing back into their units and departing the area, as Sheridan had hoped, she watched the burly man lead the Bucholzes across the swale on foot. He pointed toward the ground and in several instances squatted down and seemed to paw at the earth. The other drivers followed the Bucholzes like ducklings.

What's going on? she asked herself.

Whatever it was, Sheridan knew she couldn't reappear on the ranch road without being seen. She'd be there as long as the three trucks were out there. And it didn't appear that anyone was in a big hurry to leave.

She scooted down the hill toward her SUV and didn't stand up until she knew she was out of their view.

Sheridan didn't want to leave her part of the plan incomplete. She couldn't bear letting her sisters down after they'd done exactly what she'd laid out to them. Not being able to visit the Bucholz Ranch and gather information left a huge hole in their investigation. And she didn't know if they'd be able to fill it.

News and gossip traveled fast in Twelve Sleep County. If the sisters left the Bucholzes until last, Sheridan didn't doubt that one way or another John and Shelby would know that Lucy and April had visited their neighbors. The whole point of coordinating the visits to all three ranches at the same time was to catch the ranchers unprepared.

Then an idea came to her.

If she couldn't use the main ranch road to get to the Bucholz headquarters, there was another way. She could get there using a backdoor approach: over the sagebrush to the perimeter of their ranch, then across the side of the mountains on Forest Service roads. Sheridan could then access the ranch compound from the other side, where those old guest cabins were located.

The cabins where she'd glimpsed someone inside. The off-limit cabins that were the reason she'd been kicked off the ranch and denied her bird abatement fee the summer before.

She could be waiting there when the Bucholzes returned, and they'd no doubt be caught off guard when they saw her. That's the situation she'd hoped for in the first place. It was sneaky and less than ideal, but she couldn't come up with anything else.

She liked it, but it was risky. She'd already opened herself up to be charged with trespassing, and her new plan was to trespass even further.

But she wanted to know, once and for all, what the Bucholzes were hiding at those cabins.

Did her dad find out a couple of days ago? she wondered. And could that be why he was shot?

Sheridan drew out her phone and tapped a message into the group text: Change of plans. Going to the HQ to wait for them. I'll explain later.

THROUGH DRY STREAMBEDS, around downed trees, and over reddening buckbrush, Sheridan maneuvered her SUV off the ranch property and onto Forest Service land to fully skirt the ranch. She used an old fire road that ran parallel to the boundary fence for five miles before crossing back onto private Bucholz land.

She took an ancient two-track that meandered along the side of a small creek that she knew led to the Bucholz place eventually. She startled a small herd of elk who were bedded down in the grass next to the creek, and they thundered through the lodgepole pines to avoid her. Sheridan was struck, as she always was, with how massive bulls could slice through close-packed tree trunks without banging their antlers on the branches.

As she neared the ranch compound, the floor near the stream narrowed and canyon walls rose up on both sides.

Finally, as the canyon pinched in even more, the first of the old cabins came into view. It was a simple one-room log structure, and it was in poor shape. The roof had collapsed inward, and misshapen open window frames gaped without glass.

She powered down her truck windows and crawled her vehicle past the first cabin toward a second one in similar condition. She jumped with alarm when a fat marmot with a brown belly whistle-screeched at her from the doorframe as she drove by, then scuttled back inside.

When the third and fourth cabins came into view, Sheridan stopped her SUV and killed the engine. She made sure she had her phone on her, and she debated whether to retrieve the shotgun from the back seat to take with her. She decided against it, reluctantly. Being an armed intruder on private property wouldn't have much of an argument going for her, and that made it more likely *she* could get hurt—or arrested again.

Instead of the shotgun, Sheridan retrieved a canister of bear spray out of her console and clipped it on her belt. No one could criticize her for having bear spray in grizzly country, could they?

In the distance, where the ranch compound was located, she could hear cattle mewling in the corrals. A light breeze rattled through the tops of the trees. Otherwise, it was eerily quiet.

Because of the marmot, Sheridan gave the third cabin a wide berth, but she could tell as she walked past it that it was as unoccupied as the first two. It was the fourth cabin, the one closest to the ranch compound, that she was most interested in.

Although it was no larger than the first three, the fourth cabin was subtly different as she approached it. The windows were intact, and the roof appeared solid. There was a small curl of smoke coming from a rusty stovepipe.

As she got closer, she noticed the outline of a perimeter that formed a large square around the structure. But instead of fencing, the perimeter consisted of a series of electronic sensors mounted on three-foot fiberglass stakes set at a ten-foot distance from each other. It reminded her of portable dog fences she'd seen before, or remote high-tech corrals used by hunting guides and outfitters to restrain their horses in the mountains.

The hairs on the back of her neck and forearms prickled and her eyes widened. She suddenly wished she'd brought her weapon.

Then the front door of the cabin opened and a figure emerged. He was a tall, gaunt man with a crown of wispy white hair. He was wearing a one-piece gray union suit of some kind and his movements were stiff, his gait shuffling. He apparently hadn't seen her standing a few feet outside of the perimeter, and his destination was the unpainted outhouse that was situated in the far corner of the square.

He took a few more steps, stopped, and slowly turned her way, as if he'd sensed her presence. When their eyes met, Sheridan felt her insides clench up.

The man looked to be in his late sixties, although it was hard to tell, she thought. His skin was almost translucently pale, and his eyes widened and his mouth gaped at the sight of her. He had small close-set eyes and a lantern jaw.

"Who the hell are you?" he rasped.

"Who the hell are *you*?" she responded.

That's when she noticed the thin steel cable wrapped around his waist like a belt. The cable trailed behind him and extended into the interior of the cabin. A thick leather collar was buckled around his neck and she could see it was attached with a silver combination lock. The collar had squarish pockets of some kind on either side beneath his ears.

The realization of what she was witnessing hit Sheridan like a bolt of electricity.

"Why are you chained up? What is going on here?"

The man narrowed his eyes and glared at her. Finally, he sighed apologetically and said, "It's for my own good, I'm afraid."

"Who did this to you?"

"My relatives. But it's okay. It's not really what it looks like."

Sheridan said, "It looks like you're chained up here like a dog so you can't get out. And what is this?" she asked, gesturing to her own neck.

"A second line of precaution," he said. Then he gestured toward the sensors around the perimeter. "They call it my 'safety collar.' If I go outside the zone . . ."

"What happens if you go outside the zone?"

He pointed at the objects on the side of his collar, then flashed both of his palms with his fingers extended and said, "*Boom.*"

"Are you saying there are explosives in that collar?"

He repeated, "*Boom.*"

"My God," Sheridan said, reaching for her phone. "I'm going to call the sheriff."

"Please don't," the man said. His tone was desperate, and there was a sudden moistness in his eyes.

Sheridan was disgusted. But she also had no cell service where she stood at the mouth of the canyon. She'd need to find open terrain or climb into the mountains above the compound to get some reception.

"Will anything happen if I come inside?" she asked.

"Naw. People can come in. I just can't go out."

"I'm Sheridan Pickett," she said. "I think I saw you last summer."

"I remember you now," he said. "You're the falcon lady."

"I'm the falcon lady. Do you mind if I come inside?"

He hesitated for nearly a minute. It looked to Sheridan that he was having a long conversation with himself. Then he looked up and said, "I'm Uncle Hank. Uncle Hank Bucholz. This is where I live now for my own good."

"Are you saying you're dangerous?" she asked.

"Yeah. But not in the way you might think." Then he pointed to his temple. "It's my ideas that are dangerous. Do you want to see proof?"

Now it was Sheridan's turn to hesitate. What did he want to show her?

"I'll come inside," Sheridan said. "But only a few feet." She meant, but didn't say, that she'd stay just outside the length of the cable if he lunged at her.

"Suit yourself," he said with a shrug. "But by not seeing my project, you'd really be missing out. It would be like going to Paris, but refusing to look up at the Eiffel Tower, or something like that.

"I'll tell you everything about this," he said as he shook the cable leash. "And then I'll let you see my masterpiece."

Now he was pleading with her. He seemed so *lonely*, she thought. Did he ever get visitors? How long had he been confined there?

Despite her feelings, she knew there was something seriously wrong about the whole situation. And maybe something seriously wrong with Uncle Hank himself.

Sheridan considered turning around and running back to her SUV. She'd seen enough to blow the whistle on John and Shelby Bucholz. But if his imprisonment was wholly voluntary, as he suggested . . .

She stepped forward and walked through the sensors.

"Come inside, Sheridan. I promise you I don't bite."

As she considered it, he said, "First, I gotta do this." Without a qualm, Uncle Hank unzipped his union suit and urinated on the grass in front of him.

"That's what I was headed out to do when you showed up," he said while he finished and zipped back up with a flourish. The odor was pungent. Sheridan waited for the smell to disperse before advancing. She tried not to act as alarmed as she was.

Then he turned and strode into the cabin. As he did, he yanked at the length of cable until it, too, was through the doorway.

Sheridan took a moment to look all around her. There was no one present to witness what was happening, or to intervene if necessary. She asked herself, "What would Joe Pickett do?"

She knew the answer.

Sheridan activated the recording app on her phone and slid it into her shirt pocket. Then she followed him inside.

A BARE BULB hung from a cord over a rough-hewn table with a single chair. Uncle Hank turned it on with a pull chain and it illuminated the interior of the cabin, which was dark except for the single window cut into the logs on the west wall.

Sheridan stayed close to the open door and took it all in. Two of the walls were floor-to-ceiling bookcases filled with hundreds of hardcover books with their dust jackets removed, so it was hard to read the titles in the gloom. The books looked old, and a few appeared ancient. There was a single bed with a metal frame, a stand with a porcelain basin on it for washing, an aged woodstove, cast-iron skillets hanging from nails by their handles, a large gravity-fed cistern, and a freestanding heater and coil fueled by a propane cylinder. There were no photos, art, or posters on the walls. The place was as neat and uncluttered as it could possibly be given its small footprint, she thought.

The cable around Uncle Hank's waist led to a heavy U-bolt that was secured to the rough-cut wooden floor. There looked to be enough cable to allow the man to access the entire perimeter inside, but no farther.

Again, the sorrow she'd felt when she first met Uncle Hank washed over her. How was it possible to live like this?

"How long have you been here?" she asked.

He poised one long finger to his chin, then said, "Three years, two months, and five days."

"My God."

He slowly shook his head, as if to disabuse her of her immediate reaction. "No, it's not so bad. They bring me supplies once a week and they pump out the outhouse every month. The electricity works and they make sure I've got fresh water and propane. I eat quite well, actually, and I sleep the sleep of the dead. It's all for my own good."

"How can that be possible?" she asked. "You're a prisoner here."

"But I'm a happy one," he said, revealing crooked yellow teeth. "Do you want to know why?"

She nodded.

"I've got my books, and I've got my privacy. I've been able to work nonstop on my masterpiece," he said as he gestured to a large leather-bound volume on the tabletop. It was at least three inches thick. "Believe me, if I was out there in the world, I wouldn't have been able to accomplish what I've accomplished. I started my masterpiece back in Scranton a decade ago, but I was never able to work on it until now."

"So you're writing a book?" she asked.

"It's more than a book," he said, opening his eyes wide for emphasis. "It's an entire philosophy of spiritual life. It's a concept that could quite literally change the world for the better. If the great powers knew what I've been doing here, the great religious leaders, no doubt they would try to stop me. But here I've got complete autonomy and privacy to think freely. There are no monks or professors to steer my thinking. That's what I mean when I say my ideas are dangerous—to some."

Sheridan didn't know how to respond to that.

He continued. "I think I've benefited from not knowing or practicing any faith in my younger years before I came here. I had no preconceived notions. So what you see before you is revolutionary," he said, gesturing again toward the volume on the table. "My masterpiece is the result of years of reading original sources and drawing my own conclusions. I can maybe let you take a look at it, but you have to promise not to copy any of it down or take any photographs. And you have to promise not to tell anyone what you saw."

She said, "Before I make any promises, I need to know more about what's going on around here. I need you to convince me why I shouldn't call the sheriff, for one thing."

"No," he said, wagging his finger. "You don't want to do that."

"First, who made you stay here? Who put that cable around your waist and set up the electronic perimeter?"

"My nephew John, of course."

"Why?"

"It's complicated," Uncle Hank said. He was anxious for Sheridan to behold his masterpiece, she thought.

"What's complicated?" she asked. "It looks pretty straightforward to me. Your nephew and Shelby Bucholz are holding you prisoner on their ranch. They've kidnapped you. If you try to escape, you'll get your head blown off. That's a very sick situation, and your relatives should be in prison for it."

He waved her off. "No, no, it's not like that at all. This is all very legal, John tells me. He's got a court order to place me in a legal conservatorship for my own good. John and Shelby are my conservators. They have complete control of me, and in a way it's the ultimate freedom. I don't have to worry about money, or obligations. I have the freedom to do what I want, like *think*. And work on my masterpiece."

"Why would he do that?" Sheridan asked.

"It's my own fault," Uncle Hank said ruefully. "I was doing meth when I showed up here. I wasn't in my right mind. I demanded my share of the ranch as per my birthright. I was a complete asshole about it, to be honest."

"What judge ordered the conservatorship?" Sheridan asked.

"I can't remember. But John was very clear about it. I could either submit to him and stay here living as free as a bird, or I could be sent away to someplace nasty. It was an easy choice for me."

Sheridan scoffed. "You never saw the legal order?"

"I didn't ask."

"Tell me more about John and Shelby," Sheridan said. "What are they up to? I saw them with some men in pickups earlier today. They were walking around with them like they were all planning something."

Uncle Hank shrugged and his eyes darted once again to the book on the table. It was obvious to Sheridan that he couldn't wait to show it to her and he was getting impatient with her questions.

"John and Shelby will soon be very wealthy," Uncle Hank said. "Shelby let that slip when she delivered food to me a couple of weeks ago. She said when it happens they'll have to move me someplace else, and I told her I might not want to go. My masterpiece isn't done yet. I need another year or so, although the winters are very hard, as you can imagine. Some days, I spend the entire time sitting in front of my heater and shivering."

"How are they going to get rich?" Sheridan asked.

"I don't know the details. I could care less, frankly. John has always wanted to be wealthy, so I'm not surprised. Even as a very young boy, he was completely single-minded about that."

"So you don't know who those other men were this morning?"

"I don't have a clue. There has been a lot of activity on the ranch the last month or so. Lots of vehicles—even a helicopter. I wish they'd all go away and leave me in peace, to be honest."

"Have you ever seen a game warden here on the ranch?" she asked. "You know: red uniform shirt, green Ford pickup."

"I've seen him. I *think* he might have seen me."

Sheridan felt a flush of excitement. "When was that?"

"Three or four weeks ago. He was talking with John and Shelby."

"Do you have any idea what they were talking about?"

"Not a clue."

"Do you know if John and Shelby had a problem with the game warden? Did they ever mention anything to you about him?"

"They don't talk to me about things like that," Uncle Hank said. "All I know is that Shelby was in a really bad mood later that afternoon when she brought me supplies. She snapped my head off when I said my jar of pickles was empty and I needed more. I didn't push it further. I've learned not to do that when she's in one of her moods."

"Was she in a bad mood because of the game warden?" Sheridan asked.

"*How would I know?*" Uncle Hank said with real irritation in his voice. "Now, do you want to look at my masterpiece or not?"

"Sure," she said. Sheridan was convinced he might either completely clam up or lunge at her. She felt a sense of his coiled-up rage. For the sake of gathering more information, she decided it would be best to go along with him—at least for a moment.

"Sit," he said, indicating the single chair.

She sat. Uncle Hank hovered behind her.

"Open it."

She reached out and opened the cover of the volume. As she did, he said, "Get ready to have your mind blown." Sheridan noted that his tone had softened again, now that she was doing what he asked.

On the first page, in handwritten block lettering, it announced *THE SACRED CONFLUENCE* by Henry Alan Bucholz. The words were underlined at least five times and with different colored pens.

The second page was a list of religions:

- Christianity
- Islam
- Hinduism
- Buddhism
- Sikhism
- Judaism
- Bahaism
- Jainism
- Shintoism
- Zoroastrianism
- Mormonism

She looked over her shoulder for an explanation. Instead of offering one, Uncle Hank whispered, "*Keep reading.*"

What followed was page after page of tiny, almost illegible writing broken up by baffling but intricate illustrations. There were demons, mutilated bodies, incomprehensible symbols and graphics, and decapitated sheep and goats. She flipped more pages without really comprehending the text. There were hundreds of pages, all filled with ink, and only a few blank sheets near the end of the volume. She found it remarkable that although the tiny text was written in freehand, there were no strike-throughs or corrections. It was as if Uncle Hank believed that every single word he had written was perfect.

"I have studied the tenets of the world's major religions," Uncle Hank announced. "And I've merged them into one perfect belief system. I've incorporated the best beliefs and discarded the stupid or inane ones."

"Wow," Sheridan said, puzzled but not really impressed.

"No one else on earth has ever attempted such a thing," Uncle Hank said as he leaned over her from behind. "This has never been done before. I've got the charity and humbleness of Christianity, the resolve of Islam, the gentleness of Hinduism, the . . ."

His words rushed out and Sheridan stopped listening. The man was truly nuts, she thought. Maybe a conservatorship *wasn't* the worst idea to keep him contained.

All she wanted now was to get away and rejoin her sisters. Wait until they found out about Uncle Hank Bucholz, and the lengths John and Shelby had gone to retain sole ownership of their ranch.

His cadence got more strident as he said, "It's the confluence of all of man's most enlightened ideas and philosophies . . ." while he placed his hands on her shoulders.

Repulsed, Sheridan instantly shrugged his hands away. "You're too close," she warned. "Back off, Uncle Hank."

He reacted as if he'd touched a hot stove, which he had. He said, "I haven't touched another human being in three and a half years."

She stood up and turned around to face him. "And you're not starting with me."

"Sheridan, please," he pleaded while backing her up against the edge of the table. "I was hoping that once you'd seen it that you'd understand. That you'd appreciate that I've let you enter a special place that no one has ever been besides me. Let me show you what the rapture of the confluence feels like . . ."

She reached to her side and thumbed the safety off the canister and hit him in the face with a red burst of bear spray. As she did, she looked to the side and gulped air. Uncle John howled and covered his face with his hands and toppled over to the floor.

Holding her breath, Sheridan quickly stepped over him and leapt for the open door. It was such close quarters inside the cabin that the cloud from the spray hung in the air. She couldn't avoid it.

As she staggered through the perimeter toward her SUV, Sheridan let out her breath and breathed freely. Nevertheless, her eyes flushed tears and her bare skin burned. Fluids from her nose flowed down her face.

Before climbing into her rig, she wiped moisture from her eyes and looked back at the cabin. Uncle Hank was still writhing and moaning on the wooden floor.

Beyond the cabin, the ranch compound was still quiet except for the cows in the corrals. The Bucholzes—and the men in the white trucks from Global Exploration—had not returned.

SHERIDAN DROVE BACK toward Antler Creek Junction the same way she'd arrived. She stopped just long enough to check her phone to confirm that the entire weird encounter she'd had with Uncle Hank Bucholz had been recorded. She saw no other vehicles on the road, although she did spot a distant helicopter moving across the terrain to the west.

When she had service on her phone, she texted her sisters: I'm out and okay, but you're not going to believe what I found out on the Bucholz Ranch.

CHAPTER TWENTY

JUST AFTER NOON, Marybeth looked up anxiously in the waiting room as Dr. Ralston pushed through the double doors from the surgery center. Ralston was still in her scrubs. Her hair was covered with a plastic surgical cap, and a mask was pulled down on her neck. Joe had been in surgery for four and a half hours, and Marybeth had been beside herself the entire time.

She tried to instantly read the doctor's expression for an early sign of how the procedure had gone. It was one of the most profound few seconds of her life, and everything, it seemed, depended on what came next.

"The surgery was successful," Ralston announced. "We removed the bullet, patched up his head, and he appears to be resting comfortably."

Then Dr. Ralston nodded and afforded Marybeth a brief smile, which Marybeth involuntarily echoed. She was flooded with relief, and she wiped away a tear.

"Thank the Lord," Marybeth said, expelling the breath she realized she'd been holding inside. "And thank *you*."

"It was remarkable, really," Ralston said as she sat down next to Marybeth and placed her hand on her knee. "Your husband was very, very lucky. The bullet was intact and we couldn't find any fragmentation. It was lodged in the dura mater on the underside of his skull. Amazingly, the bullet didn't hit any major blood vessels, so the post-op swelling and bleeding are minimal. Those are two things we always watch for."

"It seems too good to be true," Marybeth said. "I mean, he was shot in the head. But he's going to make it?"

"All signs are positive," Dr. Ralston said. "So much has to do with luck and circumstances."

To demonstrate, Ralston raised her chin toward the ceiling and placed her index finger a few inches above her left eyebrow.

"The bullet entered here," she said. "Either your husband looked up at the exact millisecond the round hit him or the windshield glass deflected it upward. The trajectory is all-important here, and we may never know what exactly happened. But the glass definitely affected the velocity of the bullet itself, so it didn't exit the skull and cause more damage. The bullet lodged a few inches from where it entered."

"This is so good to hear," Marybeth said. "Joe isn't known for his luck."

"Well, he had it this time," Ralston said. "We all feel pretty good about it as well. There are so many factors involved that we need to account for: the bullet entry and exit site, the area of the brain damaged by the trauma, the caliber of the bullet and the weapon, the range of the gunshot distance . . ."

"So there's no brain damage at all?" Marybeth asked.

"I didn't say that," Ralston corrected. "The trajectory of the bullet clipped the top of the cerebrum—the frontal lobe. It didn't tear it up like it could have, but it definitely plowed a small path."

Marybeth shook her head. "What will that mean?"

Dr. Ralston raised her eyebrows. "I can't say for sure. The human brain is like how Churchill described the Soviet Union: a riddle wrapped in a mystery inside an enigma. But believe me when I say I've seen much, much worse damage."

Marybeth again released a long sigh of relief. Then she briefly closed her eyes and thought about what Dr. Ralston had told her yesterday.

"The frontal lobe," she said. "That's where personality characteristics are located, right? Things like decision-making, knowing the difference between right and wrong, ethics and morality?"

"Yes."

"Do we know . . ."

"We don't," Dr. Ralston said. "The next few days are critical as he emerges from the coma. There's a possibility some of his functions may be affected. Neurological recovery is different for every patient. It may require several months or even years.

"Or," Ralston said with a squeeze to Marybeth's hand, "he may just wake up and wonder where he's been the last few days."

"Can I see him?"

"Give us an hour or so to get him into his recovery room," Ralston said. "Then you can be with Lucky Joe when he wakes up."

"Thank you again," Marybeth said. "You saved his life—and mine."

Dr. Ralston flushed and looked quickly away. "It's nice to hear you say that. I appreciate it. We've got a great team here, and everyone performed very well."

"You are just so wonderful," Marybeth said while embracing Dr. Ralston. "We're so fortunate that you're here."

Ralston wiped a tear from her cheek. "How embarrassing, but thank you," she said. "I guess neurosurgeons are people, too."

She stood up. "Now get some rest," she said to Marybeth. "I know you probably haven't slept much since you got here."

"I will," Marybeth said. "But first I need to call our daughters and give them the good news."

"Of course, but please don't overdo it," Ralston cautioned. "There could still be complications. We're not completely out of the woods yet."

Sheridan felt her phone vibrate in her pocket and she drew it out and read the screen.

"It's Mom," she announced. April and Lucy looked up anxiously from the kitchen table, where they'd gathered. The three sisters had come together just minutes before. They were eager to share what they'd learned, but the call from Marybeth put all that temporarily on pause.

"Is he out of surgery?" Lucy asked Sheridan.

"Hold on," Sheridan said as she connected the call.

"Sheridan, are your sisters with you?" Marybeth asked.

"They're both here."

"That's fantastic. Please put this on speaker so I can talk to you all at the same time."

Sheridan did so, and held the phone out. The anticipation level within the room was beyond belief.

"I just talked to Dr. Ralston," Marybeth said. "Your dad is out of surgery. The doctor said everything went very, very well. It sounds like your dad is fortunate because of where the bullet entered his skill. She said damage to his brain could be minimal. We can't get too excited yet, but this is the best news we could have hoped for."

Sheridan found herself beaming. It was as if a weight had lifted from her shoulders. Lucy wiped away sudden tears. April whooped and pumped her fist as if her team had just won the game with a last-second shot.

Then all three sisters started asking questions at once.

Sheridan asked her mother about the wound itself, and how it was possible that there was very little brain damage.

Lucy asked how long the recovery process would take, and if there would be lingering problems of any kind.

April asked how soon Joe would be able to regain consciousness and reveal what exactly had happened that morning two days ago.

"Hold it," Marybeth said. "Slow down. Let's do this one at a time."

Sheridan joined her sisters and she placed her phone on the tabletop.

For the next twenty minutes, Marybeth briefed them on what Dr. Ralston had told her and she tried to answer the questions as best she could.

When they were through and Marybeth said she had been given the okay to visit Joe in his recovery room, Sheridan said, "Mom—there's something we need to tell you. We waited until now because you had enough on your plate."

Marybeth hesitated before asking, “And what is that?”

“We spent the morning interviewing everybody at the three ranches,” Sheridan said. “Lucy went to the Double D, April went out to see Lisa and Lainie McElwee, and I drove out to the Bucholz place. We did it all at once and we’re about to compare notes and come up with some theories.”

“You all went there by yourselves?” Marybeth asked, clearly alarmed.

“And we all came back in one piece,” Lucy said.

“Although it was close,” April added.

Sheridan thought it best at the moment not to weigh in with what she’d discovered.

“I’m glad I didn’t know about this,” Marybeth said. “I would have tried to talk you out of it.”

“That’s why we didn’t tell you,” April said with a laugh.

Sheridan said, “We’ve invited Nate and Sheriff Sondergard to come by tonight after the three of us have discussed everything we learned. We’ll see if they agree with our conclusions.”

“I’m glad Nate is coming,” Marybeth said. “I don’t know much about the new sheriff.”

“It’s cool,” April cut in. “He’s sweet on Sheridan. He’ll do what she tells him to do.”

Sheridan flipped her sister off, but silently so her mother wouldn’t know, and April grinned diabolically.

“Seriously,” Sheridan said to the phone, “do you have any idea when Dad will regain consciousness? We have so many questions to ask him about what happened.”

“So do I,” Marybeth said. “And no, I don’t know. The doctor

couldn't say for sure. And we don't know how much he'll be able to remember. All I can tell you is that I'll be there when he does wake up."

"What if he's all out of it?" April asked. "What if he's all goofy, you know? Like a five-year-old?"

Sheridan and Lucy shot her a look.

"Anything is possible," Marybeth said with a sigh. "We simply won't know until it happens. He's been lucky thus far and we can only hope and pray that it continues."

"I'll say another prayer for him," Lucy offered.

"Thank you, sweetie," Marybeth said.

WHEN THEY CONCLUDED the call, Sheridan sat back in her chair and looked at her sisters. "We've got a lot to talk about before Nate and Steve come over. So what do you two think?"

"It was the McElwees," April said. "They're running a big-ass drug distribution center out there on the ranch. There are at least three armed cartel guys hanging around. Not only that, they're doing something really weird to their cattle and the resident elk herd. I think Dad figured out what they were doing and was headed out there to get more proof so he could nail them. They knew about it, so they ambushed him."

"You might be wrong," Lucy said to April. "It could have been the Thompsons. Michael Thompson is up to his eyeballs in at least two big scandals, and he needed Dad to sign off on some kind of development. His foreman, Clay Hutmacher, is in it with him, even though he was supposed to be Dad's friend. And knowing Dad the way we do, he wouldn't have a problem telling Thompson that they might not see eye to eye. Thompson is desperate, and he might have hired some shooters to make sure things went his way."

Sheridan paused before saying, "I put my money on the Bucholzes. John has some kind of scheme going on that Dad might have bumbled onto. John and Shelby are desperate, too, but they seem to think they're about to hit some kind of jackpot. And they have some big secrets they're keeping, including the fact that they've got John's pervert uncle imprisoned in one of their cabins. The guy is chained up there, and if he tries to escape, his head will literally explode."

"My God," Lucy said. "We've got a lot to talk about. I think I'll need a glass of wine now."

"Get two glasses," Sheridan said.

"I'll get the whiskey," April announced.

CHAPTER TWENTY-ONE

Dusk was casting massive shadows on the western flanks of the foothills that rose up from I-90 as Deputy Bowkley and James Dale O'Bryan crossed the state line and entered Montana from the south. They were now on the Crow Indian Reservation.

Bowkley was behind the wheel of his personal 2015 GMC Yukon. He was in his street clothes: jeans, motorcycle boots, black T-shirt, and black leather vest. His cap read **GO AHEAD AND TRY ME.** He had full-sleeve tattoos on both arms.

O'Bryan was still slightly embarrassed to be wearing his fresh-out-of-the-box cowhand clothing. He wished Bowkley would have alerted him that it wouldn't be necessary to dress up when he retrieved him at the motel in Winchester two hours before.

"Bring your weapon," Bowkley had said to O'Bryan.

"Always," O'Bryan had responded, patting his coat pocket.

Bowkley had said very little since then. He drove cautiously, keeping to the speed limit even in Montana when it rose to eighty miles per hour and the state troopers were notoriously lenient to drivers going even faster. Even so, O'Bryan guessed that the deputy didn't want to risk being picked up and cited en route to Billings, which was still two hours away. They wanted no record of their trip to Montana if they could help it.

It was the same reason why Bowkley had instructed O'Bryan to turn off location tracking on his burner phone.

It was a lonely drive, O'Bryan thought. Except for a few semi-trucks, there had been very little traffic on the interstate. Montana was as empty as Wyoming.

"Can I ask you a question?" O'Bryan said to Bowkley.

"Sure. But I may not answer it."

"You said when I met you that you'd recommended Peddy and me to your boss. What did you mean by that?"

Bowkley let the question hover for a few moments. Then he said, "I've been in law enforcement for a very long time. If you do what I do and you're smarter than the people you work with and you work for, you realize after a while that you're never going anywhere. You bust your ass nailing pukes so the rest of society can just carry on like you don't exist. There's no appreciation, you know? 'Defund the police' and that kind of bullshit. And you realize there's no pot of gold at the end of the rainbow."

O'Bryan urged him to continue by nodding his head.

Bowkley said, "So one day you're talking to a big-shot drug kingpin that you've been assigned to escort to court every day. You've established an interesting rapport with him over the months he's been locked up while the trial is going on. He's rich, and he's really connected. You ask the guy if he knows a couple of names of guys, shooters, who could be hired to off somebody. It's sort of a joke question, but he takes it seriously.

"He says that for a hooker, a bottle of bourbon, a carton of cigarettes, and an officer to look the other way, he might share a couple of names. And you just happened to be duty officer that night.

"So he gets what he wants and he comes through with the names of a couple of freelancers."

"That would be me and Peddy, I guess?" O'Bryan said.

"Yeah, but he didn't tell me what an asshole Peddy was," Bowkley said with a sneer.

"So who hired *you*?"

"That's not a good question to ask. Let's just say that if everything comes through like it's supposed to, I'm set for the rest of my life. No more pukes, no more busting my ass for people who pretend I don't exist. Fuck 'em, I say. It's time I got what I'm due."

With that, Bowkley turned to O'Bryan with a hard, cold glare. "So don't fuck this up for me, buddy boy."

"Why don't you get on your phone and book us each a motel?" Bowkley said a few minutes later. "Find a couple of places that are cheap and close to St. John's Hospital, and use false names. And don't use Jason Witten and Marion Barber, for Christ's sake."

"Two different motels?" O'Bryan asked.

"That's what I said. So if the cops start asking motel owners if two men checked in the night before the hit, they'll have to say no."

"Ah, got it. What if they want a credit card to hold the rooms?"

"Give 'em your card number. We can pay cash when we check in. So don't worry about that."

O'Bryan dug out his cell phone and winced. "There's no signal here."

"It's spotty. This is the res. You should get something when we get closer to Lodge Grass."

"I've never been on the Crow Indian Reservation before," O'Bryan said.

"It's not much, believe me," Bowkley said with disdain.

"Isn't this where Custer's Last Stand is located?"

"Yeah, up ahead. But it's called the Little Bighorn Battlefield National Monument now because the wokesters made them change the name. And it'll be closed by the time we get there."

"Damn. I've always wanted to see it."

Bowkley sighed. "It's some hills and sagebrush and a concrete monument where Custer's body was found. That's about it. Oh, and National Park bureaucrats in their Ranger Rick hats letting you know that the Indians have *their* version of what happened, too. And wouldn't you know it, the Indian version is all about a very noble pushback against the evil white oppressors and yada yada yada. There, I just saved you a trip."

"I'd still like to see it. I saw the movie."

BOWKLEY HAD BEEN an hour late to pick O'Bryan up, he'd said, because he'd had to meet with their employer.

When O'Bryan asked the deputy if the two of them were in the clear in regard to what had happened to Peddy, Bowkley assured him they were.

"I told him Peddy was an out-of-control asshole. He needed to be taken care of."

"What did you say about me?" O'Bryan asked.

"I said you were reliable. But I also said I'd keep a close eye on you."

Then Bowkley turned his head to O'Bryan and smiled. O'Bryan got a chill that ran through his bowels.

THREE MILES LATER, O'Bryan saw that Bowkley was slowing down on the highway and eyeing a turnoff up ahead of them that led to a gravel road going east.

"Gotta make a pit stop," Bowkley said.

"I could use one myself," said O'Bryan.

The gravel road was marked with signs indicating that ahead was something called the Arrowhead Petroleum Project, with warnings not to proceed on the private road. Bowkley ignored them and drove to the pad of the nearest pump jack that was working its grasshopper-like head.

Bowkley pulled up near the pad and killed the engine. It was obvious that the oil well was new and that the construction materials used to build it had not yet been completely cleaned up. They parked next to an oversized dumpster half filled with scraps and shards of metal and plastic pipe.

O'Bryan got out to urinate on the gravel. While he did, he looked over his shoulder to see Bowkley lean into the cab of the SUV and fish something out of the center console. O'Bryan looked over to where they'd come. They were out of the view of the highway.

In front of the dumpster, Bowkley shredded the pages of a small spiral notebook and tossed the scraps into the container.

Then he smashed the face of a cell phone and broke it up into parts. That also went into the dumpster.

When he looked over and saw O'Bryan observing him, Bowkley said, "I've been wanting to get rid of those things for a couple of days now."

"A notebook and a cell phone?" O'Bryan asked.

"Not anymore."

"Are you gonna tell me who they belonged to?" O'Bryan asked.

"The guy you and Peddy didn't finish off," Bowkley said.

"So HOW ARE we gonna do this?" O'Bryan asked.

"Simple. We find his room and make sure he's alone. I'll keep watch while you go inside and do the deed. Just make sure it's *right* this time. No more fucking screwups."

"What do I do? Smother him with a pillow? Turn off his medication? Cut his throat?" O'Bryan asked, trying to keep any panic out of his tone. "I assume we don't want to mess with gunshots."

"No gunshots," Bowkley echoed. "Keep your gun in your pocket."

"So . . ."

"The boss came up with an idea. Reach under your seat."

O'Bryan hesitated for a few seconds, then he did as asked. He removed a thick black plastic clamshell container with a handle and placed it on his lap.

"What's this?"

"Open it up."

O'Bryan unfastened the two plastic clips on the front of the container. What he found inside, resting inside foam padding, looked vaguely like a handheld electric drill. Except instead of a drill bit, there was a fitting with a thick one-and-a-half-inch hypodermic needle.

"What is this thing?" he asked.

"It's a livestock vaccine-dosing gun," Bowkley said. "It's used on the ranch to vaccinate cattle. It runs on lithium batteries and you can inject a couple hundred cows with it in a day. Just stick it in the hide and pull the trigger."

O'Bryan removed it from the clamshell box. The gun had a digital display screen on the top of it.

"Power it up," Bowkley said to O'Bryan. "There's a switch on the side."

When he did, the display came to life showing the level of battery power and digital counters to set the dosage of the shot and to record how many doses had been administered.

"What's in it?" O'Bryan asked.

Bowkley took his eyes off the road as he turned his head again. "A pure fentanyl solution. It's a hundred times more powerful than morphine. It's set to administer a ten-milligram dose. Two milligrams is fatal in adults. You could take out half of Billings with it if you wanted to."

"Where did the fentanyl come from?"

Bowkley chuckled at that. "Twelve Sleep County is swimming in it. Same as the rest of the country."

O'Bryan studied the gun. It seemed simple enough: stick the needle into flesh and pull the trigger.

"Our employer thinks this will work better than anything else for our purposes, and I agree with that," Bowkley said. "They'll figure it out, eventually, when they do the autopsy. They'll know that it was an overdose of fentanyl. But it's a hospital. They'll assume some nurse fucked up big-time. We'll be long gone and a whole lot richer by the time they suspect anything else."

"Are you sure it works?"

Bowkley smiled a mean smile in response.

FIVE MILES LATER, O'Bryan noted that Bowkley had tapped on the brake pedal to release the cruise control and the SUV was slowing down. He looked ahead to see a sign that read **LODGE GRASS EXIT.**

"What, do we need gas?" he asked.

"Nope."

O'Bryan settled back. Montana State Route 463 was a two-lane with narrow shoulders. It went straight west from the interstate. In the distance was a smattering of homes and buildings choked with cottonwood trees.

Lodge Grass, he noted as they wound through it, was from another world. As they crossed the railroad tracks into town there were finely appointed single dwellings mixed in with single-wide trailers and lawns scattered with cars and pickups that didn't look like they'd run in years. The streets had names like Wolf Lays Down and Strong Enemy Drive and Old Grey Blanket Road. There was a single clapboard grocery store that needed paint and a gleaming health-care clinic surrounded by a tall chain-link fence. Except for stray dogs that literally slept in the middle of the street and a scrum of young children chasing each other through a dirt playground with sticks, there were no other signs of life.

Bowkley drove through Lodge Grass and took a county road that continued northwest. There were loose cattle on the road and a few abandoned vehicles. When O'Bryan saw a sign saying that St. Xavier was twenty-six miles away, he asked, "Where are we going?"

"Hunting," Bowkley replied.

Before O'Bryan could ask what they were hunting for, Bowkley swung wide in the road so he wouldn't hit a man who had his thumb out trying to catch a ride. The man shot by O'Bryan's passenger window, but O'Bryan could see the hitchhiker was Native and in his forties. He wore a high-visibility orange plastic vest and a slouch hat.

Bowkley slowed down to a stop, then reversed until they came abreast of the man. Bowkley powered down O'Bryan's window and leaned across the bench seat.

"Where are you headed?" Bowkley asked.

"Saint X," the man said. "I got a house there."

"We're going that direction. Jump on in."

The man paused for a few seconds, weighing his options. He had probably not expected to be offered a ride by two Caucasian men on reservation grounds. Then he opened the back door and swung inside. The man was dark-skinned with remarkably sharp cheekbones and a wide rubbery mouth. There was a look of animal caution in his eyes, O'Bryan thought.

"Do you work on the highway?" Bowkley asked. "I noticed the vest."

"Flagger," the man said. "We're working up by Crow Agency. We've been there since summer. But tonight, my ride had to go see his girl play basketball in Hardin."

"Then it's your lucky night," Bowkley said.

"Thank you, mister," the flagger said.

"I always thought being a flagger on the highway would be a damned boring job," Bowkley said. "Is it?"

"Yeah, but it's a living."

"What's your name?"

"Leonard."

Bowkley said, "Leonard the Indian Flagger." O'Bryan wasn't sure why the man said it, and he was as confused as Leonard. Was it to mock him?

Then Bowkley leaned over and quickly retrieved the vaccine gun from the clamshell container on O'Bryan's lap. He reached over the back seat and plunged the needle into Leonard's shoulder and pulled the trigger, which made an audible *click*.

Leonard was as surprised by the sudden move as O'Bryan was. So surprised that he hadn't even raised his hands to ward off the gun. Leonard stared at the instrument as Bowkley withdrew the needle from his shoulder.

"What the fuck did you just do?" Leonard asked. "What is that thing?"

Bowkley said nothing as he fitted the gun back into the foam of the case.

A second later, the flagger seized up as if a massive bolt of electricity had hit him. White foam formed around his lips, and his eyes went wide. Then he collapsed and shuddered and slumped over dead.

"It works," Bowkley said. "Now help me roll him out of here. No one will think twice about a drug overdose on the res, believe me."

O'Bryan was still buzzing with both adrenaline and regret when Bowkley's phone burred between Crow Agency and Hardin. They were back on I-90 headed north.

Bowkley took the call and held the phone to his face. His only responses were "Really?," "I understand," and "How much?"

When he punched off, O'Bryan looked over expectantly.

"Slight change of the overall plan," Bowkley said. "Forget about the motel rooms. After we do this thing in Billings tonight, we're going to get the hell out of there and beat it back to Saddlestring. Those three cunts have turned out to be a bigger problem than we realized."

CHAPTER TWENTY-TWO

"SO WE'VE GOT a dilemma," Sheridan stated as she looked around the dining room table at the Pickett home later that night.

Sheriff Steve Sondergard sat at the head of the table and Nate Romanowski slouched at the other end. Sheridan addressed them both. "The three of us have interviewed all the ranchers we suspect. And each of us thinks we have uncovered enough suspicious stuff to believe that any one of them might have ordered or done the ambush two days ago.

"As I promised," she said to Sondergard, "we'll share everything we found out with you. And you have agreed to do the same. Hopefully we can come up with a consensus on the best way to proceed."

Sondergard nodded to acknowledge the arrangement. Nate said nothing and showed no indication of what he was thinking. No doubt, Sheridan thought, Nate wasn't sure yet if he trusted the new sheriff. As far as she knew, they'd never met. Nate was instinctively suspicious of law enforcement and he had many good reasons over the years to come to that opinion. Sondergard had reacted with surprise when Nate was introduced at the table. It wasn't a warm greeting. The sheriff had no doubt already heard some stories about the outlaw falconer, and obviously they weren't stories that had warmed his opinion of the man.

"So you're the vaunted Nate Romanowski," Sondergard said.

"I am."

"Why are you here?"

"They asked me."

"Do you have some kind of special law enforcement experience?"

"I've been arrested and shot at by federal law enforcement," Nate said. "And I've held my own as well."

"Care to elaborate on that?"

"Not tonight," Nate said, dismissing him. "I think I've got a few years before the statute of limitations kicks in."

Sondergard looked over at Sheridan for some kind of explanation.

"He's my boss and a family friend," she said. "Nate has a very unique way of looking at things."

"We'll see," the sheriff said, raising his hands in surrender.

Nate had of course brought Kestrel, who was currently absorbed in watching *Bluey* again in the family room.

After briefing Sondergard and Nate on the news from Marybeth about Joe's condition, she turned to each of her sisters and gave them the floor. In addition to recapping their conversations with the Thompsons and McElwees, they played snippets of the interactions from their phones and showed the few photos they'd surreptitiously taken before and after the interviews.

After concluding her presentation, Lucy said: "My feeling is that Michael Thompson and even Clay Hutmacher view our dad as standing in their way. To them, he's an impediment. Brandy, too. Thompson perceives himself as above the law, and I can see him ordering the ambush to prevent my dad from nixing his development project, whatever it is. As I told my sisters, Thompson just reeks of desperation. I got the feeling that he's circling the drain unless he can pull off one more thing. And Brandy, I think, would do anything to stay on top."

Sondergard said to Lucy, "Deputy Carroll talked to them before you got there. He didn't come away with the same impression as you did, to be honest. He said Thompson was arrogant and condescending, but from what I understand he's always that way."

"What do you think he's got planned out there?" Lucy asked. "He wouldn't tell me, other than to hint that it's some big deal."

Sondergard said, "I've heard from a couple of county commissioners that Thompson has made some calls requesting a block of time at a future meeting. He wants to show up with his lawyers and pitch some kind of big presentation. His appearance hasn't been scheduled yet because Thompson insists that the public and the press can't be there. That's a no-go according to state public meeting laws, so the commission and Thompson's people are negotiating. But I have no idea what he plans to present."

"Whatever it is, I think he'll do anything to make it happen," Lucy said.

"Yes, but that doesn't help us figure *this* out," Sondergard said, indicating the case at hand. "Because when it comes to the timeline of the ambush the other morning, he's got a hell of a tight alibi. It turns out he was flying from Atlanta to his ranch that morning. His wife was with him. We confirmed that with the FAA and our airport manager. His alibi is solid."

"It's solid if you think he pulled the trigger himself," Lucy said. "But I don't think that for a second. Thompson is the type to order it done and stay an arm's length away from the actual act. I could see him giving the order to Clay Hutmacher, though. Clay *was* here at the time, and he knows enough people in this valley to know who he could hire to pull this off. Or maybe Clay was one of the shooters."

"I thought Clay Hutmacher was Dad's friend," April said.

"He was," Sheridan responded. "But when Clay Junior died, it broke the old man. He hasn't been the same since it happened."

"Is there any evidence that Clay was involved?" Sondergard asked Lucy. "Other than the fact that he followed you when you left the ranch? That alone doesn't tell us anything. Did he say anything to you that implicates him?"

"Not really," Lucy said. "But he seemed guilty of *something*."

Sondergard nodded, but it was obvious he wasn't convinced. Nate showed nothing.

The sheriff said, "I have an open mind on this, but you've got to give me more in regard to the Thompsons. If we want to get a search warrant for his premises or something—maybe to try and find the rifles that were used—I need more to take to a judge."

"What about what he says about our dad?" Lucy asked.

"That isn't much, is it?" the sheriff asked. "He and Hutmacher simply say that your dad can be stubborn. That probably offends you, but from what I know of him, that's completely true."

APRIL WAS NEXT. When she was through, she said, "The McElwees are running a large-scale drug distribution center, and I think they're working directly with one of the cartels. I think our dad suspected what was going on out there, and if that isn't motive to want him out of the picture, I don't know what is."

Sondergard didn't dispute that. He said, "I'm going to reveal something here that can't leave this house. Does everyone agree with that?"

Nods all around from the sisters. Sondergard paused, looking directly at Nate. Finally, Nate nodded his head and blinked his eyes, agreeing to the deal.

"Good," the sheriff said. Then: "We made a decision not to really interview the McElwees in regard to the shooting."

"What?" April asked, quickly angry. "Why in the hell wouldn't you go talk to them?"

"I did talk to them for about ten minutes," he said. "Look, give me a second here to explain. We've heard the stories about the McElwee sisters from a CI we trust."

"CI?" Lucy asked.

"Confidential informant," Sondergard said. Then: "The sheriff's department initiated a joint investigation with the FBI and DEA before I got here, but the ball got dropped after the last sheriff left. A task force like that involves a lot of bureaucracy and sign-offs, and it isn't moving as quickly as we'd like it to. But the McElwee sisters are on our radar.

"For now, though, we decided not to go out there and interrogate them," he continued. "We don't want to tip our hand until we're ready. From what I've heard, the McElwees are well-connected in regard to the LE community. We're keeping this under wraps until we're ready to go out there in full force. But we don't want them to know about it before we do."

"I think that's a bullshit reason," April said. "Our dad got shot."

She gave a disapproving glance at Sheridan as if to scold her for being somewhat involved with the new sheriff. Sheridan glared back.

"Believe me, I know why you're upset," Sondergard countered. "If it were totally up to me, we would have brought the sisters in yesterday morning. But the feds were adamant, and they're leading the investigation. So we deferred for the time being."

"Not good enough," April said, smoldering. She sat back hard in her chair and crossed her arms across her breasts. "I could see those gangbangers setting up the ambush," she said. "And what they're doing chasing cows around on foot is beyond me. But those boys aren't ranch hands, that's for sure. And by the time you and your buddies decide to raid the place, they could be gone and the sisters could clean up and play innocent like they've done before."

"It's a risk," the sheriff said. "But it is what it is. I value the new information you've provided."

April rolled her eyes and sighed.

"AND NOW WE have John and Shelby Bucholz," Sheridan said to deflect from the tension in the room between April and Sondergard. Before she began, Sheridan noticed that Nate had a half smile on his lips. Apparently, he'd been quietly amused by the argument.

"I talked with them personally," Sondergard interjected. He apparently wanted to prove, especially to April, that he *had* been working on the case. "They came into the department voluntarily and we spent about forty-five minutes together. Nice folks, I'd say. They said they were gathering cattle the morning of the ambush. When I asked them if anyone could corroborate that, they gave me the names of two locals they'd hired to help them. Both of the guys were a little sketchy, but they confirmed that they'd been out on the ranch helping out John and Shelby that morning."

Sheridan looked hard at him and said, "Steve, you're wrong about them. They're *not* nice folks."

Sheridan then recapped her drive to the Bucholz Ranch, the convoy of vehicles she'd observed, and the forced confinement of Uncle Hank. When she showed photos of the man on her phone, even April was fascinated and seemed to have put her dispute with the sheriff to the side.

"It's kidnapping if nothing else," Sheridan said. "There are probably about a half dozen other serious charges to bring against John and Shelby. So of course I wonder if Dad caught a glimpse of him when he visited the Bucholz Ranch a couple of weeks ago. Was he going out there that morning to confirm what he'd seen? Did John and Shelby set up an ambush to stop him?"

"Wow," Sondergard said. "That took a turn I didn't expect. John and Shelby completely fooled me."

"That's what they do," Sheridan said.

"Are you sure there are explosives around this guy's neck?"

"There's a locked collar around his neck for sure," she said. "I have no idea if they're real explosives. But *he* believes it."

"But why would they do that to him?" Sondergard asked. "Why keep him confined like that?"

"He claims it's for his own good, like I told you," she said. "But I think it's more complicated than that. He must have some kind of legal claim on the ranch that John and Shelby want him to grant them. Otherwise, why keep him alive? But it's all too twisted to figure out."

Lucy raised a finger in the air. "Maybe it's all about his masterpiece," she suggested. "Maybe he told John and Shelby that he'd sign over the ranch to them, but not until his work is finished. That would be a reason to keep him around."

"That makes sense," Sheridan said. "I never thought of that." She was impressed with her youngest sister and reminded once again that Lucy had matured. Sheridan too often tended to think of Lucy as the child she once was, she realized.

"What about the white trucks you saw?" Nate asked Sheridan. His entry into the conversation made all three sisters and Sondergard turn their heads to him.

"Do you mean the Global Exploration trucks?"

Nate nodded.

"I don't know how they fit in," Sheridan said. "I did a quick Grok search before you all got here." She scrolled on her phone to find what she was looking for, and she read aloud from the screen: "'Global Exploration (United States) is primaily a uranium miner, but is expanding into rare earths via the Aliende Project in Brazil and the Roundtop Mesa Mill in Utah. Headquarters are in Houston, Texas, and they have a market cap of three point one billion dollars.' There isn't really a lot more information that I could find before you got here."

"Uranium?" Sondergard asked aloud. "Do we have that here?"

"This state has a lot of it," Nate replied. "Along with everything else."

"So what are they doing on the Bucholz Ranch?"

"No idea," Sheridan said. "Did John or Shelby mention anything about an energy company looking at their ranch when you talked to them?"

"No."

"See how they are?"

THEY DISCUSSED THEIR findings and theories for forty minutes. Nate again receded into silence.

Sondergard said he'd investigate the situation at the Bucholz Ranch in regard to Uncle Hank. He said he'd wait for his new deputy to return from his day off.

Lucy introduced the idea that perhaps all three ranches had colluded in the ambush, since all of the ranchers seemed to have motives for going after their father. April disagreed, saying that the McElwees had such animus for their neighbors that she couldn't see them cooperating on anything at all.

Finally, Sheriff Sondergard sat back in his chair and said, "I'm impressed. My guys didn't get near this much. I've got a lot to think over."

"We aren't done yet," Sheridan said to him. "Did you locate the missing notebook and cell phone?"

He shook his head. "I put Deputy Bowkley on that one. I haven't heard anything either way."

For a while, Sheridan had started to wonder if someone in Sondergard's own department had actually found the items—and not told him. Which made her wary.

Although she wanted to trust Sondergard completely, she wasn't there yet. He'd need to convince her over time, she thought. That he had withheld the information about the investigation into the McElwee sisters showed he was capable of misdirection and deception. Or maybe that was just a prerequisite for being a county sheriff.

"WHEN DID YOU say your father might regain consciousness?" Sondergard asked.

"We don't know," Sheridan replied. "We're waiting for the call from our mother."

"If he could shed some light on this, like where he was going that morning . . ." As his sentence trailed off, Sondergard looked hard at Nate.

"You haven't said much. You listened to everything tonight. What is your theory as to who could have done this? Do you have one?"

"Yes."

"Can you enlighten us?" The sheriff was clearly annoyed, Sheridan thought. She hadn't seen that side of him before.

Nate paused a long time. He looked over Sondergard's shoulder and said, "Kestrel's out for the count. I need to take her home."

"But what is your take on this case?" Sondergard pressed.

"We won't know until Joe wakes up and tells us who did it," Nate said.

"That's it? I thought you had special powers."

"I never claimed I did," Nate said softly.

Sondergard grinned, but not in a kind way. "Sheridan says you have this unique way of looking at the world. I'm just wondering what it is."

There was more than a little aggression in Sondergard's tone, Sheridan thought.

Nate again paused a long time before responding. Finally he said, "Every year, I fill all my hunting tags: elk, deer, pronghorn, wild turkey, and all the waterfowl I can eat. I used to get asked a lot why I was such a successful big-game hunter. People asked me that question because they might have observed me getting into my drift boat with a simple bow and arrow and floating down the Twelve Sleep River. By the time I rowed into the river access near Saddlestring, my boat could barely float because of the weight of all of the dead game in it."

"Yes?" Sondergard said, prompting for an explanation.

"They asked me, how do you hunt from a boat?" Nate said. "I told them I *don't* hunt from a boat. I connect with my surroundings, and I let the animals come to me. Simple as that."

"What are you saying?" Sondergard asked. He was clearly perplexed. He looked to Sheridan. "Is that some kind of secret code language?"

Sheridan shrugged.

"I have a little girl to get home," Nate said. He stood up and walked into the family room and scooped up Kestrel.

THREE AND A half hours to the northwest, Marybeth was fighting sleep in a chair next to Joe when the supervising night nurse entered the hospital recovery room. She'd introduced herself as Barbara Peters, and Marybeth found her to be pleasant and professional.

"Has there been any sign of consciousness?" she asked Marybeth.

"Not yet. He's sleeping very peaceably, though."

The top of Joe's head was swathed in bandages that stretched down to his eyebrows. Tubes sprouted from his body like an old potato growing roots. Wires attached to probes snaked out from beneath the covers and connected to several banks of electronic gear.

Nurse Peters walked to the side of Joe's bed and glared at the monitor above the headboard that displayed his vital signs. Then, after a few seconds, she hit the side of the monitor with an open hand in a gesture much like smacking a television that refused to work.

"Well, *shoot*," she said. "It's not showing his oxygen level. They told me they'd fixed this machine, but apparently not."

She turned to Marybeth and said, "I think we'll need to move him into a room where everything works. I'll go check on availability."

With that, she turned on her heel and strode out of the room.

Marybeth was fine with that. Joe shared a room with a middle-aged man named McWilliams, who was apparently recovering from surgery as a result of a car accident that happened on the interstate near Laurel, Montana. McWilliams was obviously heavily medicated and his head was bandaged up as well, but at least once an hour he opened his eyes, stared at Marybeth with wide-eyed appreciation, and whispered, "*Hey, you, sweetheart. Why don't you come over here and sit on my face?*" And, "*Come over here and lay on top of me and wriggle around a little.*"

Then his eyes would close and he'd fall back asleep and leave Marybeth both insulted and annoyed. Until the next time he came to.

Nurse Peters showed up with an attendant a few minutes later.

"We're going to move your husband down the hall," she said. They unplugged him from the machines in the walls, but they didn't remove his IVs from the stands with rollers. The attendant pushed Joe's bed out into the hallway while Nurse Peters rolled the stands along beside him. Marybeth followed.

The new room, three doors down from his old one, had no other patient in it. Marybeth's first thought was she hoped the hospital wouldn't charge them extra for a single room, but she didn't say it.

Nurse Peters and her colleague fitted all the loose couplings into monitors and rebooted the equipment. The screens lit up, and Peters observed them carefully and said, "That's better. Everything's working like it should be." Then, "Try and get some sleep, Mrs. Pickett."

The new room allowed Marybeth more privacy and fewer lewd suggestions. She settled into a reclining chair and was asleep beside Joe in minutes.

Marybeth slept deeply, and she didn't hear the footsteps outside in the hallway from two men who'd accessed the ward from the elevator.

SHE WAS JOLTED awake by a commotion in the hallway about a half hour later. Marybeth saw Nurse Peters jog by the open door and shout something over her shoulder. Another nurse quickly followed her.

Marybeth rubbed her eyes and sat up. Joe's condition was unchanged, and he didn't stir. She rose and stepped out into the hallway. To her right, the floor receptionist behind the counter said to another nurse, "I don't know what happened. I was talking to some guy for a few minutes. He said he was lost in the hospital and I gave him directions to the cardiac unit, where he said his father was. I told him visiting hours were over, but he was quite insistent. But I didn't see him go down there into that room, I swear."

Nurse Peters emerged from a room to Marybeth's left. She declared, "We've lost Mr. McWilliams . . ."

As she said it, she looked up and met eyes with Marybeth. The declaration had obviously not been for the visiting wife of a recovering patient, but for the other personnel in the hallway. Nurse Peters was embarrassed, and she said to Marybeth, "I'll need you to step back inside for a few minutes. I'm sorry, but we've got a situation."

"What happened?" Marybeth asked. "He seemed okay a couple of hours ago."

"Yes, he did. I don't know what happened. Some kind of seizure, I think. His vitals were steady until they lit up like a pinball machine . . . then nothing."

Emergency room technicians appeared and rushed down the hall in front of Marybeth. She recognized that one of them wielded a heart defibrillator.

Ten minutes later, Marybeth went back to the doorway as orderlies wheeled a gurney down the hallway into the room. The patient, McWilliams, was obviously dead. Yellow foam clung to the sides of his mouth.

Only then did she realize that the whiteboard attached next to the room had not been amended earlier. It still read:

T. McWILLIAMS
J. PICKETT

CHAPTER TWENTY-THREE

Two Days Before

JOE AWOKE IN the predawn dark to see that the old digital clock on his nightstand was blinking *12:00—12:00—12:00*, meaning the power had gone out during the night at some point. As he checked his phone, he felt the house tremble as hard wind buffeted the side of it from the north. It was 4:45 a.m.

He padded over to the window and parted the curtain. Outside, it was a surprise November maelstrom. Dense clouds of poker-chip snowflakes tumbled through the blue-white illumination of their single outside pole light, and he could see drifting across the road.

"Joe, what's going on?" Marybeth asked, her voice thick with sleep.

"Blizzard," he said. "Big one."

"Oh great," she moaned as she rolled over.

"I think you can sleep in this morning," he said.

In a way, he thought as he made coffee, it *was* great.

Joe was exhausted from being in the field at least twelve hours a day for the last month straight checking hunters, hunting camps, hung carcasses, wounded animals, trespass complaints, and landowner issues. The blizzard, which hadn't been predicted and had arrived with massive strength, would force all of the hunters to stay in their tents, mountain camps, and hotel rooms until it eased up. There was no point in chaining up his tires and going out there only to get stuck in three-foot snowdrifts.

Joe was almost hopelessly behind on his office work. There were dozens of emails to answer, reports to read, and directives from headquarters in Cheyenne that he hadn't even opened. In a couple of hours, he would contact dispatch and let them know of the weather situation and that he'd be available to respond to urgent calls if necessary. Otherwise, he planned to spend the day on the huge amount of catch-up work that had been accumulating since the hunting seasons opened up.

As he did every morning, he opened his weather app on his phone, and then checked the Department of Transportation site. Every highway in northern Wyoming was closed. Nothing would be coming or going for a while. The schools were also closed, as were county and local offices. That meant Marybeth's library would be closed for the day as well, as he'd predicted.

He knew day-to-day life could be hard on a game warden's wife during hunting season, when he was often gone before she got up and not back until after dinner. It was worse now with the girls out of the house, more lonely he was sure. He'd always felt guilty about it, but Marybeth rarely complained.

So why not surprise her?

Joe looked through the refrigerator and pantry. During hunting season, those locations became a mystery to him. But there was flour, eggs, butter, milk, and half a pound of bacon. He'd let her sleep in, he thought, then he'd make her breakfast and deliver it to her in bed. Then he'd feed her horses in the barn and clean up the manure. She could take it easy for a change.

Then, maybe later . . .

STILL IN HIS robe and slippers, Joe sat down at his desk with a mug of coffee. He was pleased to find out that most of his unopened emails were perfunctory, and he mass-deleted them. He loved deleting emails, and it made him smile.

His new supervisor had requested an activity log for every month, and he was over two months behind. So he retrieved his spiral notebook and opened it next to his keyboard so he could bullet-point his actions in chronological order. While rifling through it, Joe was reminded of the many unresolved questions he needed to follow up on and that he'd postponed until he had the time.

Today, he thought he had the time. And almost all of the issues had to do with several local landowners.

The Double Diamond Ranch.

The Bucholz Cattle Company.

McElwee Land and Cattle.

He began with his visit to the McElwees and the photos he'd taken and the notes he'd scribbled down that day.

First, though, he opened an email from the state lab in Laramie. They confirmed that the soil sample he'd taken from the corral of the McElwee Ranch contained elk blood as well as an "unknown toxic substance" that would require further testing.

Then, on the screen of his phone, Joe enlarged the labels he'd seen on the containers within the house trailer on the hillside. Then he carefully keyed them into a search engine: sodium hydroxide, phenethyl bromide, tert-butoxycarbonyl, acetone, xylazine, propionyl chloride.

They were precursor chemicals used in the manufacture of fentanyl. He guessed that would turn out to be the "unknown toxic substance."

Joe sat back and shook his head. There was no doubt that Twelve Sleep County was awash in the drug, as were so many other rural counties across the country. But he'd never imagined that it might be being manufactured locally. But it all fit: the remote location, the beakers, the cookware, the "ranch hands" who didn't look like ranch hands.

He scrolled through his phone and found the contact details for Rick Orr, a special agent for the FBI that he'd met recently. Orr, unlike so many feds Joe had encountered over the years, seemed on the level.

Since it was two hours later in the eastern time zone, Joe punched Orr's cell phone number. After twenty seconds, the man picked up.

"Joe Pickett," Orr said. "I didn't expect to hear from you again. Especially this early in the morning." His voice was groggy.

"It's five thirty here," Joe said. "I figured you'd be up by now."

"I would have been a couple of months ago before I retired and moved to Florida," Orr said. "Now I get up when I want to, do a little fishing, drink a little bourbon, and try not to even think of D.C."

"Sorry about that. I didn't realize you'd moved on."

"It's okay," Orr said. "They didn't exactly throw me a big party. I was a thorn in their side, as you know. They were more than happy to see me go. So what's up? Is Romanowski in trouble again?"

Joe chuckled and said, "Not that I know of. No, I was hoping you'd help me out with a matter I'm investigating. It's a little out of my league."

"I'll try, and if I don't have the answers I still have a few friends in the bureau I could call on. I do try to keep up with things, even though I'm officially off the clock. You know, it's hard to completely walk away."

"I get it. It's about fentanyl," Joe said. "I think someone is making it here. I was wondering if you found that to be unusual."

Orr hesitated. Joe could almost visualize the man gathering his thoughts. Then he said, "A year ago, I would have said yes. I don't think I'd say that now. And in a way, it makes sense to me when I think about it."

"How so?"

"Fentanyl is big business, as you probably know. It used to be that China produced all of the ingredients, the precursor chemicals, and sent them to labs in Mexico, where it was manufactured and later distributed in the U.S. The CCP had deals with the cartels, especially the Sinaloa cartel.

"But the situation has changed, or is changing," Orr said. "We're in a cold war with China, as you know, and we've really cracked down at the border and disrupted the distribution of pills. It makes sense to me that instead of doing all the manufacturing in Mexico and sending finished product to the U.S., they'd develop a work-around."

"A work-around?" Joe asked.

"Ship the precursors directly to bad guys in the U.S. and cook it up here. Avoid the border completely. Of course, you'd still need experienced people who know how to make it. But I could see it happening. Instead of shipping the finished product, the cartels send people who know how to *make* the finished product. And the CCP changes the way they ship chemicals.

"You see, Joe," Orr said, "the dirty little secret is that there are thousands of undocumented Chinese nationals all over the country. They're mostly military-aged men, and they walked across the border with all of the others and vanished into the interior of the country. We know this because of many verified reports of Chinese trekking through the Darién Gap along with all the other immigrants.

"I'm not current enough on the issue to know if the feds are locating and deporting them. In the meantime, who knows? Maybe they've formed a network to transport fentanyl precursors around the country to new labs."

"And that kind of manufacturing could be done in the middle of nowhere?" Joe asked.

"I'd say yes," Orr said. "There might be quality issues, but I've read where the chemists don't hesitate to test the purity of the drugs on dogs, pigs, or cattle. If the animals die, they change the formula a little. That kind of thing."

Joe sat up. "They test fentanyl on animals?"

"Probably people, too," Orr said. "I wouldn't put it past them. But it can't be great business to kill *all* of your customers. So yeah, they do animal testing."

"So a ranch with livestock and wild game could be a really good location for fentanyl production?"

"I can't say for certain, of course," Orr said, "but yes, a remote ranch would probably be ideal. Especially if it's near to an interstate highway where the chemicals could be delivered."

Joe recalled the "drunk" elk reportedly tied up in the McElwee corral. And suddenly it made more sense.

"Thank you, Rick," Joe said. "You've been a big help."

"I have?"

"You have no idea," Joe said.

MARYBETH SAT UP in bed and smiled slyly when Joe arrived in their bedroom with pancakes, bacon, and coffee on a tray. There were also two empty plates and silverware placed in a cigar box because he couldn't find a better container.

"Oh my," she said. "What brought this on? What did you do, Joe?"

"This time, nothing," he said, slightly offended. Then: "We're snowbound."

"It's a snow day? How lovely."

When he clumsily placed the tray on the covers beside her, she deftly reached out and saved the tureen of coffee from spilling onto the quilt. Joe sat on the foot of the bed.

"The pancakes might be a little dry," he said. "I'm out of practice." Joe used to make pancakes for their daughters on Saturday mornings, but it had been years since all of them had been in the house together.

"I'm sure they'll be fine. What's it like outside?"

Joe briefed her on the weather and the road closures. He said it looked like the storm would keep up until midnight, but that the next few days were supposed to be sunny and mild.

Marybeth slid two pancakes onto a plate and buttered them. "So what's on your agenda for today, then?"

"Paperwork. I'm way behind."

She said, "I need to start on my budget proposal for the county commissioners. I'm glad I brought my laptop home."

While they ate, Joe filled her in on what he'd discovered on the McElwee Ranch, and what Orr had told him. Marybeth said she was surprised to learn that the sisters had apparently elevated their criminality.

"Do you think the three guys you saw out there are cartel members?" she asked.

"They fit the profile."

"So what's next?"

"I'll talk to the new sheriff when he moves into his office," Joe said. "Then it's his responsibility. I'll assist if he wants me to, but we'll see."

After they'd finished, Joe said to her, "You know, we've been here quite a few years. But there are still a lot of things I don't know about the people in this county. Especially the old-timers, the third- and fourth-generation ranch families. There's a lot of history between them and a lot of old feuds. A lot of secrets. Like the McElwee sisters. I mean, I knew they were dodgy, but I always considered them small-time. It's hard to get a handle on some of the people unless you've been here as long as they have."

"That's true," Marybeth said. "Some roots run deep around here. If it wasn't for my patrons at the library, a lot would get by me. There are always undercurrents, even in a place that looks peaceful and boring from the outside."

Joe nodded. It was true. If it weren't for Marybeth's library intelligence network, he'd know vastly less about the locals than he did.

"I think I need to talk to Lorne Trumley," Joe said. "He's an old-time rancher and he's bordered the McElwees and the Bucholzes for generations, and he's not far from the Double D. He's crusty and opinionated, but he's a good man. He also pays attention to what's going on around him, even if he doesn't gossip a lot about it. I'm thinking he could shed some light on a few of the questions I have about his neighbors."

Marybeth agreed. "Good idea. I don't think there's any love lost between Lorne and his neighbors, but he's an honest broker. I knew his wife before she died, and she was a sweetie. She was a member of three different book clubs at the library."

"I've also got a couple of other leads to follow up on," Joe said. "If the roads aren't too bad into town, I may be gone for a few hours today. I need to talk with George Haggarty about some aircraft I saw flying over the Bucholz Ranch."

George Haggarty was the longtime manager of the Saddlestring Airport FBO, or fixed-base operator. He'd be aware of the private aircraft in the area, and he lived in a small house within the airport grounds.

Joe asked, "Do you know what's good about blizzards?"

"Breakfast in bed?" she said with a grin.

"Other than that. The good thing about a blizzard is that it freezes everyone into place. People are easy to find because they're stuck there."

As HE ROSE and gathered up the dishes for the tray, Marybeth asked, "Have you considered talking to the Coffee Chicks?"

He paused. The self-named Coffee Chicks were a group of up to six local women in their seventies and eighties who convened every morning at the Burg-O-Pardner restaurant in Saddlestring. They maintained a table far removed from the Main Street Mafia. The Coffee Chicks' unofficial leader was a woman named Elizabeth "Bitzy" Scicluna, who had been the county clerk for three decades before recently retiring. Other Chicks included ranch wives, former waitresses, grocery store clerks, postal workers, and clerical staff for doctors, lawyers, and accountants.

"If anyone knows what's going on with the Thompsons, Bucholzes, and McElwees, it would be the Coffee Chicks," Marybeth said.

"I never thought about them," Joe said.

"That's why I'm here," she said playfully. "No one is more plugged into every aspect of the valley than those ladies. And you know about the Burg-O-Pardner. It's like Waffle House—it never closes. If those Chicks need to wade through snowdrifts on foot, they'll be there today."

Joe nodded. "I might just go see them."

"Don't get stuck," she cautioned.

"Oh, I probably will," he said. "That's nothing new."

THE SNOWPLOWS WEREN'T yet out on the county road from the Pickett house and game warden station to the town of Saddlestring. Joe knew he was lucky that most of the drive was in heavy timber on both sides without openings where the wind could whip across the road and create snowdrifts. Nevertheless, despite chaining up his front wheels and engaging the four-wheel drive, he nearly bogged down in a few places. The only way he got through them was to gun the engine and blow through.

Joe was driving the only vehicle on the road that morning, and he hoped the tracks he'd cut would hold in place for his return trip. Biscuit beside him seemed to enjoy the adventure, especially when he slammed through snowdrifts and the pickup was momentarily blinded in snow.

THE ROADS IN Saddlestring weren't much better, although there were at least a few tracks. Joe stopped to help pull a woman in a sedan from the borrow pit after she'd made an "emergency trip" to the grocery store for peanut butter and toilet paper, only to find out the store was closed.

Because the airport was located on a bench above town, the entry roads were more windswept and passable. Joe drove past the darkened airport terminal to the adjoining FBO complex that consisted of a small cinder-block building and a collection of private hangars.

George Haggarty was a large man in his midsixties with broad shoulders, a square oversized German head, sharp blue eyes, and a carpet square of close-cropped white hair. He peered out from inside the door of his house through a three-inch opening after he'd heard Joe knock on it. The portico leading to the house created a strange wind-tunnel effect that swirled snow up from the ground.

He looked puzzled until he recognized Joe.

"For God's sake," he said. "What are you doing out on a day like this?"

"May I come in?" Joe asked, wincing against the snow.

"Of course, of course," Haggarty said, stepping back and opening the door fully. He closed it quickly behind Joe to prevent more snow from blowing into his house.

Haggarty was wearing jeans and a thick chamois shirt and an apron. He had a dripping spatula in his hand, and Joe could smell meat cooking in the adjoining kitchen.

Haggarty's house was spartan—an overstuffed chair and couch facing an old television, a few volumes in a board-and-brick bookcase, and several military- and aviation-related framed photos on the walls. On the mantel above a roaring fireplace was a shrine of sorts to his late wife, Thelma, who had died a few years before.

"When I heard you knock, I was afraid some fool had landed on the strip," Haggarty said. "I was afraid you were a wayward pilot about to ask for a place to stay until this storm blew through."

"Nope, I drove," Joe said.

Joe didn't know Haggarty all that well, although he'd met him a few times before going up with Game and Fish–contracted pilots to do deer, elk, and antelope herd surveys. Haggarty had retired from the U.S. Air Force after a full career. He was now a one-man show at the FBO, managing not only the private airplane hangars but the fuel facilities, a small private waiting lounge for passengers and pilots, and other day-to-day maintenance.

"I'm frying up some brats in the kitchen," Haggarty said. "They're elk brats with cheddar cheese and jalapeño. I made them myself. Want one?"

"No, thanks," Joe said. "I already had breakfast."

Haggarty suddenly frowned. "Hold on—are you here to ask me about the elk I harvested?"

"Not at all."

"It was perfectly legal."

"I never thought any different," Joe said.

"So what brings you here?" Haggarty asked. "Don't tell me you're thinking of going up in this weather."

"Nope. I'd be okay if I never went up again, to be honest." Joe was terrified of flying in small planes. Every time he did, he thought the experience took another couple of years off his life.

"It's safer than driving around in your truck, that's what I always tell people," Haggarty said. "Except maybe today."

Joe said, "I was hoping you could tell me about some private aircraft I've seen flying around the valley in the last couple of weeks."

"I probably can," Haggarty said. Then: "This is the only game in town when it comes to fuel and maintenance. Follow me—

I've got to get those sausages turned before I burn this place down."

HAGGARTY SAWED THROUGH three fat sausages and ate them at his kitchen table while Joe described the helicopter he'd seen as best he could.

"The strange thing about it," Joe said, "was that it had this long pole-like thing stretching out from the front of it. There was a football-shaped nose on the end of the pole. It reminded me of a wasp when I saw it."

Haggarty nodded. "It sounds to me like an Airbus AS350 Écureuil. Single-engine utility chopper with a fenestron tail. Used a lot by law enforcement, airlifting folks to hospitals, and survey companies. It's a dandy aircraft."

"And the pole thing mounted on the front?"

"Probably used for geophysical surveying or finding mineral deposits. You say the helo was flying really low in a grid pattern?"

"Yup."

"Then the pilot was probably mapping the area to isolate mineral deposits. I've seen a few of those machines come through here over the years. They're usually owned or leased by energy exploration companies."

Joe stroked his chin. "What do you suppose they were looking for?"

"Your guess is as good as mine," Haggarty said. "That's the kind of question I don't ask the pilots, because they won't tell me the answer anyway."

"I'm impressed," Joe said. "You really know your stuff."

Haggarty finished off his bratwurst and sat back in his chair, content. "I do know my stuff," he said. "But I also know that helicopter you just described is sitting in one of my hangars right now. An energy company leased the building for six months to house it." Then he smiled.

"What's the name of the company?"

"Global Exploration, out of Texas," Haggarty said. "I don't know much about them and, like I said, they don't tell me. All I know is that their check cashed, and that always makes the airport board happy."

Global Exploration. The same company name Joe had seen on the heavy-duty-equipment trucks driving through the Bucholz Ranch.

"Can I take a look at it to make sure it's the helicopter I saw for sure?" Joe asked.

"I'm not sure I should open up the hangar without the permission of Global Exploration," Haggarty said. "Some of our clients are real sticklers about confidentiality. They don't want locals to know what they're doing, you know?"

"I get that," Joe said. "But I don't want to start up the helicopter and fly it. I just want to *look* at it. I mean, I saw it in the sky. Why can't I look at it on the ground?"

Haggarty stroked his chin, weighing Joe's request.

"If Global Exploration has a hangar here, it's public record, right?" Joe said. "Isn't the lease with the county airport board?"

"It is," Haggarty conceded.

"Then this is all on the up-and-up," Joe said. "Unless you want me to come back with a search warrant or something."

"We don't need to do *that*," Haggarty said.

"You can come with me to verify that I don't do anything in there I shouldn't," Joe said.

"I'll get the keys," Haggarty said with a sigh.

Joe's hat, parka, and jeans were coated with snow as Haggarty unlocked the metal door to Hangar #3 and shouldered the door open. Biscuit had come with them, and the Lab shook snow from her back. Joe closed the door behind them as Haggarty located the light switch.

"There it is," Haggarty said.

Joe stamped his boots and brushed off snow as he approached the helicopter. It was larger in person than he thought it would be, and it sat like a huge sleeping damselfly. The rotor blades sagged from the spindle on top.

The pole mounted under the cockpit stretched out nearly twenty-five feet and it had a gleaming white oblong orb on the tip of it.

Joe touched the pole. It was solidly mounted.

"Maybe don't touch that thing," Haggarty cautioned.

Joe pulled his hand away as if burned by it. "Can I look inside the cockpit?"

"I can't see how that would hurt anything," Haggarty said. "Just don't crawl inside with your wet clothes." Then: "I don't know what you think you're looking for."

"Neither do I," Joe responded.

He opened the door to the cockpit and leaned inside. There was a single pilot's seat, as well as a sidewise seat behind it that faced a wall of small computer screens.

It was obvious what the setup was. A pilot operated the aircraft, while a tech guy sat behind him and monitored the instruments. A long thin paper printout hung from a digital printer like an extended white tongue. Joe used the light from his phone to see the document better.

At first, all he could discern from the printout was that it was filled with scientific gibberish—all symbols, numbers, and what looked like geographic coordinates.

"What are you doing in there?" Haggarty asked from behind him.

"Reading stuff I don't understand," Joe said. As he said it, he shifted his body so Haggarty couldn't see over his shoulder while he snapped several quick photos of the printout with his phone.

"What's it say?" Haggarty asked.

Joe read it to him. It said: 43°97′58″ N, 106°88′70″ W. Then: Nd 2.4%, Pr 2.4%, Dy .08%, and Tb .07%.

"What in the hell does that mean?" Haggarty said.

"Darned if I know," Joe said, withdrawing from the cockpit and pocketing his phone.

"All I know," Haggarty said, "is that we ought to get out of here before we get drifted in."

BACK IN HIS pickup with Biscuit, Joe called up the photos he had taken inside the cockpit and sent them to Marybeth.

Can you make any sense of this? he texted. Then: Off to see the Coffee Chicks.

"So what do you suppose these guys have found?" Joe asked Biscuit. "And what do John and Shelby Bucholz know about it?"

CHAPTER TWENTY-FOUR

As Marybeth had predicted, the sign in the window of the Burg-O-Pardner flashed **OPEN—OPEN—OPEN**. Joe pulled into the unplowed parking lot beside the building. There were only two other vehicles in the lot—a jacked-up Jeep near the back door and a five-passenger Polaris Ranger in front mounted with tracks.

Joe told Biscuit to stay inside, then he swung out and squinted against the snow driving into his face. Torrents of snow streamed down from the flat roof of the restaurant like an intermittent waterfall and he stepped through it and opened the door.

As always, the Burg-O-Pardner smelled of fry grease, baked goods, and tobacco smoke. But in this case, there was a rare emptiness inside. Five women sat together at a large round table in the corner of the restaurant, their heavy coats piled up on a nearby four-top. The cook leaned out over a half door to the kitchen. His forearms displayed multicolored tattoos and an unfiltered cigarette dangled from his lips. He looked bored and slightly annoyed.

"My goodness," one of the women cried out when Joe arrived, "it's the game warden."

"Are you here to check our licenses?" another of the Coffee Chicks asked provocatively. "Does this mean a full body search?"

"Oh, Bitzy," another said with a laugh. "You should hope for so much."

"As a matter of fact," Joe said as he approached the table and removed his hat, "I am here to talk to you all, if you don't mind."

The women looked at each other, obviously intrigued.

"Have a seat," Bitzy said, gesturing to an empty chair. "Not all of us made it today in this storm. We're missing Lisa and Mary Katherine."

"Thank you," he said, setting into the chair. The Coffee Chicks looked at him anxiously, if playfully. They knew they weren't in trouble.

"We all know who *you* are," said Bitzy Scicluna, who was dark-eyed and wiry and clearly in charge. "We've often discussed your storied exploits. But I don't know if you know the rest of the Coffee Chicks."

"Kind of," Joe said. "But not formally."

In addition to Bitzy, the rest of the women at the table were all in their seventies or eighties. There was Cheryl, the plump and rosy-cheeked former manager of the Holiday Inn. There was Betty, who once managed the fairgrounds and 4-H program for the youth of Twelve Sleep County, even though she was never the official director of either. There was Shawna Johnson, who had recently sold a home-cleaning company called Shawna's Magic Maids that had serviced the valley for forty years. And there was Debbie, who still ran a fourth-generation ranch near Winchester with her ailing husband.

"Unlike the Main Street Mafia," Bitzy said with a nod toward the empty head table where the town fathers had coffee every morning, "we are tough and resilient when it comes to dealing with Mother Nature. We don't let a few snowflakes ruin our day. On a day like this, I just get in the Ranger and drive around and pick up the members of our crew. It isn't so hard. If our pioneer ancestors could survive this kind of weather, we can, too."

"It'll be over by tomorrow," Cheryl said. "November storms don't last."

Betty said, "We're not a bunch of softies. I hear they closed schools *last night* based on the weather report. Can you believe that?" she asked the others.

Then the Chicks talked over each other for a while, detailing the hardships they'd experienced due to Wyoming weather "back in the day."

Joe waited for the topic to finally wind down, and he said, "My wife, Marybeth, said you'd be here."

"Your wife should join us when she can," Bitzy said. "We like her and she'd be more than welcome."

"I'll let her know," Joe said.

"She's the best thing that ever happened to that library," Debbie offered. The others all murmured their agreement.

"I'll get right to it," Joe said. "Marybeth told me this morning that the Coffee Chicks are more plugged into this community than anyone else. She suggested I ask you for your opinions on a few of the local folks I'm dealing with. I'm not asking you to sign affidavits or testify in court about anyone. It's not like that. But I think I could really benefit from any background you can provide."

The women shared long looks with each other. Then Bitzy said, "We're not merchants of gossip."

"I appreciate that," Joe said. "I was thinking of you more as local oracles."

Which made Bitzy cackle with laughter. "Oh, nice one, Mr. Joe. Flattery is always appreciated."

Bitzy raised a finger and turned to the cook, who was watching them from the half door. "Corky, we need some lunch menus."

"I'm thinking about closing," Corky said. "There isn't much going on today, and I don't want to get stuck on the way home."

"You've got valued customers sitting here, Corky. You can close after our lunch."

"I'm buying," Joe told him.

"You bet you are, Mr. Joe," Bitzy said.

Corky sighed and stubbed out his cigarette. As he delivered the menus, he grumbled, "The menu hasn't changed in twelve years, ladies. You all know what's on it already."

WHILE CORKY MADE and delivered salads, soup, and sandwiches—and a cheeseburger for Joe—Joe outlined the parameters of his three distinct investigations without getting into too much detail. "Like I said, I'm not here looking for dirt. I play things by the book. I'm just looking for insight. If you know good things about the subjects involved, I'd love to hear that, too."

The Coffee Chicks all warmed up to the topic and joined in with their observations about the Thompsons of the Double D, the McElwee sisters, and John and Shelby Bucholz.

"That's the thing with those three ranches out there," Bitzy said. "We've talked about it many times before. It's like God took a wagon filled with common sense, decency, and integrity and distributed them in equal measure among the ranches in the county. But when it came to that stretch of Antler Creek Road, He ran out of all the good things before He got there."

Joe listened and nodded and made a few notes in his spiral notebook. He found, as he always had, that when he had an open blank page in front of him, the people across from him simply felt compelled to fill it.

ON THE McELWEE sisters, rancher Debbie said that she and her husband had tolerated Buck, the father, even though he "was a horse thief and known outlaw." But when it came to Buck's two wild daughters, they'd cut all ties to them years before.

She said, "The sisters don't hesitate to ask for help or to borrow equipment or labor, but they never reciprocate. Plus, they have very, very loose morals. And no compassion, in my opinion. They could care less if their cows starve in the winter, or if a horse needs doctoring. They've always had bigger things on their mind."

Bitzy added that over the last few years, the sisters had started registering and licensing large vehicles at the county courthouse DMV to their ranch corporation. "We were wondering what they were up to," she said. "We thought they were starting up a trucking company or something."

Joe didn't mention his new suspicion that the McElwee sisters were hosting the manufacturing and distribution of fentanyl, but Debbie's and Bitzy's observations bolstered his theory.

SHAWNA JOHNSON, THE former owner of the home-cleaning service, provided especially valuable information to Joe, because unlike the others, she'd actually been in their homes.

On the McElwees, Shawna said she'd fired *them*.

"It was a nightmare some days," she said. "We were always picking up empty liquor bottles and drug paraphernalia around the house. And we never knew who would show up and wander through the house when we were out there. Once, I bumped into a naked man who claimed he was an artist. He had paint all over his skin and just one name, although I forget what it was. Plus, there were out-of-state 'businessmen'"—she did air quotes with both hands as she said it—"who looked more like gangsters to me. I'd just go about my business, but it's hard to ignore the fact that groups of people are smoking weed and doing dope in the living room at any time of day. Some days, I'd leave that place and just find myself trembling, it was so bad."

"The businessmen," Joe asked. "Could you tell where they were from?"

"Mexico, or some other country like that in South America," Shawna said. "A couple of them could barely speak English. Oh, and how Lisa and Lainie sucked up to them! It was disgusting."

ON THE THOMPSONS, Shawna also had inside knowledge. She said that Brandy was a narcissist who never looked her in the eye, and that Michael looked her in the eye, but only to intimidate her.

"They wanted their mansion to be perfect," Shawna said. "And that's okay as far as it goes. But we live in the rural West. A lot of the roads aren't paved, and there's the weather. You can't have that kind of white-marble tile just a few steps away from the mud outside and keep a pristine home."

Shawna leaned toward Joe and said, "Did you know about the cameras?"

Joe said he didn't.

"Michael had them installed," she said. "There are hidden cameras in every room."

"You're kidding," Joe said, recalling the layout of the public rooms he'd been in on the ranch.

"And there were some other secrets, of course," Shawna said while arching her eyebrows and turning her heard toward Cheryl, the former manager of the Holiday Inn.

Cheryl said to Joe, "I'd never talk about this if I still worked there, but I don't anymore."

"What's that?" Joe asked.

"We had a special arrangement with Brandy—her own corner suite that she kept on retainer with us. When Michael was gone, which was often, she'd come into town. Let's just say she hosted a lot of men in that suite, including some names you might know from the tabloids and the internet."

Joe sat back, surprised. He said, "I'd probably not be familiar with the names, actually. Marybeth might, but I wouldn't."

"Not all of them were celebrities or finance guys," Cheryl said. "Some were local."

"Tell him," Shawna said.

"Clay Hutmacher," Cheryl whispered.

Joe was genuinely surprised. "Do you think Michael knew?"

"I doubt it," Cheryl said. "They were very sneaky."

"We think the cameras were the reason Brandy did her dirty business away from the house," Shawna added.

"Well, what do you know," Joe said. "I never picked up on that, and Clay didn't mention anything to me."

But it perhaps explained Clay's almost irrational loyalty to the Thompsons, Joe thought.

"And Michael Thompson is either a crook or he's in real financial trouble," Betty weighed in. "He wanted to host this big fundraiser for the 4-H kids out at the fairgrounds, which was odd for him because he'd never showed any interest in them before. But he did a big event last summer, and invited all these big shots he knew from around the country. I heard they raised over two hundred and fifty thousand dollars, which was impressive. But to this day, I don't think the 4-H kids have gotten a check from him. That's pretty low, if you ask me."

Joe turned to Bitzy and asked, "Do you know anything about the development Michael Thompson is planning for his ranch? Did he apply for building permits and such?"

"He has," Bitzy said, "but it's all hush-hush. Since I'm not in the office anymore I don't know the details. All I know is that it's supposed to be huge, and a couple of the county commissioners are in with him on it. Thompson also claims he has contacts in state government that will help grease the skids. My speculation is that it's going to be some kind of multimillion-dollar resort."

That tracks, Joe thought, but didn't say. He wondered if Thompson's machinations had all been recorded by his in-house video system. And what else might be on those tapes.

On John and Shelby Bucholz, there was less insight overall from the Coffee Chicks. Shawna had worked for them years before, but when they delayed payment or the checks bounced, they'd parted ways.

Debbie said, "I've met them a bunch of times at county stockholder meetings. They're smiling glad-handers, but there's something going on there if you ask me. John, especially. He talks big, like he's got the world by the tail, but if you see their place, you wonder why they've let it go to seed like it has if they're so successful. Plus, as I think you know, their names are always on a list near the cash register at the hardware store, the feedstore, and so on. 'Don't accept credit on these people,' the list says. Which means they don't pay their bills on time or at all."

For Joe, it was information he'd heard before. What he *hadn't* heard before came from Cheryl.

"A funny thing happened at the hotel a few years ago," she said. "An older gentleman checked in. If I remember correctly, his name was Henry Bucholz. Just to be friendly, I asked him if he was related to John and Shelby, since the last name isn't a common one. He took me aside and said John was his nephew and that he, Henry, was actually the primary owner of the Bucholz Ranch. Anyway, the guy was *really* creepy. He carried around this huge book under his arm everywhere he went.

"I was at the front desk when he said he was going out to the ranch," Cheryl said. "It was a day or so later when I realized he'd never come back. We checked his room and he'd left everything in it—clothes, shaving stuff, his suitcase. I called John and asked him if his uncle was okay, and John said he didn't know what I was talking about. We put Henry Bucholz's belongings in the lost and found, and I pretty much forgot about him until now."

"Did you think to call the sheriff?" Joe asked.

Cheryl shrugged. "For what? The bill was paid in full, and John claimed he didn't know who the man was. And you know what the sheriff was like then," she said, rolling her eyes.

Joe couldn't help but think of the figure he'd seen in the rundown cabin at the Bucholz Ranch. Could it have been Henry Bucholz?

CORKY WAS LOUDLY shutting down the kitchen to make the point that he was ready to close the Burg-O-Pardner when Joe thanked the Coffee Chicks for their time. "This was very helpful," he said, closing his notebook and sliding it into his breast pocket.

"It was?" Bitzy asked. "Really?"

"You helped fill in some blanks for me."

"Don't be a stranger," Bitzy said. "Or better yet, tell Marybeth to come by and join us. Frankly, she's probably a better fit with this crew."

Joe smiled. Bitzy was correct.

"Don't get stuck out there," Bitzy said as Joe headed for the door. "I don't want to have to pull you out of a snowdrift."

"I'll do my best," Joe said.

"And don't wreck your truck," Bitzy said to giggles from the other four ladies. "We know all about your record in that department."

In the time Joe had been in the Burg-O-Pardner, the storm had increased in intensity and the roads were worse. He pulled a car from a snowdrift on the street, and the young couple passing through thanked him and asked where they could get a hotel room for the night. Joe suggested the Holiday Inn, and then thought about the exclusive corner suite Brandy Thompson kept there.

He called Marybeth and said, "I'm on the way."

"Good," she said. "It isn't getting any better outside. Was it worthwhile?"

"Absolutely," Joe said. "I need to sort a bunch of things out, but it was absolutely worth my time to come to town. Your Coffee Chicks are . . . amazing. They do know everyone and everything. They want you to join them, in fact."

Marybeth laughed. "I'll wait a couple of decades until I retire, if you don't mind. But I'm glad they could be of help."

"Learned some things at the FOB, too," Joe said.

"I'm researching those photos you sent me," Marybeth said. "I'm learning a lot myself. I can't wait to fill you in. Are you still planning to go visit Lorne Trumley?"

"Nope," Joe said. "I would get stuck if I tried, I'm afraid."

"Let us celebrate your rare moment of caution and common sense," she said.

"Apparently, God ran out of that somewhere along Antler Creek Road," Joe said. When she didn't reply, he said, "I'll explain later."

THE TRACKS HE'D made that morning had largely filled in with fresh snow, but there was enough of an indentation in the cover to use as a guide to stay on the road to his game warden station. As he drove, he punched up Lorne Trumley's house phone. The rancher answered on the second ring.

"I hope you're not out and about today, Joe," he said.

"I'm headed home as we speak, Lorne."

"Well, don't get stuck."

Joe rolled his eyes. How many times had he been told that in just the past few hours?

"It sure screws up shipping cattle tomorrow," Trumley said. "It'll probably take them at least a day to clear the roads after this. In the meanwhile, I've gotta pay for putting up semitruck drivers in motels for extra nights."

After lamenting the snowstorm for a few minutes more, Joe got right to it. "Lorne, I'm doing some follow-up on a few of your fellow ranch owners. Specifically the Thompsons, the Bucholzes, and the McElwee sisters. I'm hoping you can help me figure them out."

"Are the three of them colluding in something bad?" Trumley asked. "If so, it would be the first time those folks ever got along."

"No. They're individually suspicious."

"That I believe," Trumley said. "I've tangled with all of them over the years, as you probably know. It's just too bad that you can't pick your neighbors."

"If you don't mind, could you fill me in on any experiences

you've had with them in the last few years? We don't need to go way back."

"I try my best to keep my head down and avoid 'em," Trumley said.

"I understand."

"Let's start with Michael Thompson," he said. "I actually haven't spoken with him for quite a while now. Probably two years or so. He's an arrogant so-and-so."

"What was it about?" Joe asked.

"Well, for a while there, I think he wanted to buy up half of the valley starting with my outfit. He knows that, like most of us out here, I'm land-rich and cash-poor. He probably looked at the Crazy Z-Bar and figured he was doing me some kind of favor.

"He approached me through one of his lawyers in Atlanta, I believe. I think he was a little shocked when I turned him down."

"Did he offer a lowball price?" Joe asked.

"No, it was pretty fair at the time. I didn't accept it because I told the lawyer that's not how I do business, at arm's length through a lawyer in another state. I told that lawyer that Michael Thompson could come talk to me face-to-face. This place has been in my family for four generations. I wouldn't sell unless I could be assured that we kept it as is: a working cattle ranch."

"What did Thompson want to do with it?"

"He never really explained that to me, but I had the feeling he wanted to subdivide the ranch and develop it into a hundred little ranchettes and sell the tracts to other Michael Thompsons. That's not something I'd want my name associated with. We've got enough Michael Thompson types around these days as it is."

"Gotcha," Joe said.

"Then he stopped calling," Trumley said. "Or I should say he told his lawyer to stop calling. I haven't heard from him since, which is okay by me."

"What about the McElwees?"

Trumley sighed. "Them sisters are crazy, as you probably know. They're all over the place, like farts in a skillet. I think they're involved in all kinds of shenanigans, but that's just speculation on my part. I steer clear of them and they don't bother me unless they want to borrow my tractor or something like that."

"What about the Bucholzes?" Joe asked. "Don't you share a pretty long fence line with them?"

"Twelve miles of it, in fact," Trumley said. "Except when it gets knocked down and my cows cross over or their cows cross over to my ranch. Which means I'll be out there fixing the fence, since John can never seem to find the time to help out."

"So would you describe your relationship with them as cordial?"

"Frostier than that," Trumley said. "Except for the last couple of months."

"Why do you say that?"

"I've known John since he was a teenager," Trumley said. "I never really saw him as someone who was passionate about the land. That's something you either have or you don't, and John never had it. Neither does Shelby. No, the only thing John has ever been passionate about was being a rich big shot."

"So what's happened in the last couple of months?"

Trumley chuckled and said, "John's put on a big charm offensive with me, acting like we're great buddies and neighbors. He and Shelby even brought me a birthday cake for my eighty-fifth birthday last month."

"Do you know why he's warmed up to you recently?" Joe asked.

"It's the damnedest thing," Trumley said. "John told me he thinks that it's important for me to retire from this tough ranching life and live it up someplace warmer, like Arizona. He's offered three times to, and I quote, 'take this old place off my hands.'

"He knows I don't have any kids that want it and I'm alone out here. So he acts like he's being compassionate. He doesn't realize that if I ever left this place I'd be dead within a week, I reckon."

"Did he name a price for the Crazy Z-Bar?" Joe asked. "Or was he just fishing around?"

"Five point seven five million," Trumley said. "And an assurance that surface rights are included. To be honest with you, Joe, that's not a bad price."

"So why haven't you taken it?"

"Because," Trumley said, "John Bucholz doesn't have two nickels to rub together. I know that for a fact. There's no way he could get that kind of cash together, and I know that there's not a bank within a thousand miles that would lend him the money because of his credit rating and reputation."

"So what is his thinking?" Joe asked.

"Your guess is as good as mine," Trumley said. "I don't think he could even come up with a low down payment. And he's nuts if he thinks I'll vacate the place and he can pay me over the next twenty years off the proceeds of my own ranch."

"That's very interesting," Joe said. Then: "Have you seen a helicopter flying around recently?"

"I've seen it, all right. The first time I saw that helicopter it was over my land. I got out of my truck with my Winchester, but it was out of range by the time I jacked a shell in."

Joe winced. "You were going to shoot it?"

"I was going to scare the pilot off," Trumley said. "I probably wouldn't have aimed right at him."

"So you don't know anything about that aircraft?"

"Not a damned thing. All I know is that it was overflying my property without permission."

"And was it coming from the west?" Joe asked. "From the direction of the Bucholz Ranch?"

"You damned right it was."

"Did you ask John about it?" Joe said.

"I called him, all right. He claimed it was news to him, but I think he was trying to blow smoke up my skirt. Then he reminded me that he still had an offer on the table if we wanted to get together and talk it over. I hung up on him."

"I've seen the helicopter," Joe said. "It's sitting in a hangar at the FOB. Is the name Global Exploration familiar to you at all?"

"I don't believe so," Trumley said. "Did they send out a landman?"

"Not that I'm aware of," Joe said. "But I think they were flying over the terrain where your ranch butts up against the Bucholz property."

Before punching off, Joe recalled something Trumley had just mentioned. "You said John specifically asked you about mineral surface rights?"

"He did. I've got them. Fat lot of good they've done me over the years."

"Thank you, Lorne."

"For what?"

"I'll let you know when I'm sure," Joe said. "But I think I'm starting to figure a few things out. By the way, have you ever heard of Henry Bucholz?"

"Hank?"

"I guess," Joe said.

"Yeah, I met Hank twenty years ago," Trumley said. "He came out to visit the ranch and look for dinosaur bones or some damned thing. He asked me if he could poke around our place for 'em, and I let him on. He showed up a couple of days later practically giddy. Said he'd found the thigh bone of a diplodocus."

"No kidding."

"I looked in the back of his pickup and I said, 'Hank, I hate to break it to you, but that's a chunk of petrified wood.' It broke his heart. Hank was a few fries short of a Happy Meal, if you know what I mean."

"Have you seen him around lately?" Joe asked.

"Nope. I haven't set foot on the Bucholz place in twenty-five years. And I have no plans to do so in the future."

Joe roared his pickup through the accumulated snow on the access road to his house to prevent bogging down. He prayed that the cow moose that often blocked his progress wouldn't materialize from the timber, and for once she didn't.

He entered his home through the mudroom and shook the snow off his parka, boots, and hat. The savory aroma of elk chili simmering on the stove and cornbread baking in the oven permeated the air. He found Marybeth at the kitchen table with her laptop open in front of her.

"I did some research on those photos you sent me from the hangar," she said. "You're going to be interested in what I found."

"What's that?"

"We can talk about it later."

"Later?"

Then he noticed that she'd set the table already and had added two candles. There was also a half-empty glass of wine in front of her. She looked up and smiled. Provocatively, he thought.

"This is nice," he said.

"We need more snow days," she replied as she stood up and approached him. "So, do you have any big plans for later?"

"No."

There was no doubting her intent. But in case there was any, she alleviated them by throwing her arms around his shoulders. "*My* plans involve you," she said.

"You're right," Joe said as she led him down the hallway toward the bedroom. "We do need more snow days."

CHAPTER TWENTY-FIVE

November 18

Deputy Bowkley and O'Bryan sped south on Interstate 90 south of Lodge Grass in the dark. As they did, O'Bryan scanned the pitch-black countryside to the west looking for distant flashing lights of emergency vehicles that could be retrieving the body of a local man who had been discovered on the side of the road. But except for a few distant porch lights, it was pitch-black out there.

"Doesn't look like they found him," he said.

"It might be a few days," Bowkley said. "Law enforcement on the res leaves a lot to be desired."

It was well past midnight, and there had been fewer than five oncoming cars in the last hour. The only signs of life were the green-eyed reflections of mule deer poised on the shoulder to cross the highway.

O'Bryan felt sleep coming on as the adrenaline rush he'd had earlier began to recede. It had all gone off without a hitch, just as Bowkley had said it would. Bowkley had distracted the night nurse with a story about being lost in the hospital, while O'Bryan scanned the names written outside each hospital room until he found the one containing J. PICKETT.

He'd slipped into the room without being seen. O'Bryan had pulled his hat down low on his head and had concentrated on looking down at his boots as he did so, knowing there were likely closed-circuit cameras mounted in the ceiling of the outside hallway. The livestock vaccine-dosing gun was inside his coat, out of view.

It had taken a moment for O'Bryan's eyes to adjust to the darkness within the room. He'd heard the rhythmic pulsing of diagnostic machines and the digital readouts on monitors emerged slowly from the gloom. Then he'd heard the labored breathing of his target from the bed. Despite two names written on the whiteboard, there were no other patients in the room. For that he was grateful.

O'Bryan had wasted no time. He'd opened his coat and grasped the pistol grip of the dosing gun, then powered it on. He wanted to do his job and get out of there as quickly as possible. He could hear Bowkley engaging with the nurse, asking for directions, pretending he was confused by which elevator to take.

Pickett's head was turned aside, exposing his white neck. O'Bryan padded to the side of the bed and gently pressed the tip of the gun to the skin.

Click.

Pickett thrashed soundlessly and arched his back. O'Bryan stepped back and powered the gun down and slid it back under his coat.

"Don't scream," he whispered.

Within a few seconds, Pickett's body went rigid and then became limp. The man's left arm slid out from beneath the sheets and hung lifelessly near the side of the bed.

O'Bryan felt nothing. He'd never met Joe Pickett, and he'd had no personal animus with the man. In fact, O'Bryan had been more affected by the sudden death of Leonard the Indian Flagger.

O'Bryan exited the room the same way he'd come in: head down, shoulders hunched, not exposing himself to the cameras.

NOW IN THE passenger seat, O'Bryan held up the dosing gun. "Should we get rid of it somewhere?" he asked Bowkley. "Like we did that phone and notebook?"

"Absolutely not," Bowkley said sharply. "We're going to need it later tonight."

O'Bryan frowned in the dark. "Tonight?"

"Tonight."

The deputy turned his face to O'Bryan. "I'm putting it all together in my head—how we're going to do it. But it's hard to concentrate when you keep interrupting me."

"Do what?"

"We're going to silence those three girls," Bowkley said. "I think you know what I'm talking about."

O'Bryan shook his head. "I didn't sign on for this. Not three young girls."

"They're not that young," Bowkley said with a leer. "One of them is a real cunt, believe me. But it is what it is. Those damned girls are figuring things out. We need to protect ourselves. I don't want to spend the rest of my life in prison, do you?"

"No, but this is too much," O'Bryan said, his voice rising. "This is . . . terrible."

"Don't you want to get paid and get out of here?"

O'Bryan nodded emphatically. "I never want to see this place again for the rest of my life. But three girls?"

"It is what it is," Bowkley said again. "And we've got to do it tonight."

O'Bryan leaned back in his seat and moaned.

"Kids are dying all over this country from fentanyl overdoses," Bowkley said. "They think they're buying cocaine or meth, and they find out too late that it's dosed with fentanyl. It wouldn't be the craziest thing in the world to find out that these three made that same mistake.

"Not only that," Bowkley said, "I can make sure I'm the first responding officer on the scene. And when I look around, what do I find? A little bag of fentanyl on the kitchen table."

O'Bryan moaned again.

"Then it's over," Bowkley assured him. "We part ways, take our money, and we'll never have to see each other for the rest of our lives."

"Don't you think it'll look ridiculously suspicious that a father and all three of his daughters die of fentanyl overdoses on the same night?"

"Yeah, it isn't perfect," Bowkley said. "But it isn't impossible, either. Fentanyl is a bitch. Like I said, people are dying of it all over the fucking nation. It's a tragedy, yada yada yada."

"Tonight?" O'Bryan said.

"Tonight. While they're sleeping. What I'm trying to figure out is how to handle their dogs. If those dogs start barking they'll wake everybody up and make it harder to get the job done."

AT THE SAME time, Sheridan sat at the kitchen table with her laptop, dutifully inscribing what she and her sisters had learned yesterday on the three ranches. When the report was complete, she planned to send it to Sheriff Sondergard as well as to her mother. Sondergard had promised to send his files on the case to her as well, but it was after midnight and he'd yet to fulfill his promise.

Sheridan's hope was that her written record, plus the sheriff's case file, would combine to present a clearer picture on the suspects and where they were at with the investigation.

Earlier in the evening, they'd talked on speakerphone with Marybeth. Their father was still unconscious, but their mom said she'd noticed a few promising indications that he was coming out of it. He'd sighed and yawned involuntarily, but he'd not yet opened his eyes.

"When he does," Sheridan had said, "ask him where he was headed that morning."

"Oh, I will," Marybeth promised.

"And call us the second you find out," April said.

When Sheridan told her mom about the investigative report she was about to compile, it jogged her mother's memory.

"Let me send you some photos he took at the airplane hangar," her mom said. "I want to see if you come up with the same conclusion I did."

After a pause, Marybeth said, "You know, I never did get to

discuss my theory with your dad. I was going to, but that's when all of *this* happened."

BECAUSE IT WAS late and her sisters had already gone to bed, Sheridan had muted her phone. So it startled her when the phone lit up and vibrated and skittered across the tabletop.

She hoped it would be her mom with good news, but the screen read STEVE SONDERGARD.

"Sorry to call so late," he said. "Did I wake you?"

"No. I'm working on the report. I've got some photos to research that my mom sent along, and then I think I'll be done." Then: "You must be working late as well."

"Ten-four," he said. "When I was out there this evening, the records on your dad's phone we'd requested from the service provider came in. We had to go that route because we couldn't look up the recent activity directly off your dad's phone."

Sheridan sat up, suddenly alert. "What did you learn?"

"Something interesting in regard to the last calls on the register," Sondergard said. "Not counting the last one, which was your mother's call to his phone that morning. Two calls preceeded that. One incoming and one outgoing. The first call to your dad lasted three and a half minutes and it was from the night before. Then the morning it happened, your dad apparently called the number back and talked for five seconds. Both from and to the same number."

"What was the number?" Sheridan asked.

He read the number: 272-320-5768.

"Where's that?" she asked as she copied down the number on her laptop.

"I just checked. It's an area code for northeast Pennsylvania. I've made a request to the provider to find out who has that number, but I probably won't hear back from them until tomorrow, when their customer service office is open." Then: "Of course, we shouldn't assume that the call was literally from Pennsylvania. That doesn't make any sense. So it had to be someone local with a cell phone they obtained in Pennsylvania. Just because the area code is out of state doesn't mean the call originated from out of state. Hell, I have a Montana area code associated with my phone and I haven't lived there since college."

"I agree," Sheridan said.

"Do you think it was a hunter? There are lots of hunters from Pennsylvania out there."

"I don't know," Sheridan said, her mind racing. "But it sounds like this person called my dad on his cell to tell him something the night before. Maybe to request a meeting in the morning. And my dad called the number back that morning to confirm that he was coming."

"That's what I came away with as well," Sondergard said. "So whoever called him could have been the shooter, or set up the ambush."

"I think a hunter would have called my dad on his office phone, not his cell phone," Sheridan said. "A hunter would look up the game warden station on the internet and call *that* number. Dad's office phone transfers to his cell if he's out in the field, which is most of the time. But the caller wouldn't know that. My dad's cell phone number isn't public knowledge."

"We might finally be getting somewhere," Sondergard said.

"Thank you, Steve. This is important."

"I agree." Then: "See, I do know how to do my job."

She could imagine him smiling as he said it.

"You should have my report within the hour," Sheridan said. "I just have one more thing to do."

IT DIDN'T TAKE long for Sheridan to research the letters and symbols on the helicopter cockpit printout that her dad had taken a photo of. As she did it, she could feel her heart racing.

Nd was the scientific symbol for neodymium, a mineral that was essential for high-strength magnets in electric cars and wind turbines.

Dy was dysprosium, a mineral that increased magnetic performance in extreme temperatures.

Tb was terbium, used for enhancing lighting on screens and displays. It was also used for studio lighting on film and television sets.

And Pr was for praseodymium, a key element in magnets and alloys.

Together, they were considered to be rare earth minerals. And although rare earths weren't exactly rare, as the name implied, high concentrations of the elements in one place was *extremely* unusual—and valuable.

Neodymium found at 2.4 percent, dysprosium discovered at .08 percent, praseodymium found at 2.4 percent, and terbium at .07 percent was a major find.

Although it was impossible to determine the value of this rare earths deposit, the value of other recent discoveries in Wyoming alone was mind-boggling. A find near a coal mine in the north-central part of the state might hold $34 billion in elements. Another near Upton was worth over $20 billion. And the Halleck Creek site near Wheatland was estimated to contain over $37 billion in rare earth minerals.

Previously, she read, most rare earth minerals came from China, but those supplies were threatened due to the tension with that country. Over ninety percent of all rare earth minerals were refined in China as well. And she found it interesting that rare earth deposits weren't all that rare. The minerals could be found all across the globe, with the biggest recent domestic finds occurring in Wyoming.

Hence, there was a modern-day gold rush and it was happening around them.

Sheridan keyed the coordinates 43°97′58″ N, 106°88′70″ W into the onX Hunt app on her phone. She generally used the app to search for falcon nest locations. The app pinpointed the coordinate locations on a 3D map and she zoomed out. The app also indicated the property lines on all of the private ranches in the county.

The coordinates revealed a location on the western boundary of the Crazy Z-Bar Ranch. And right on the other side of that property line . . .

Then two things hit her at once.

She quickly opened up another window and furiously keyed the phone number Steve had given her into the search engine. The 272 area code was from northeastern Pennsylvania, all right. But specifically it covered Williamsport, Scranton, Wilkes-Barre, and Monroe County.

Scranton.

"And who is from Scranton?" Sheridan asked herself out loud.

Sheridan pushed back quickly from the table and stood up. The enormity of what she'd found hit her hard. She quickly texted Marybeth:

> I think I've figured it out. Call ASAP.

After pressing SEND, she paced around the kitchen. Her mind was reeling. Should she wake her sisters and blurt out her theory? Or wait to bounce it off her mother first?

Then Sheridan's phone lit up with an incoming text. She anticipated that the message was either from her mom or Sheriff Sondergard.

It was from neither. It was from an unknown number, but not an unknown person.

> Sorry for the late hour. This is Deputy Bowkley from the Twelve Sleep County Sheriff's Department. We may have a break in the case, but I need to discuss it with you in person. I can come by in the next hour. Please kennel your dogs so they won't wake everybody up when I get there.

IN THE BILLINGS hospital room, Marybeth heard her phone chime with an incoming text at the same moment that Joe moaned and turned his head toward her. She froze in place while he opened his eyes. It took him a few seconds to focus on her face. His expression was slack.

"Joe?" she whispered.

His lips pursed, and he continued to simply stare at her.

Then he frowned and croaked, "Who in the hell are you and why are you sitting there?"

"Joe," she said softly, "it's me. Marybeth."

"*Marybeth who?*" he asked with a snarl.

Horrified, she dropped her head into her hands. For a moment, she couldn't breathe.

Then she felt a soft grip on her knee. She opened her fingers to peer through them to see that Joe had reached out from beneath the sheets to touch her. He was grinning.

"You are a sight for sore eyes," he said. "How long have I been out of it, sweetie?"

"*Joe*," she hissed through gritted teeth. "That was *not* funny."

"Probably not," he conceded as he reached up and touched his bandaged head. Then: "Boy, I've got a bit of a headache."

"You were shot in the head, so no wonder," she snapped. "Do you remember anything about it?"

"Yup," he said. "A couple of guys ambushed me. I saw the first couple of rounds hit the truck. I stopped and was trying to get out of there when everything went black."

"But you're feeling normal now?" she asked.

"Under the circumstances, I'd say I'm feeling pretty good."

She reached out to him with tears in her eyes. A great weight had suddenly lifted.

"It's been really strange, the last couple of days," he said. "I could actually hear some of your conversations, but I couldn't react. I felt like I was trapped inside my own body.

"I heard the doc say my personality might be changed," he said. "So I thought I'd lighten the mood with a joke, you know?"

"*It was not funny*," she said again. Then she leaned in close to him. "Joe, what were you doing that morning? Who were you going out to see on Antler Creek Road?"

Joe said, "I was going out to the Bucholz Cattle Company ranch to see a guy named Henry Bucholz. He claimed that he'd been kidnapped, and he was being held against his will. It was such a crazy story that I thought I needed to check it out. He called me the night before and said to come out first thing the next morning. It was a setup."

Marybeth nodded along. It all made some sense now, and she wondered if her daughters had come to the same conclusion.

"There was a really strange thing about that call," Joe said. "I thought the voice on the other end sounded a lot like John, even though it was a Pennsylvania phone number. Like John was trying to disguise his voice. That's why I called back the next morning as I was going out there. But it went straight to voicemail."

Before Marybeth could react, she sensed a presence behind her and she turned her head. Dr. Ralston was framed within the doorway, watching it all. She was beaming.

CHAPTER TWENTY-SIX

O'Bryan watched the Pickett house from behind the thick trunk of a spruce tree in the dark. He was eighty yards away, but he could clearly see the oldest daughter pacing past the kitchen window. It was the only room in the house with lights on.

On the way to Saddlestring, O'Bryan had found a photo on his phone of the Pickett family that came from the local library website under "Meet Our Staff." Marybeth Pickett, the director of the library, stood proudly with her husband, Joe, and their three adult daughters. The photo looked to O'Bryan like a campaign photo.

Although he'd fleetingly glimpsed the three daughters the day before in the woods when they'd pinned Peddy and him on the road, it helped to know which one was which.

O'Bryan recognized that the oldest daughter, Sheridan, was the one pacing inside the kitchen. That meant the middle one, April, and the youngest, Lucy, were asleep somewhere in the house. There were three vehicles parked out front. One had Montana plates.

As he watched, Sheridan stopped suddenly and looked at her phone. Then she called out something, probably the names of the dogs, and ushered her animals down a dark hallway.

Deputy Bowkley had obviously just sent the text, and this was O'Bryan's cue to move.

He drew the dosing gun out of his coat and powered it up while he approached the house. He entered the backyard through a short gate and sidled along the exterior toward a back door. A horse whinnied from a barn somewhere out in the dark behind the house, and the cry startled him.

As Deputy Bowkley had theorized, the back door was unlocked. O'Bryan opened it silently and stepped inside the kitchen. There was an open laptop on the dining room table and a sheaf of loose papers scattered beside it. The oldest daughter was still in the back of the house, presumably locking her dogs into their crates. No dog barked or rushed him, for which O'Bryan was grateful.

He quickly moved to the staircase and climbed the steps. He balanced on the balls of his feet on each stair to reduce the sound of his footsteps and carried the dosing gun loosely at his side.

At the top of the stairs, he paused and let his eyes adjust to the gloom. Bowkley's description of the layout of the game warden station was more than helpful. There was a large bedroom downstairs down the hallway, and two more bedrooms on the second floor. O'Bryan could see four closed doors ahead of him, two on each side.

O'Bryan hated every second of his life at the moment, he thought. And he hated Bowkley and his employer for putting him into this situation. He had nothing against the three women, just as he'd had no beef with their father. Yet here he was, standing in the dark hallway of an unfamiliar home, trying to guess who he'd kill first when he started opening doors.

THE PLAN WAS simple, as laid out by Bowkley as they'd driven south. Bowkley would send a text to Sheridan implying that he had important information to deliver to her in person and asking the woman to put the dogs in their crates for the night. While she did it, O'Bryan would secretly enter the home and find April and Lucy in their bedrooms, where he'd administer lethal doses of fentanyl. While he was engaged, Bowkley would come directly to the house in his uniform and knock on the front door. Bowkley would then subdue Sheridan until a dose could be delivered to her as well.

Then, after, O'Bryan would hide out until Bowkley reported to his office that he'd discovered the bodies of all three sisters in their home. All had apparently died from a bad batch of fentanyl. Then both O'Bryan and Bowkley would get rewarded for their work and O'Bryan, at least, would leave this godforsaken state and never look back.

O'BRYAN REACHED FOR the knob on the first door on the right. He turned it slowly and pushed it open. It was a bathroom. Crumpled towels covered the floor and the counter was covered with plastic bottles of hair and skin products.

He backed out and closed the door and turned to the room on the other side of the hallway. It had to be a bedroom.

O'Bryan grasped the dosing gun in his right hand while he opened the door with his left. Immediately upon entering the room, he knew he'd guessed correctly. Moonlight from a gap in the curtains revealed the lump of a figure in a bed ahead of him. He could hear her soft breathing.

It was the one with the crazy-colored hair, he saw. April. She was turned on her side away from him, but her white neck and shoulder was exposed. He inched toward her and raised the dosing gun.

That's when he heard someone enter the room behind him and a female voice say, "Don't take another step and drop that thing in your hand, whatever it is."

OUTSIDE, BOWKLEY SETTLED back in his seat behind the wheel of his SUV and checked his watch. It had been three minutes since he'd sent Sheridan the text. He'd changed into his uniform outside the vehicle and gotten back in. O'Bryan had walked off in the dark toward the house.

Bowkley was worried about O'Bryan. He wasn't sure he could trust him. The man had obvious reservations about his assignment. Would he chicken out? If so, Bowkley would use the dosing gun on *him*, he vowed to himself. And another body would be disposed of in Savage Run Canyon.

Lost in thought, Bowkley didn't notice the figure approaching his SUV from the trees bordering the road until his driver's-side window exploded inward. When he turned toward the shower of glass, he glimpsed a long-barreled revolver swinging through the opening and instantly crushing the bridge of his nose into flat pulp. The sharp pain of the impact resulted in an eruption of yellow and orange spangles that blocked his vision.

As Bowkley cried out and reached up to stanch the gout of blood from his nose, the man threw open the door and pulled him from his seat and outside the vehicle. Bowkley was hit again in the side of his head with the butt of the gun and was spun face down into the long grass. The deputy was momentarily stunned, and he could do nothing to prevent his attacker from removing his weapon from its holster and tossing it away into the trees. Then he felt the sharp pinch of his own handcuffs being closed around his wrists.

His assailant reached down and flipped Bowkley onto his back, then leaned down on his knee with all of his weight on the deputy's chest. As the spangles in Bowkley's eyes faded, he could see that the man above him was big and blond and his eyes were cold.

Nate leaned down into Bowkley's face and bared his teeth as he spoke. "If any of those girls get hurt, I'm going to tear you apart with my hands and feed you to the wolves."

"You can't do that," Bowkley spat through a mouthful of blood from his broken nose. "I'm a cop."

Nate leered and grasped Bowkley's right ear and twisted it a full forty-five degrees. The pain was unbelievable and the sound of the cartilage popping was loud.

Bowkley screamed.

"I knew you'd eventually come here," Nate said. "All I had to do was wait and you'd come straight to me. Now, tell me who hired you."

"No one hired me," Bowkley said. "I was responding to a call from the Pickett house—"

Nate twisted his ear off and flipped it onto the deputy's chest as if it were a poker chip. Then he grasped the man's left ear and prepared to do the same.

"Who?" Nate asked.

After Bowkley confessed, Nate asked, "Who is with you and where are they now?"

At that moment, there were three sharp gunshots from inside the house.

Pop-pop-pop.

SHERIDAN TORE UP the stairs from putting the dogs away and thumbed on the light switch in April's bedroom to find a dead man on the floor with three gunshot wounds in his chest. April was scrambling out of her bed to retrieve the handgun she'd placed for the night on the top of a chest of drawers.

Lucy was pointing her .38 revolver at the body splayed out at her feet. The room smelled sharply of gunpowder. She was obviously stunned.

"I heard him coming up the stairs and when I confronted him he gave me no choice," she said. "He lunged at me and I remembered April saying just to point it and pull the trigger."

Sheridan stepped past Lucy and knelt down near the body. She recognized the object near his hand as a vaccine dosing gun, and her first thought was that Lucy had made a terrible mistake. Then she saw the butt of a conventional handgun sticking out of the man's belt, and she recognized him as "Marion Barber."

Nate thundered up the stairs and burst into the room with his

.454 Casull held out in front of him in a shooter's grip. He paused when he saw the scene inside April's bedroom.

"Who shot him?" he asked.

"Lucy," April said.

"Good girl," Nate said to Lucy. "But I think you can lower the gun now."

In a kind of trance, Lucy quit pointing it and let the revolver drop along her thigh. Then she handed it back grip-first to Sheridan and said, "I never want to hold a gun again."

"Who is he?" Nate asked Sheridan. "Do you know him?"

"I don't know his real name," Sheridan said. "But I recognize him from yesterday."

"He was one of the guys following us," April added.

Nate said, "He worked for John Bucholz. And so does the one-eared deputy I left outside."

At that second, a group text arrived on all three girls' phones. It was from Marybeth:

> Your dad is conscious and talking. He seems okay! It was John & Shelby.

April looked up from her phone to Sheridan. "Maybe you should call your boyfriend."

CHAPTER TWENTY-SEVEN

Five Days After

JOE LEANED BACK in a lounge chair in the living room with the television on, toggling back and forth between *Clarkson's Farm* and fly-fishing shows on the Outdoor Channel. He was wearing his robe, slippers, and flannel pajama pants. He was bored out of his mind.

It was midafternoon after an emotional morning. Both Lucy and April had said tearful goodbyes. April drove off north to Bozeman to resume her work at Dewell Investigations, and Lucy had driven south to Laramie and the University of Wyoming. Marybeth had arranged for Lucy to see a UW trauma counselor about the shooting, and Lucy had reluctantly agreed, even though, she claimed, she'd already come to terms with it.

"I was protecting our family," she'd said. "Isn't that what we do?"

Joe told both girls how proud he was of them and that he was honored to be their father. He also mentioned that he wouldn't miss their gentle probing questions over the last few days in attempts to assess his mental acuity. He was fine, he told them. He'd need more than two holes in his head to make a real difference.

And it appeared thus far to be true, he'd told Marybeth the night before. Although he did have sharp headaches from time to time and some of his dreams had been harrowing, he did feel almost normal again.

Or so he hoped.

Sheriff Sondergard's SUV drove up outside, accompanied by Sheridan's vehicle. Joe started to push himself up to answer the door when Marybeth came into the room from the kitchen.

"I'll get it," she said. "You sit down. That patch in your head needs to heal."

He'd been told by Dr. Ralston when they left the Billings hospital to take at least two weeks to "relax and recover," which were two traits he'd never mastered.

Joe grumbled and sat back down.

"John and Shelby Bucholz are in custody," Sondergard said as he sat down on the couch opposite Joe with his hat in his hands. "We also rescued Henry Bucholz. It turns out that explosive col lar was real. We're detaining Uncle Hank until we can figure out what to do with him."

Sheridan came in and greeted her dad with a kiss, then sat next to Sondergard. Marybeth crossed her arms and listened in while leaning against the bookcase.

"John Bucholz is a zombie," Sondergard said. "He can't believe that his entire future has come crashing down around him. He knows he's never going to get it back."

"Was Shelby involved?" Joe asked.

"She was involved with keeping Henry prisoner," the sheriff said. "She knew about the mineral deposit. We don't know how much she knew about the hit men John hired to kill you. But she's turned on John to save herself. She explained it all to us.

"It was all about that discovery of rare earth minerals," Sondergard said. "John bet everything on it—everything. He couldn't wait to be a billionaire. He gambled that he'd be able to acquire the ranch from Uncle Hank, pay Global Exploration for finding and exploiting the mineral reserves, and pay off Bowkley, O'Bryan, and Peddy for doing his dirty work.

"But there were two problems with that scheme: you and Lorne Trumley."

Joe arched his eyebrows. It was painful to do so.

"Global found that eighty-five percent of the mineral deposit was actually on the Crazy Z-Bar Ranch. The remaining fifteen percent was on John's property on the other side of the boundary line."

"Ah," Joe said. "So that's why John tried to make nice with Lorne recently. He wanted to buy the Crazy Z-Bar for the mineral rights without tipping his hand. Maybe he had a way to borrow money in secret, I don't know. But with that rare earth discovery in his back pocket, he might have figured he could pry loose some mysterious hedge fund money or something."

"We're still trying to confirm that," Sondergard said. "But I think we will."

Sondergard said, "Luckily, my former deputy Bowkley is singing like a bird as well, especially after he found out that John never actually had the money to pay him. Bowkley feels betrayed, and he's willing to testify against the Bucholzes and cooperate with us in nailing them. I think a lot of what Bowkley is saying is bullshit, but it'll be hard to prove."

"Like what?" Joe asked.

"He says it was all O'Bryan and Peddy, and that Bowkley tried over and over to rein them in. He says O'Bryan and Peddy did the ambush, which I believe. Then he says O'Bryan murdered the deer hunter and burned the trailer down, then offed Peddy. He also claims that O'Bryan is responsible for a fentanyl overdose death on the Crow Indian Reservation, and in your old hospital room in Billings. I've seen the security footage from the hospital and I think Bowkley isn't lying about that last one, at least."

"How did John get to know Bowkley?"

"Apparently, Bowkley picked up John for speeding through Gillette. Somehow, they got to talking. John told Bowkley he was a big shot and he was about to make a very big score. Bowkley asked how he could be a part of it, and John told him about the job here in the department. John wanted someone on the inside who could keep him in the loop, and Bowkley was all over that."

Joe asked, "Where did they get the fentanyl? Did you figure that out?"

"They could have bought it anywhere, I'm sorry to say," Sondergard said. "But I have my suspicions. That vaccine dosing gun was analyzed by the lab and it contained enough pure fentanyl to kill everyone in Twelve Sleep County. But we do know that the gun itself belonged to the Bucholz Cattle Company."

Sondergard held forth for several minutes while Joe, Marybeth, and Sheridan listened. Joe was impressed with the new sheriff and his attention to detail.

"They tried to kill my entire family," Marybeth said after the sheriff paused. "I still can't wrap my mind around that."

"So why Joe?" Marybeth asked. "Why was Joe John's other problem?"

Sondergard said, "John thought you were about to talk with Lorne and blow the whistle on the discovery, since you'd seen Global Exploration on the ranch. If you spilled the beans on what they were doing out there, the whole scheme might collapse. So he decided to hire a couple of guys to take you out before you told anyone. John had already taken Uncle Hank's phone away from him, so he used it to call you and set up the ambush."

"So Henry wasn't involved in any way?" Marybeth asked.

Sondergard shook his head. "Uncle Hank doesn't know what the hell is going on. In fact, he keeps begging us to take him back out to that cabin so he can finish his masterpiece."

"Poor man," Sheridan said. "Perverted, but kind of sad at the same time."

Joe said, "To be honest, I wasn't sure what was going on out there on the Bucholz Ranch. I was just bumbling around. But I was beginning to suspect it was something big, especially when I found that helicopter in the hangar. But I didn't put everything together at the time."

Sondergard said, "The execs at Global have confirmed that the helicopter was equipped with a really sophisticated piece of equipment. Apparently that goofy thing on the front of the aircraft is a kind of high-tech metal detector that can locate rare earth minerals in the ground. It can also penetrate the soil to see how big the deposit might be. And from what they told us, this discovery is just massive. It's no wonder John Bucholz got a little crazy when he found out."

Sondergard turned to Sheridan. "Oh, and the helicopter is sometimes flown at night. That explains the 'spacecraft' that nearly landed on Earl Wright."

"So he wasn't completely crazy after all," Sheridan said.

"Nope," the sheriff said. "But you'd think he would have known the difference between a flying saucer and a helicopter."

"We really thought it was the McElwee sisters," Marybeth said.

"For good reason," Sondergard said. "The feds raided their ranch two days ago and uncovered a large-scale fentanyl distribution network. They also arrested three suspected members of the Sinaloa cartel. The sisters had a pretty good motive, I agree.

"Oh, and one other thing," he said to Joe. "One of the cartel guys admitted to the feds that they sometimes tested their fentanyl on livestock to see how potent it was. The way they did it was to sprinkle some on salt blocks and watch how the animal behaved. But in one case, a bull elk came down from the mountain and licked the salt block before they could stop it. That's probably what the archery hunter saw."

"I'm glad you got them," Joe said. "I hope the feds put those guys away for a long time."

"And the Thompsons?" Marybeth asked.

"Michael has lawyered up, so we really can't talk with him," Sondergard said. "We've heard he's hired Global to prospect on *his* ranch. Thompson's probably hoping they discover more rare earth deposits so he can buy his way out of all of his troubles. And knowing how that guy operates, he'll probably pull it off."

"Probably," Joe agreed. Then: "Congratulations on all of your hard work on this. You and my daughters cracked it."

"We did," Sondergard said. "I just wish I wouldn't have hired one of the bad guys. That's on me."

THEN SONDERGARD PAUSED for a long while and stared at the top of his boots. Joe assumed the sheriff had something to say, but was reluctant to do so.

Finally, Sondergard said, "Your friend Nate Romanowski."

"Yes?" Joe said. He noticed that both Marybeth and Sheridan had tensed up.

"Well, he did some real damage to Deputy Bowkley. He literally tortured him for information. They had to sew an ear back on the guy at the hospital. There's no other way to look at what happened than first-degree assault, attempted murder, and maybe even kidnapping. Even if the guy had it coming to him."

"What are you asking?" Marybeth said in an arch tone.

Sondergard looked up and sighed. "I guess I'm asking that you tell him not to do that kind of thing anymore."

Joe smiled. "I've been telling him that for years. It's never worked."

AFTER JOE AND Marybeth shook Sondergard's hand and thanked him again for his hard work, the sheriff and Sheridan left the house together. When they did, Marybeth and Joe exchanged a look.

When Sheridan came back to retrieve the phone she'd accidentally left on the couch, Joe said, "So, are you two an item?"

Sheridan smiled and narrowed her eyes. "I'll get back to you on that. But for now, you need to relax and recover."

"I'm getting a little sick of hearing that," Joe grumbled.

ACKNOWLEDGMENTS

The author would like to thank the people who provided help, expertise, and information for this novel.

Renee Jean of the *Cowboy State Daily* provided invaluable information and insight into Wyoming's burgeoning rare earths discoveries and mining.

Thanks also to Theodore H. Schwartz, MD, author of the fascinating *Gray Matters: A Biography of Brain Surgery* (Dutton, 2024). Dr. Schwartz helped keep me on the straight and narrow when it came to bullet wounds to the head and medical procedures, although I still took some liberties that are not his fault and any errors are mine alone.

Sources for some of the themes included the *New York Times*: "This Is What Makes Us Rich" and "How Mexican Cartels Test Fentanyl on Vulnerable People and Animals" by Natalie Kitroeff and Paulina Villegas.

Special thanks to my first readers, Laurie Box, Molly Box McCarty, Becky Box Reif, and Roxanne Box Woods.

A tip of the hat to Molly Box and Prairie Sage Creative for cjbox.net, merchandise design, and social media assistance.

ACKNOWLEDGMENTS

It's a sincere pleasure to work with professionals at Putnam, including the legendary Neil Nyren, Daphne Durham, Ivan Held, Alexis Welby, Ashley McClay, Molly Pieper, Rob Sternitzky (who knows Joe Pickett's world better than I do), and the incomparable Katie Grinch.

And thanks once again to our agent and friend, Ann Rittenberg.